"I feel like I've be
prove it."

"Watched? Where?"

"Everywhere. It's been g... ... .. a few weeks now. I felt it a few times before I went on leave from my job, and now that I've been home, it's happened more frequently. Even when I'm in the house."

"When was the last time it happened?"

"Earlier. Tonight." The same fury she'd sensed in him before was back, darkening his hazel eyes to a fiery amber. "When I was walking around downtown."

"And you didn't think to mention it?"

"I forgot. And when I thought about it again, it didn't seem relevant to what I saw in the alley."

"It's all relevant, Evangeline. And when you add on that we've got a serial killer on the loose, ignoring your instincts is the worst thing you can do."

"Troy, you don't need to make this your problem. The GGPD is dealing with a whole lot worse right now."

"You are my problem. The moment I took the call to come help you tonight, you became my problem."

She wanted to be his partner, not his problem.

* * *

The Coltons of Grave Gulch: Falling in love is the most dangerous thing of all...

* * *

Dear Reader,

Welcome back to Grave Gulch, Michigan. A lot has happened in the past five months to our intrepid Colton clan, from kidnappings to secret babies to the realization that a serial killer is on the loose in Grave Gulch.

Detective Troy Colton has been managing it all. His nephew was returned home unharmed, and so far, the Grave Gulch PD has managed to keep all of his cousins and their new loves safe. No small testament to Troy's hard work and dedication.

Evangeline Whittaker has always been a well-respected member of the district attorney's office. She's an ADA with an impeccable record—one that has been tarnished since she defended the case that put a killer back on the streets.

Now someone wants revenge. Only they've gone about it in the most diabolical way, ensuring Evangeline will experience maximum pain as a killer stalks her from a distance.

Troy's always had an attraction to the ADA but has kept those feelings at bay. But now, Evangeline needs him. Needs him to get to the bottom of what's happening to her. And, maybe, just needs *him*.

As a killer gets ever closer, Troy and Evangeline will be tested. Can he keep her safe? Can she trust herself to know where danger is truly lurking? And can they find their way through it all to love?

I hope you're enjoying the Coltons of Grave Gulch. As always, I've had such fun being a part of this series and coming back to the world of the wonderful and dynamic Colton family.

Best,

Addison Fox

COLTON'S COVERT WITNESS

Addison Fox

Special thanks and acknowledgment are given to Addison Fox
for her contribution to The Coltons of Grave Gulch miniseries.

Recycling programs
for this product may
not exist in your area.

ISBN-13: 978-1-335-62898-5

Colton's Covert Witness

Copyright © 2021 by Harlequin Books S.A.

This edition published by arrangement with Harlequin Books S.A.

For questions and comments about the quality of this book,
please contact us at CustomerService@Harlequin.com.

Harlequin Enterprises ULC
22 Adelaide St. West, 40th Floor
Toronto, Ontario M5H 4E3, Canada
www.Harlequin.com

Printed in U.S.A.

Addison Fox is a lifelong romance reader, addicted to happy-ever-afters. After discovering she found as much joy writing about romance as she did reading it, she's never looked back. Addison lives in New York with an apartment full of books, a laptop that's rarely out of sight and a wily beagle who keeps her running. You can find her at her home on the web at www.addisonfox.com or on Facebook (www.Facebook.com/addisonfoxauthor) and Twitter (@addisonfox).

Books by Addison Fox

Harlequin Romantic Suspense

The Coltons of Grave Gulch

Colton's Covert Witness

The Coltons of Mustang Valley

Deadly Colton Search

The Coltons of Roaring Springs

The Colton Sheriff

Midnight Pass, Texas

The Cowboy's Deadly Mission
Special Ops Cowboy

The Coltons of Red Ridge

Colton's Deadly Engagement

The Coltons of Shadow Creek

Cold Case Colton

The Coltons of Texas

Colton's Surprise Heir

Visit the Author Profile page at Harlequin.com.

For Olivia, Izzy and Callin.
With love.

Chapter 1

Evangeline Whittaker stared down the main street of Grave Gulch, Michigan, and wondered when the whole world had gone sideways. Although her eyes were protected from the early-evening sun by oversize sunglasses and a floppy hat, no amount of shielding her gaze could stop what she saw through the lenses.

The citizens of Grave Gulch, now protesting outside the city's police department—a common sight over the past few months, due to an increase in local crime—with signs and heavy shouting, eerily audible even though she was several blocks away.

Protesting…and the subtle yet unrelenting pressure from the knowledge that a killer was in their midst.

Although the GGPD was doing its job, people were fed up and anxious by the latest details pouring out of the news cycle. Only, instead of the news showing a random family dealing with a bad situation in a faraway place, this time, it was local. *As local as you could get*, Evangeline admitted to herself as she stepped aside to allow a couple to walk past her on the sidewalk.

There had been three dead bodies discovered in Grave Gulch in a matter of six months. All found with a gunshot to the chest and all seemingly random until you searched beneath the surface.

But once you looked below, it was easy to see the similarities, Evangeline thought on a hard shudder.

All male. All shot while alone walking their dogs. All in their fifties.

Enough similarities that the GGPD had been forced to admit the one thing that was guaranteed to send people into a panic: Grave Gulch had a serial killer on its hands.

Add on the trauma of discovering a well-loved grandmother, Hannah McPherson, was a toddler kidnapper, the GGPD's lead forensic scientist, Randall Bowe was assisting criminals he deemed "worthy," and the discovery and subsequent takedown of a drug kingpin running his business in town, and all of Grave Gulch's residents were scared. The fear either they or a loved one would be next on a killer's list swirling deeply beneath it all.

Hadn't she felt the same sense of concern? Sure, she might be eternally single, but she had a family. And while her mother was quick to lock up good and tight each night, her father often had a mind of his own when it came to how he wanted to live his life. Or worse, his unique brand of screaming obstinacy whenever he felt the world around him wasn't bowing to his wishes.

A persistent worry, the two of them, but one she couldn't overly concern herself with now. She had enough to contend with on her own. Forced leave from her job. That doggedly odd sense that she was being watched—even in her own home—that hadn't let up in weeks. When you added on the mess that was currently the Grave Gulch County DA's office—one she'd managed to find herself smack in the middle of—life was on an out-of-control roller coaster at the moment.

How had it happened so quickly?

She'd spent well over a dozen years in the district attorney's office, keeping her head down and doing her job. Doing it damn well, as a matter of fact. Yet somehow, she'd failed to see a problem right in front of her face.

And now she had tangible responsibility for a serial killer out on the streets and preying on innocents.

Evangeline had spent innumerable sessions with her therapist over the years, dealing with the ever-present twin feelings of despair and responsibility. She'd worked long and hard to ensure that those feelings, a leftover gift from her father's parenting failures, didn't veer into her professional life.

But there was no help for it now.

Three people were dead and a killer was on the loose because she'd not properly prosecuted him. Not on purpose—she let out a frustrated breath—but still on her watch.

On her work.

Damn Randall Bowe and his mishandled—and *criminal*—approach to evidence keeping. And damn her for not digging harder.

Round and round she went, on the endless circle of arguments in her mind. Yes, the GGPD's forensic scientist had often tampered with evidence or flat-out overlooked it, but as a prosecutor she shouldn't have simply assumed a GGPD employee was acting in good faith.

Yet she had.

The blowback had been awful. The cases where she'd used Bowe's evidence—or lack thereof—as part of her legal argument had put them all in this mess. Even worse, she'd failed her boss, Arielle Parks. Arielle was both mentor and friend and it was an endless source of embarrassment and pain to Evangeline that her mistakes reflected so poorly on the district attorney.

And underneath the roiling thoughts in her mind was a bigger one. The lone thought she never seemed able to get past.

How could the world be full of so many awful people?

At this stage of her life, she should know the answer. She'd learned the lesson young, hadn't she? So, in a lot of ways, it should have stuck by now. Yet it hadn't. She lived a life steeped in reason and lawfulness and it still amazed her how many people saw the world as a place to get away with things.

A place to take their anger out on others.

Or selfishly reap whatever benefit they could derive for themselves, no matter the cost to others.

On another hard sigh, Evangeline blew out a breath. *Maudlin much?*

She'd come out because her condo had begun to feel stifling and, at those persistently odd moments, creepy. She couldn't explain it, but even in the confines of her own home, she'd been aware of a relentless sense of being watched.

She'd sensed it for about a month, the feeling growing stronger by the day. At first it was just a fleeting sense, that someone caught her eye too long on the street or a strange sense someone was lingering in the parking lot of her condo complex, even if she couldn't define why she felt that way.

But it had grown worse.

A persistent scraping at the base of her neck, rippling the nerves to her scalp, had become a regular occurrence.

She'd initially blamed it on the pressure at work, the mishandled evidence causing any number of errors in her caseload. Finally, though, Evangeline had had enough of sitting home feeling stuck and decided to head out for a bit of fresh air and some dinner. Yet as she walked, watching the people and trying to appreciate some of the early summer warmth, the fresh evening air wasn't doing much for her mood. That strange sixth sense continued to crawl up and down her spine.

A feeling that had done nothing for her already dour mood.

It was early June, which meant the days were getting longer and longer. And here she was, the space between her morose thoughts getting smaller and smaller so all she focused on was her mistakes. She'd left her home because she needed dinner and a reprieve from the increasing claustrophobia induced by her own four walls, but she'd find no break if all she did was keep covering the same ground over and over in her mind.

With a glance at one end of the street at the protesters, Evangeline turned and headed the opposite direction. She briefly toyed with the idea of going to sit down and have a bite at Mae's Diner, but the last few times she'd gone out, someone had inevitably recognized her from the news. Something dark and uncomfortably swirly had settled in her thoughts today and she didn't want to risk adding to her bad mood. A slice at Paola's Pizza would be the better bet. Hot, gooey dough and cheese was always a mood lifter, and the entire transaction at the counter would take no more than five minutes, ten tops.

She might have to head back to the glum quiet of her condo but at least she'd have pizza.

As she headed in the direction of the restaurant, that strange sense skittered over her once more. It was subtle and if she weren't so on edge she'd likely have ignored it, but was it possible she was being watched?

The public had recently made no secret of its disdain for the DA's office, and while she believed she'd acted in the best interests of the residents of Grave Gulch County, that didn't mean everyone saw it that way. She and her colleagues received threats from time to time. It was unpleasant, but it was a part of the job.

Evangeline crossed the last block for Paola's, once again trying to shake off the miserable mood. Pizza. *Pizza*, she kept reminding herself as she put one foot in front of the other.

It was only as she crossed the last alleyway before the row of storefronts that led to Paola's that something caught Evangeline's attention in the distance. Two people, struggling at the end of the alleyway. The fading summer sun backlit them both so that Evangeline couldn't clearly make out their faces, just snatches of their features as they fought.

Downturned, angry mouths as they shouted.

Slashed eyebrows.

Waving hands.

What she could clearly see was the larger form of the man struggling to hold the arms of the smaller, slender figure—a woman, dressed in a white blouse and dark slacks.

An urgent need to help rose up inside of her and she'd nearly started toward them when the distinct shape of a gun filled the man's hand. Before Evangeline could utter a word or even gurgle the start of a scream, the unmistakable sound of a gunshot rang out.

From where she stood she could see the clear stain of red spread across the white blouse, just before the small woman fell to the ground in a heap.

Rooted to the spot, Evangeline stared down the mouth of the alley in horror at what she'd just witnessed. An overwhelming urge to help warred with an innate sense of self-preservation.

It was only when that large, still-faceless figure turned toward the woman on the ground and lifted her by her feet, dragging her through the alley, that Evangeline pushed herself into motion.

Digging into her oversize bag, she fumbled through the endless depths until she finally got a grip on her cell phone. Hands shaking, she ran back in the direction of the protesters she'd seen earlier. What had felt menacing a little while ago now seemed like a haven of humanity. Scores of people who could help her and keep her safe from the dark, faceless threat at the end of that alleyway.

She clumsily fingered the screen of her phone, whose face remained locked no matter how many times she tried to swipe and enter her password. It was only as the comforting sound of voices grew louder that she finally managed to get her phone open.

With the desperate hope that she wasn't too late, she jabbed 911 into the phone and tried to summon up a calm she didn't feel.

"Nine-one-one. What's your emergency?"

As the operator's voice flowed through the line, Evangeline wondered if she would ever find that calm again.

* * *

Detective Troy Colton listened to the dispatch coming over the loudspeaker in the conference room where he and a fellow detective, Brett Shea, had holed up for a work session. As he comprehended the urgency of the summons, he tossed his pen onto the table. The move offered no comfort, but the endless screaming outside the Grave Gulch Police Department had grown tedious in the extreme and his patience had increasingly waned as the afternoon wore into evening.

And now they had a witness claiming someone was shot in an alley downtown?

He stood and pulled on his sport coat over his weapon harness. Brett had already snapped to attention, along with his K-9, Ember. The black Lab was a tracking specialist. She'd come to full alert and moved to stand beside Brett in the span of a heartbeat, despite Troy's previous assessment that she'd been fast asleep in the corner of the conference room.

"Let's swing by and ask Mary if she has any other details." Brett was already nodding as he and Ember followed Troy to the door. "We'll have her notify Melissa, as well."

The GGPD's front desk clerk was young but her sweet face and endless excitement at being a newly-wed didn't diminish her ability to be both serious and on her game at every minute. "Detective Colton," Mary Suzuki addressed Troy as he and Brett walked up. "Dispatch is still on the line. Should I patch them through?"

"Sure." Troy nodded. "And get Melissa on this, as well. I know it's the chief's day off and she's earned every bit of it, but she's going to want to know something's going on. I'll call her after Brett and I figure out what's happened."

He loved his cousin Melissa and respected her implicitly as the head of the GGPD. He'd never keep her in the dark, but it killed him to think that all her years of hard work couldn't even give her a reprieve on a night off with her fiancé, Antonio Ruiz.

"It's the job, Troy," she'd say back to him. He could already hear her voice, threaded through with responsibility, thrumming in his head.

But he still hated to ruin her evening.

Wasn't that why he and Brett had volunteered to take the late shift? The entire department had been working tirelessly to get serial killer Len Davison off the streets. He and Brett figured they'd tag-team it and see if they could spark any questions between them that might push them all in a new direction.

Mary watched him with alert eyes as he took in the details from the 911 operator. A female caller had seen another woman shot in one of the alley entrances in downtown Grave Gulch. He shifted the phone back to Mary, instructing her to stay on the line as he and Brett headed out. The affirmation from the operator that an ambulance was en route rang in his ears.

"It'll be faster there on our own two feet," Troy said as he headed for the exit. "But we need the cruiser."

He knew it was the best choice, especially if they needed to give chase. But the time it would take to get through the melee outside the precinct and into town would cost precious seconds a shooting victim didn't have.

Brett nodded. "Let's go."

Troy ignored the protesters as they ran for their vehicle. He well knew the reality of how badly the woman shot in an alley needed them. And if the thought of an innocent person lying in a pool of blood set off an unpleasant string of images of his own mother, he'd just have to push them down.

He and his sister had been much too young to have actually seen the evidence of Amanda Colton's murder. It was only years later, as a GGPD rookie cop, that he'd had access to the crime scene photos. They were painful, but a confirmation that finally put to bed what had lived in his imagination since childhood. Even with that terrible reality, his mother's sudden and violent death was a constant presence in his mind. It drove him to enter law enforcement, and he knew it did the same for all of his Colton family members in the field, as well. Sometimes bad things happened. And even worse, there were times when the bad person who did those things was never caught.

The cop lived with the cautionary tale.

The son lived with the painful reality that was his life.

Evangeline paced the sidewalk, still on the phone with the 911 dispatcher. The voice on the line was soothing and calm, but Evangeline felt neither. All she could do was stare down the mouth of the alley, imagining the dead body lying just beyond view.

She'd suggested that she go down to check for a pulse but the dispatcher had remained adamant that the police were on their way. Evangeline should remain in place or, even better, seek shelter in a nearby shop. The operator had already scolded her for leaving the sea of people farther down the sidewalk and cautioned Evangeline against going anywhere near the crime scene. A terrible sense of cowardice filled her, even as she knew the reality of the situation and the logic in the dispatcher's orders.

The victim had taken a gunshot at close range and likely hadn't survived, she knew. Add on that Evangeline had no medical training to help, and she had to face the bigger risk that the woman's assailant was still there, trapped in the alley and waiting to make his move to escape.

"Police are in range," the other woman reassured her just as the sight of two men and a K-9 came into view.

Evangeline had lived in Grave Gulch for most of her life and recognized one of the cops on sight. She'd known Detective Troy Colton for years, even though they'd only spoken a handful of times and then only in relation to cases Evangeline was prosecuting.

But oh, goodness, the man was a looker.

Tall and broad, he moved with purpose. He was fit and competent, his large frame as impressive for the solid, muscular build as the kind-hearted soul who lived inside. His eyes were a tawny, golden hazel that had the ability to actually weaken her knees and his skin was a warm brown.

Yes, she'd always had a bit of a crush on Troy. But what were the odds he'd be the one to show up here in her moment of horror and need?

"Police are on scene," Evangeline relayed to the dispatcher. "I'm going to hang up now."

The operator seemed inclined to argue but Evangeline cut the connection before she could be persuaded otherwise. The adrenaline that had pumped so fiercely through her system hit another uptick as she waved on the men now running toward her. "There! Down the alley. Hurry, please!"

"Stay here, ma'am," a man she didn't recognize ordered her as he and his dog raced down the alley.

"Please stay here, Evangeline," Troy said, no less urgently, even as he slowed. "Don't follow us."

"The killer might still be down there."

"All the more reason for you to stay put."

Troy was already off, following the other cop, so that all she could do was holler at his back. "Be careful!"

A quiet voice brought Evangeline back to the moment, even as her gaze still lingered on Troy's retreating back. "Sweetie, are you all right?"

She turned to find an older, kindly-looking woman. The stick holding her protest sign was dangling from her hand, and her eyes were full of concern. "I couldn't help but overhear you mention a killer. What's going on?"

Although Evangeline saw nothing but support and help in the woman's rheumy blue gaze, she eyed the sign warily. As an officer of the law, she believed deeply in the right to protest in peaceable assembly. As one of the objects of those protests, however, she found her inherently broadminded nature wavering.

"Um, I needed some help."

"You said 'killer.'"

"It's—" She broke off, struggling for the right words. "I thought I saw something. The police are investigating."

"Willie!" The older woman hollered to someone across the street, waving the man over with her free hand. "Get over here!"

Whatever kindness Evangeline believed she'd seen in the woman was nowhere in evidence. Instead, she saw the obvious thrill of being in the thick of things coupled with an already heightened sense of purpose that had brought her into the streets in the first place.

"Get Evan and Sally, too!" she added before the man had a chance to cross the street.

The dispatcher's words echoed around in her mind, warning her to keep her distance, while this person dragged more innocent, vulnerable people closer to the threat.

"What are you doing?"

"If a killer's on the loose, you can be damn sure I want a front seat to his arrest."

Chapter 2

Ember let out a series of hard, sharp barks as Troy crossed the last few feet into the alleyway. He stopped short at the T-shaped entrance; the sidewalk alley that fed into the broader area running behind the various shops and buildings was empty. With the precision honed over years of training, he lifted his service weapon, sweeping the area, only to find his initial assessment was correct.

"No one's here." Troy gave the alley one additional sweep before dropping his gun.

"Nope," Brett said as he ordered Ember to his side, the two of them trotting back from the end of the alleyway that gave access into downtown.

"But dispatch said a woman had been shot. There's no one here. No body." Troy reviewed the ground, quickly taking in the area that would have been visible from Evangeline's position on the main street. "No blood."

His gaze roamed the alley again, even though he knew what he'd see. He'd lived in Grave Gulch his entire life and while he hadn't spent that much time walking the town's alleyways, he knew how they were structured. The long, thin corridors served the functional aspects of the town's businesses, just wide enough for delivery trucks and garbage pickup to pass through.

A killer could have escaped through one end of the alley or the other, but dragging a body through the area would still have left a mark. Not to mention that it would have captured the attention of people back out in the main walking areas of town. Only there was nothing. No shell casings, no blood. Not even a sign of a struggle in overturned trash cans or knocked-in recycling receptacles.

"I don't understand." Brett moved close, Ember at his side. "The call was legitimate. And I realized we passed by her quick, but Evangeline looked scared out of her mind as she pointed us down the alley."

Troy had seen it, too: the black eyes, even from a quick glance, that were obviously wide and terror-filled. The strong, straight pose that had seemed crumpled up on itself somehow. Defeated, almost.

He'd known Evangeline Whittaker for quite a while now. She was strong, smart and tough as nails. Her reputation as a fair but tenacious member of the DA's staff had taken a serious hit over the past few months. A situation he could appreciate since the GGPD's had taken a hit, as well. But fair or not, their citizens had a right to be upset.

And Evangeline's actions in the courtroom sat squarely in the midst of their unhappiness.

Was it possible this was some sort of stunt? A way to drum up sympathy and to take the heat off the bad press directed her way?

As a trained detective, Troy knew he had to consider all the angles. Yet even as he did consider the very real possibility Evangeline had made the entire thing up—a situation only corroborated by the lack of evidence and indication that anything had even happened—something in him fought the suggestion. Hadn't he learned that lesson the hard way? Randall Bowe had tampered with evidence, ensuring things weren't what they appeared on the surface.

Recent events aside, he'd also spent years observing that she was incredibly good at her job. A role that, if done right, required honesty, thoroughness and overall decency. He'd always been impressed by her, on the occasions where he was part of a case she was prosecuting.

And she's gorgeous.

That lone thought whispered in, hardly subtle and completely inappropriate for the moment. Yet even as he couldn't deny the images of her that always sprang to mind when he heard mention of her, Troy pushed them aside. Especially when he considered the scared woman, shuttered behind a large floppy hat and big sunglasses, that he'd spoken to on the sidewalk.

The long waterfall of dark hair he normally pictured, along with the eyes that were the color of her hair and the firm cut of her cheekbones had no place in this situation.

Nor did they have any bearing on her possible guilt or innocence.

Which meant it was time to talk to her and find out what was going on.

Brett had already started for the alley exit with Ember, and Troy turned to follow.

Which made Brett's heavy shout, along with Ember's corresponding bark, deep and angry, that much more jarring.

Especially when his fellow detective and his K-9 partner took off at a run, straight for Evangeline.

The crowd pressed in around her. The anger Evangeline had only heard from a distance earlier as she'd observed the protesting residents had an entirely different quality as it hemmed her in from all sides. Snippets of fuming remarks and heated utterances grew louder and louder, the frustrated citizens' anger reigniting at the chance to focus on a new object.

No longer a person, she thought frantically. She was increasingly not a person to them, but rather, a target for all that ire and fear.

That's the one from the DA's office that put a killer on the streets.

I thought she was fired.

What right does she have to stand out here talking about killers when she's the reason Len Davison's on the loose?

Over and over, the remarks flew, picking up steam along with the head nods and the angry faces and the stifling press of bodies.

She hadn't told the older woman what she was waiting for or why she'd mentioned a killer to the police, but the crowd had made up a story of their own. That and the continuing fear, coursing through all of Grave Gulch, that a serial killer was on the loose.

"Excuse me! Break it up!" An authoritative voice rose up over the comments of the citizenry.

That voice was joined by a second, ordering everyone to move on and disperse.

The whirling blur of humanity slowly stood down, the individuals' movements too sluggish for Evangeline's taste. But even in the lingering panic, she couldn't deny that they were moving along. As her panic receded, she could make out faces again. Some she recognized, some she didn't, but the whirling rush of fear had stopped spinning quite so quickly.

"Evangeline. I mean, Ms. Whittaker…" Troy Colton started in. "We'd like to talk to you."

"Did you find her? Is she okay? Did you find the man who shot her?"

"Shot who?"

The other man she didn't recognize posed the question and it only managed to re-spike her waning reserves of adrenaline yet again. "The woman! The one I called nine-one-one for!"

"There's no woman, Ms. Whittaker."

She whirled to look at Troy, the face she'd so recently thought sexy and competent now set in hard lines. "What do you mean, there's no woman? I saw it. A man and woman were fighting. Right there at the end of that alley." Her hand flung out toward the entranceway between the two buildings. "He shot her. I saw the spread of blood all over her white shirt myself."

A hard shaking settled in her bones, rattling her body as the adrenaline faded, leaving nothing behind, not even the reserves of strength she'd been subsisting on for the past few weeks. "I saw it."

Troy's gaze hadn't left her face and she saw the pity that shifted his mouth from grim to something far worse. Doubt.

"There's no one there?"

He glanced at the crowd that still surrounded them. The protesters had moved back to give them room, but they hadn't left the area. And they were all within ear-shot of everything taking place.

"Why don't you come with us? We'll take your statement and try to figure out what's going on."

What was going on?

And why did she suddenly feel as if the world had fallen away beneath her feet?

Mary had radioed for additional backup and the two officers on duty who'd taken her call helped disperse the rest of the crowd. Another team was sent to scout the entire downtown area, checking for anyone on the run or bearing any resemblance to a beefy man in a hat.

Troy commandeered use of the police vehicle while the pair working the crowd stayed to make sure everyone went on their way, promising to send someone back for them. The other cops on duty only nodded, even as they assured him that they could walk, based on their proximity to the precinct.

Brett and Ember took the cruiser they'd driven over from the precinct to cover off the area around the alley and corresponding routes that fanned out from there. So it was only a matter of settling Evangeline in the back and heading to the GGPD.

He'd been deliberate and careful in his movements and she was obviously uncuffed, but it still struck him that having to sit in the back of a police cruiser might make her feel like a prisoner. She remained quiet on the quick ride, and every time he glanced at her through the rearview mirror her face remained wan and pale, her wide eyes determinedly focused on the still above-average-size crowd out and about downtown Grave Gulch on a Sunday night.

Troy considered what he knew about her, beyond his knowledge of her prowess in the courtroom.

She had been a part of the Grave Gulch County DA's office for a number of years, her case record impeccable up until the issue with the town serial killer, Len Davison.

Davison's actions had caught them all off guard, his escalation a situation the GGPD was trying desperately to manage. The entire department had gathered as much information as possible and were all working around the clock to catch the man, but his methods so far had been unpredictable.

So had his connections.

What their chief, Melissa Colton, had originally assumed was mere sloppiness coming out of the CSI department had taken a dark turn earlier in the year. Their chief forensic scientist, Randall Bowe—responsible for working some of the most challenging cases the GGPD managed—had been falsifying evidence. Or flat-out not collecting it.

Troy had seen that truth himself when he worked with Melissa to comb through Bowe's files. Or what little they could get their hands on, seeing as Bowe had fled with his hard drive and hard copies of his work back in January. The GGPD's tech guru, Ellie Bloomberg, had managed to recover quite a bit and it all supported what they'd already come to suspect: Bowe had been mishandling and destroying evidence.

They'd spent the ensuing months combing through all of Bowe's cases, searching for inconsistencies and falsehoods. All while going after a serial killer, as well as dealing with the normal amount of crime in Grave

Gulch. His cousin Jillian, a junior member of the CSI team and Bowe's scapegoat prior to his skipping town, had been putting in serious overtime, trying to find whatever she could in the files. She'd done an amazing job working through the evidence, but the department still had a lot of holes.

Holes, Troy thought as he walked Evangeline into an empty conference room, holes that had caused problems for the DA's office, too. Belief in Bowe's evidence had caught all the prosecutors short and had resulted in several mishandled cases, including Len Davison's.

And it was that mishandling that put a serial killer on the streets. A fact she would be well aware of and, likely, feel some responsibility for.

"Can I get you anything, Ms. Whittaker?"

"It's Evangeline, Troy. We know each other. And no, thank you. I'm okay."

Troy recognized the shock and fear that still mixed beneath her gaze. He walked over to the small fridge in the corner of the conference room and snagged two bottles of water despite her polite decline. "Why don't you have some water anyway."

She accepted the bottle with a quiet thank-you before her gaze tripped around the room. It was covered with notes, maps of Len Davison sightings and crime scene photos. Concern for her rode low in his gut. "I'm sorry you have to see these things."

"No, it's fine. And they're all images I've seen already."

"I guess you would have."

Although the DA's office had to request crime scene photographs through normal legal channels, it wasn't a surprise that she had seen the images of Davison's victims.

"I still can't believe this is happening in Grave Gulch." She murmured the words before firmly turning her back on the photos and taking a seat at the long conference room table.

"I'm sure people say that everywhere. Any crime is a shock, but something of this nature is what people expect to see in movies or experience in books that keep them reading late into the night. They don't expect it in their backyard."

"I guess you're right."

Although Troy, Melissa and his fellow officers had all been dealing with a lot—along with the town's considerable ire at how the evidence for Davison's case had been handled—he knew they weren't alone. He'd heard plenty of rumblings that the Grave Gulch County DA's office was having a hard time, too.

Troy's cousin, Stanton, and Stanton's new love, Dominique, had seen it firsthand. Dominique's connections as an investigative journalist, along with her contributions to the local prison with creative writing skills courses, had led her to realize one of the convicts she worked with hadn't gotten a fair trial. Charlie Hamm's case was more testament to Bowe's shoddy work, but it had been one more mark against the DA's office, too.

Well aware that blowback was pressing hard against Evangeline, Troy asked, "How have things been at work?"

"I wouldn't know. I've been on enforced leave for a few weeks now."

News traveled quickly, especially in the county's police and legal circles, but this one had been kept close to the vest. He'd heard the barest whisper Evangeline was on leave, but when he hadn't heard it over and over as a continued item of gossip, he'd assumed that she was cleared. "For how long?"

"They haven't put an end date on it yet, but my boss is quite sure I will be back in a few more weeks." Evangeline opened the bottle of water and took a long, draining sip. "I'm not so sure she's right."

"Why is that?"

"Because the good citizens of Grave Gulch County don't appreciate ADAs who put serial killers back on the streets."

"They don't appreciate police departments who keep corrupt forensic specialists on the payroll, either."

Troy wasn't quite sure why he said that, because it smacked of disloyalty and the airing of dirty laundry. As a Colton, he avoided doing both. Yet there was something about her. Something in those big eyes and slim, fragile shoulders that spoke to him and made him want to offer her some comfort.

It was interesting, because in all the time he'd known her—and, admittedly, they didn't know one another well—Troy had always seen Evangeline Whittaker as strong and capable. She was slim, but there was a core strength to her that infused her very essence.

The woman sitting opposite him looked defeated.

Which made what he had to do that much more difficult.

"Are you ready to talk about what you saw in the alley?"

"I already told you what I saw. You don't believe me."

"I didn't say that."

For the first time since he came upon her on the street, he saw a spark of fire light the depths of her eyes. "No, you don't."

"We didn't find a body, Evangeline. No sign of a struggle. No shell casings. No blood."

"I know what I saw."

"Then why don't you take me through it. Step by step, tell me what happened."

He pulled a blank notepad from the table and took notes as she began to speak. Her legal training had obviously kicked in, because she shared the information in clear, concise terms and with minimal embellishment.

Troy wrote it all down. Her decision to go out and get dinner, just to get out of her condo for a bit. The waning light as the summer afternoon turned into evening. Even the tone and tenor of the crowd protesting down near the GGPD. She captured it all.

It was only when she described what she saw in the alley that Troy's doubts crept back in. He wanted to believe her. The fear in her voice and the rising tension as she described the man and woman struggling were real. Just as real as the tremors that gripped her voice when she recounted that man pulling a gun.

"She was wearing a white shirt, Troy. I saw the blood spreading on it. I know what I saw."

"Can you describe what he looked like?"

"Had a ball cap on and he was arguing with her. Yelling. He looked so angry. He was bigger, and clearly male from his size and build. And in the way he had a grip on her, I could tell they were fighting."

"Could you hear what they were fighting about?"

"No." She shook her head. "I just knew they were fighting."

Troy flipped through the pages of notes. The steady cadence of her voice still whispered in his ears as he reread the words. Again, he took in the clear, concise descriptions. Her consistency in narrating the scene as

ality of knowing Len Davison was out on the
he had always taken pride in working hard at
d being a model employee. Yet over the past
hs, all of that hard work and all of that effort
ike it was for nothing.

uestions she had seen other people's eyes. The
s that had rattled around in her own mind.
now, the questions she saw in Troy Colton's se-
azel gaze.

was a good cop. A good detective. She had
around him long enough to know those things
ue. She had to trust him, even if his initial re-
left her feeling vulnerable and alone.

dog didn't pick up any scent at all?" she fi-
ked.

not based on Brett's text."

oesn't make sense. Any of it. I know what I
d even if the woman did survive, there would
evidence of it. Troy, the man shot her at point-
nge."

ite that weird sense of being followed and the
iveness of feeling trapped in her own home,
ine *knew* what she had seen. She didn't doubt
How did you doubt watching two people fight
ther one pull out a gun and shoot the other?
s the minutes ticked past, the inevitable ques-
pt in.

here some sort of stain already on that white
mething she hadn't noticed at first glance.
hat fight been some sort of strange role-playing
the two of them?

rse, was it just two people, fed up and irritated
that had been going on in Grave Gulch, sim-

well as what had transpired before she happened upon
the alley. Even her account of the altercation had the
distinct marks of someone who was skilled at noticing
other people.

Abstract recognition of clothing. A sense of proportion between the two people having an argument. The
ability to read and recognize they were fighting, without hearing their actual words.

She had been an observer. An astute one, too.

So where was the blood? A body? Or a sign one had
ever been in that very spot she described?

His phone buzzed and Troy dug it out of his pocket.
Brett's name filled the screen above his text.

Headed to precinct. Ember never found a scent.

It figured.

One more odd detail in an evening full of them. He'd
spent some time in his career around K-9s but hadn't
been in such close proximity to one on active duty until
Brett joined the GGPD a few months prior. He'd easily
seen the bond between Brett and Ember. Even more,
he'd come to understand just how well trained the animal was. If she didn't pick up the scent of blood or gun
residue it was because there wasn't any to find.

"What's that look for?" Evangeline's voice was low
but he heard the threads of suspicion and doubt all the
same.

"My partner's K-9 wasn't able to scent any evidence
in the alley or in the streets surrounding the area."

"I know what I saw."

Troy stared down at his notes again, surprised to see
where he'd abstractly doodled on the words. The phrase
"white shirt, blood spreading" was underlined and he'd

written and rewritten the word *blood*, emphasizing its presence on the page.

Much as he wanted to believe her—and he knew himself well enough to know that somewhere deep inside, he did believe her—it wasn't that easy. Nor was it going to be easy to convince his fellow officers as well as his chief that this was a lead they needed to follow.

But as he sat there, staring into the dark depths of Evangeline Whittaker's eyes, Troy recognized the truth. This woman needed his help. He'd spent his life wishing there had been someone there to help his mother in her moment of need.

He'd be damned if he left Evangeline alone in hers.

chilling r
streets. S
her job a
few mon
had felt l

The q
question

And
rious, h

He
worked
were tr
sponse

"Th
nally a

"N

"It
saw. A
be som
blank

Des
oppres
Evange
herself
and an

Yet
tions c

Was
shirt?

Had
betwee

Or w
with al

Chapter

He didn't believe her.

Over and over, that truth bore
Evangeline wanted to scream with
all. She knew what she'd seen.

What she'd witnessed.

That woman had been shot in
that left no question murder was th

But there was no evidence. N
Nothing that would indicate what
tually happened.

Although adrenaline still pu
heavy, syrupy waves, Evangeli
focus. Yes, she had been edgy
weeks. That feeling of being wat
pressive and cloying. Not to men

She also had to acknowledge
tremendous amount of stress w

ply having a fight? But even then, the dog would have found a scent.

"Why don't we look at this from a different angle?" Troy said. "Was there anybody else around you when you saw the altercation in the alleyway?"

"No, there wasn't. I was avoiding the protest happening at the opposite end of town and decided to go a different direction to get a slice of pizza."

"So, no one was near you?"

"No, not at all," she said.

"What made you look down the alleyway at all?"

Evangeline recognized the tactic. She had used it herself, many times, questioning a witness. It was an effort to get her to re-create the scene, and also give Troy an opportunity to see where there might be holes in her story.

"I understand how suspicious this looks. But I know what I saw. You're not going to trip me up or get me to say something different."

"That wasn't my goal," Troy said.

"Oh no?"

"No, actually I'm trying to see if we can find anyone to corroborate your story. Because while I recognize we haven't found a lick of evidence, I saw your face when Brett and I arrived. And I know you, and I don't believe you're making up fake calls to nine-one-one about women being shot in alleys."

"Oh."

"Yeah. Oh."

Evangeline considered his words, and that small moment of heat that had risen in his eyes when she had suggested he was trying to trip her up. Was it possible he *did* believe her?

Or more to the point, that he was on her side?

It had only been the past few weeks, since she was put on extended leave, that Evangeline had realized just how alone she was. Her job was consistently busy and she took a deep pride in doing it well, but the time spent with her own thoughts had been rather revealing.

She talked to her mother regularly, on their twice-weekly calls, but those remained light and airy, with Evangeline unwilling to say anything that might ruffle her. Her mother had spent far too many years dealing with the fallout of her father's behavior, and Evangeline had no wish to add to the now stress-free life she led post-divorce.

Her father was different. They exchanged bland, cordial emails and the rare phone call to celebrate an annual holiday. A decision that suited them both but kept her life somewhat stress-free, as well.

Or, it had.

The Davison case and the truth that had come out of Randall Bowe's deception had upended every bit of order she had managed to create in her adult life. Order that she now realized was dependent on keeping others at arm's length. A fact that made the creepy sensation of being watched or the long, endless days with nothing to do suddenly overwhelming.

"Why don't I drive you home?" Troy's offer interrupted the direction of her thoughts and she was grateful for it.

"You don't have to do that."

"Sure I do. I can swing by and get you something to eat, too. You never did get dinner."

The offer was thoughtful and a reminder of all she'd always believed about the good and upstanding Troy Colton. He was a consummate professional, focused on his job, but also unfailingly kind. A man who took care of others with a simple ease that often went unnoticed.

Only, she had noticed.

She'd noticed him often, burying her little crush on the attractive detective with a focus on work and a line of questions on whatever case they might be discussing. It would never do to show that side of herself. The one that was woman first, lawyer second.

She had been raised in a home that had proven women couldn't have it all. She'd taken that learning into her own life and career and had never deviated from those beliefs.

It was only now, when she'd been forced to question all she held close, that she had to wonder if she'd been wrong all along.

Because it felt incredibly good to have a nice, thoughtful man to lean on.

Troy waited until Evangeline was buckled into the passenger seat of his SUV before he turned on the ignition.

Although there were still a few things he wanted to look into on the Davison and Bowe cases, based on the way his evening had gone Troy knew it was time to call it a day. He had connected with Brett shortly before heading out of the precinct to let him know he was done for the day, and Brett's response was all Troy could want in a partner. After asking after Evangeline, Brett had promised he was going to put another couple of hours in on the Davison case and would follow up with an email on any notes he made.

They weren't formal partners yet, Brett's recent arrival in Grave Gulch ensuring he was still getting the lay of the land in the department, but the two men had found a good, working rhythm with each other. Troy knew the addition set Melissa's mind at ease and his own thoughts had improved since he'd realized he had such a qualified person to help work through various cases.

It made it easier to leave tonight and take Evangeline home. He'd decided it was important to do that in his own car instead of in a police vehicle. As he pulled out of his parking spot, he briefly glanced at her face. She looked considerably less tense than when she had sat in the back of the cruiser.

"What are you hungry for?"

"You really don't have to get me dinner."

"I think I do. Especially since I'm stopping for something myself."

"Okay. Well, what do you want to eat, then?"

He fought the smile at the ease with which she'd shifted the conversation—*just like a lawyer*—and went with honesty on his part. "A burger is always a good idea."

"That is an excellent point. A burger sounds great."

And he knew a local place that did pretty good carryout. Troy dialed them from his in-car dash, his phone quickly connecting. In a matter of minutes, he'd ordered two cheeseburgers and added the fries for good measure.

Based on the directions she'd shared, it wasn't far to Evangeline's condo and he was grateful for the extra time needed on the food prep to observe her a bit more. After navigating his way out of downtown, Troy turned into the parking lot of the burger joint. Cutting the ignition, he turned to face her.

"How have you been holding up?"

She hesitated for the briefest of seconds, as if weighing how much she was going to say, before she spoke. The trembling, upset tones he'd heard back at the precinct had faded, replaced by a layer of something he could only interpret as resignation.

"I'm fine. It's been a bit jarring not waking up on a schedule every day, but I'm doing okay."

"Honestly, I was a bit surprised when you mentioned that you were still out of the office. I heard the lightest rumblings when you went on leave but since I hadn't heard anything else about it, I'd assumed you were cleared to return."

"You did?"

"Yes. Which is good because it means your personal business is being kept private. As it should be."

"It doesn't make it any less embarrassing."

Troy heard those notes of frustration once again lining her voice and he had to admit he would feel the same if the position was reversed. For him, being a cop was a calling. He had worked so hard to make detective and strived every day to make sure that he lived up to the responsibility of the badge.

While he knew a lot of his professional drive came from emotionally processing his mother's murder, it wasn't just Amanda Colton's premature death when he'd been just a child that had affected him. The Coltons believed in justice, honesty and the value of hard work. It was important that they conveyed back to the public that their trust was placed in capable hands.

He wore the badge with honor and he had learned early in his career that others in the GGPD felt the same. He had certainly always believed that of his counterparts in the DA's office, as well.

It was what made the situation with Randall Bowe so terrible. Yes, the man might be CSI, but he still had the responsibilities of a cop. Of protection. Of honesty. Of integrity.

And he'd betrayed all of them.

Evangeline let out a light sigh. "Embarrassing or not, thank you for telling me that. I assumed everyone knew about my situation."

Her words pulled Troy out of the angry thoughts that always accompanied any mental wanderings about Bowe. The man had proven himself scum and it was Troy's biggest wish to see him arrested and prosecuted to the full extent of the law. "You're welcome."

"You look sort of upset for a guy who's about to eat a juicy cheeseburger. You want to talk about it?"

Troy shifted in his seat to look fully at Evangeline. She still had the big floppy hat on but had tucked her sunglasses away somewhere. The look didn't diminish her beauty. Instead, the long waves of dark hair that had escaped her hat now fell down her back, soft, enticing and eminently touchable.

Shaking off the thoughts he had no business having, he keyed in on her observation. "Was I that obvious?"

"Kind of. Your face got a little squinty and your lips fell into a straight line. I figured something upset you."

"What isn't upsetting lately? Something is happening in Grave Gulch and it has been since the start of the year. My sister's little boy, Danny, was kidnapped. Twice." Troy shook his head, the mental anguish that Desiree had lived through not once, but twice, still fresh in his memory. "Then there's the obvious situation with Davison and with Bowe. But even beyond the two of them, there have been some incredibly strange things that have happened to my cousins, too. There's this general sense of unrest and unease and it's becoming increasingly difficult to process."

It felt good to say the words. To actually let out all of the things that had been bothering him the past several months. But it was because it felt good that Troy realized he should say nothing.

Police business was one thing. Family business was another. And the Coltons had certainly dealt with their fair share of both. His nephew's recent kidnapping as well as his cousin's run-in with a drug kingpin. It had all felt overwhelming at times.

Evangeline's voice was gentle and pulled him back from the dark direction of his thoughts. "Although I haven't been as closely in the loop as usual, I was very happy to hear that everything worked out okay for your sister. And also happy to hear she's engaged."

"Thank you. Desiree had a tough time there for a while. Her son, Danny, was at the heart of it all, at serious risk as a kidnapping target. Stavros has changed her life. Both their lives."

"I can't imagine anything scarier for a mother. Or for your family."

He saw the genuine compassion in her face and recognized that even in the midst of her own troubles that day, Evangeline could still think of others.

Wasn't that one of the things he was struggling with?

Of all the things they had discovered about Randall Bowe over the past few months, his lack of compassion for others had been the worst.

Recently, some of the GGPD had noticed a pattern—that Bowe's behavior appeared tied to the ending of his marriage. Although they were still technically married, the relationship was now over. Melissa's discussion with Bowe's wife had confirmed that, his wife confessing that things had gone bad after her infidelity.

The GGPD had determined that it was that betrayal

that indicated which cases Bowe played with in the CSI files. A cheating spouse or a relationship gone sour? Consistently, Bowe tampered with those files.

It indicated someone who not only lacked compassion for others, but who could only assuage his own feelings of anger by hurting other people.

Danny's initial kidnapping, from the wedding of Mary Suzuki, had been the first clue that ultimately broke the case wide open. The note that came after his nephew's kidnapping had been very clear. The GGPD needed to reopen a case that had been handled improperly if they wanted the boy back. The kidnapping was an act of desperation by the grandmother of a woman whose case had been mishandled from the start. Everleigh Emerson had been innocent of her estranged husband's murder, but the evidence had been fairly clear-cut against her.

Or it had *appeared* clear-cut.

In the rush to get Danny back, Troy and the rest of the GGPD had listened to the warning in the note and done what was asked of them. From there, it was only a matter of reading Randall Bowe's files more closely, and then they'd begun to find inconsistencies.

As tactics went, Troy was still seething over the approach taken to use his nephew as bait, but no one could argue with the outcome. Bowe's crimes had been uncovered. Everleigh was innocent of murdering her husband, had never cheated on the man as Bowe had believed, and remained equally innocent of any involvement in Danny's kidnapping. A fact that had brought her even closer to his family.

When the man who had actually murdered her husband came after Everleigh, Troy's cousin Clarke had put all of his PI skills into finding the real killer and keeping her safe. So safe that Everleigh was about to become a Colton, her and Clarke's intense time together having led to love.

He couldn't help but compare that situation to Evangeline's.

Confused at the direction of his thoughts—she was hardly a victim like Everleigh—Troy brushed them aside with brisk efficiency. It was fine to think this woman was attractive. It was another to let those thoughts of her cloud his judgment when it came to handling cases.

Instead, he fell back on his training and the polite veneer he used in any and all situations. The "Colton polish," as he'd heard fellow townsfolk refer to it, never failed. "Thank you for that. I know my sister really struggled to find any sense of peace and normalcy for a while. It helped that the motive for kidnapping Danny was discovered and dealt with."

"How? I mean, I know he was kidnapped but I never heard the reason why."

Troy was surprised Evangeline didn't know the story. "I guess the GGPD and the DA's office aren't talking as much as I thought."

"Maybe that's part of the problem," Evangeline muttered.

"You think?"

For the first time since he came upon her outside the alleyway, Troy saw a spark of the Evangeline he knew and admired. It lit the depths of her eyes and framed her voice in a layer of passion and determination. "We're matched resources, right? Law enforcement captures the criminals and the DA's office prosecutes them. Yet here are two very intimate issues that neither of us knew details about. You barely knew I was on leave, save for a few light whispers. And I had no idea your nephew's case had been solved. Twice."

"I'm sure Arielle was trying to give you your privacy with respect to your leave." Arielle Parks, the well-respected Grave Gulch County DA, was under a ton of scrutiny herself. He could only imagine she wanted to shield her staff as much as possible.

"And I am more grateful for that than I can say. But it still doesn't change the fact that our organizations should be talking more."

He was prevented from saying anything by the ping on his phone that said the order was ready.

As he got out of the car to go retrieve their burgers, Troy couldn't help but take Evangeline's impassioned words to heart. It had meant a lot to him to sit and talk with her, openly and honestly, about all that had happened in Grave Gulch since the new year.

More than he would have ever thought possible.

Evangeline directed Troy through town and back toward her condo complex. She'd lived in the elegant building for about three years now, her home a product of years of saving as much as possible and then the satisfaction of building a place in the world that was all hers.

She directed him to a parking area in front of her building and then quickly got out of the car before he could come around to help her. It was hard to explain, but she felt as if they had reached some sort of intimacy as they sat and talked while waiting for the burgers. She knew Troy Colton, obviously, but didn't actually *know* him. To talk the way they had, in the car and before, while they sat at the precinct, had meant something. Even there, he was in full cop mode but he never made her feel badly.

That ability to talk, engage and, ultimately, to understand—that was a skill. One she knew was incredibly valuable for someone in law enforcement. Because in the end, wasn't that all anyone wanted? A fair shake. The feeling of being listened to.

The feeling that they mattered.

Of course, she acknowledged to herself, it also helped that she wasn't accused of anything.

Yet, a small voice whispered in her ear.

"Evangeline?"

She turned to see Troy's expectant face staring up at the building. "Sorry, I was woolgathering. I'm right down this way. The third door."

"I guess I've been a bit presumptive." Troy held up the brown paper bag. "But I assumed we would have dinner together."

"Oh, yeah, sure, that would be great."

It's not a date. It's not a date. It's not a date. She mentally whispered those words to herself over and over as she unlocked the door, flipped on the lights and invited him into her home.

"Here, let me take that."

"Oh, no, ma'am, this is door-to-door service. Just direct me to the kitchen."

She smiled at that and pointed down the small hallway that led to her kitchen. "Right down there, then."

It was simple, but his silliness was enough to set her back at ease. This wasn't a date and she was perfectly capable of sharing a meal with a man. But that didn't mean it couldn't feel nice to have a houseguest. Someone to talk to.

Something that would break the monotony of what she had been living with for the past few weeks.

Evangeline followed him into the kitchen, heading

for the cabinet where she kept plates. Troy had already torn open the bag, the scents of cheeseburgers and fries filling the room with a delicious aroma that had her stomach growling.

"That smells amazing. Burgers were an inspired idea."

"They usually are." Troy smiled. "I also find they help on the days when I had a really big adrenaline rush and need an energy pick-me-up. Are you doing okay?"

The concern was completely unexpected. "Yeah, I'm okay."

"All right. I just wanted to check." He turned back to the burgers, busy setting the wax paper–wrapped halves onto plates.

"I can tell by your tone of voice that you don't believe me." The words came out more accusatory than she'd intended, yet Evangeline found she couldn't quite pedal them back.

"I believe you. My question is if you believe yourself."

"What is that supposed to mean?"

"You've been under a lot of stress. It's okay not to have all the answers, or to be perfect."

Although she had appreciated the sharing of confidences in the car, this felt like a bit too much intimacy. And it cut a little too close to home. "You don't know anything about my life, Troy. I'm telling you I'm okay, because *I am* okay."

She eyed him but refused to engage any further. She'd spent her life trying to one-up her father in conversation and when confronted like this, all she wanted to do was back off and curl up into herself.

In the courtroom, she never backed down.

In her personal life, she backed away so quickly she left proverbial tire tracks in the dirt.

"All right, then." He shrugged before handing her a plate. "You're okay."

The "damn right" was on the tip of her tongue but she held it back, refusing to give him any satisfaction.

Settling in at the table, she had just pulled a napkin onto her lap when his phone went off. He set his plate on the table and dug his phone out, frowning as he stared down at the face. "Excuse me."

Troy left the kitchen, all signs of the lighthearted dinner companion who'd followed her into the house vanishing.

All she saw was the stiff and stoic back of a cop.

How had their conversation turned so quickly? One minute he was teasing her about door-to-door service and the next she was backing away like she'd been stung by a rattlesnake. Of course, she couldn't quite forget the personal snapback in between.

Way to welcome your guest, Whittaker.

She left her burger on her plate, unwilling to start eating before he came back, but she did sneak a fry as his words drifted toward her from the hallway.

"What did CSI say about the alley?"

CSI?

He hadn't mentioned putting CSI on anything. Sure, Detective Shea and his K-9 had looked into the surrounding area but they'd sent more cops down there, too?

And what would they have back in hand so quickly? She understood the processing of evidence took time. No matter how riveting a TV crime drama, securing evidence simply didn't work the way it was portrayed in entertainment. Add on the fact that Sunday night at the GGPD wasn't exactly crawling with CSI experts on duty and his questions to whomever was on the other end of the phone were a puzzle.

It was only when he walked back into the kitchen, grim-faced, that Evangeline felt those frissons of fear she'd finally managed to force back on the ride home rise up again in full force.

"What happened?"

"CSI combed the alley for evidence."

"You didn't tell me that." The accusations were back but Evangeline didn't care. Was this the way he operated? A few nice words and dinner, all while keeping a suspect on the hook?

For the first time, she saw the heat and sparks of anger fire up under her direct gaze. "I didn't need to tell you that. It's part of my job and as an assistant district attorney, you're well aware of that. In fact, if I hadn't sent out a CSI team your office would be on my ass for violating proper protocol."

He was right.

Damn it all, he was 100 percent right.

And still, she felt a tiny sting of betrayal she couldn't quite define.

"And suddenly CSI works overtime on a Sunday night?"

"They do when a serial killer is on the loose in my jurisdiction."

Damn. Once again, he had an answer. And once again, she had to admit it was the right one. More than right. It was proof the GGPD was determined to take any and all action to get a killer off the streets.

"Our jurisdiction, Troy. We're in this together."

He nodded, even as his face remained grim. "Yes. Ours."

She appreciated his ready agreement, even as she couldn't get past the broader issue at hand. "Killer or no killer, CSI can't process evidence that quickly."

Troy sighed but his gaze never left hers. Never dropped in the split second before he delivered bad news. "They can when there isn't any evidence to process."

Chapter 4

Troy hated to have such irrefutable proof, but he knew the investigators and was sure they had done a thorough job.

He'd always believed in them, but Randall Bowe's betrayal had lit a fire under the entire team. Even though no one else in Grave Gulch's CSI division was suspected of colluding with Bowe, they all had something to prove.

And they'd all been working overtime to prove it.

"It's just like Detective Shea said. Before." Evangeline's voice was low, the distinct notes of defeat lining her words. "His K-9 didn't catch a scent, and CSI is saying nothing is there, too."

"Yes."

"Which means you think I'm lying."

"No, I didn't say that."

"You're thinking it, which is the same thing."

Her burger and fries still sat on her plate, untouched. Dark circles rimmed the fine skin beneath her eyes and a defeated slump rounded her shoulders.

"No, I'm not. Quit putting words in my mouth and quit assuming you know what I'm thinking."

"What else could you be thinking?" she asked. "I called in a murder and not only did you not find a body, but you haven't found a bit of evidence that suggests there ever was one."

She was right. Empirically he knew that. Yet bodies didn't suddenly disappear. And well-respected members of the community who worked in positions of authority simply didn't go around seeing murders where none existed. "Then something else is going on."

"What else could possibly be going on? I know what I saw, Troy. I know what murder victims look like. And I saw one. Yet there's no one there."

"Then we figure out the angle."

"What angle? There is no angle."

He sat down as if he hadn't heard her. She was on edge and he'd spent enough time around people to know that part of defusing a tense situation was to avoid further engagement. This woman had a great legal brain and sooner or later it was going to get its way past her anxiety.

In the meantime...

Well, in the meantime he had a new focus. And that started with getting some food into her.

"You're going to eat right *now*?" Her high-pitched voice was just shy of a screech, which only reinforced his tactic.

"Yes, I'm hungry. You should be, too."

"How am I going to eat?"

He shoveled in a fry and kept his tone light. Irritatingly so, if he had to guess. "One bite at a time."

"Why?"

"To keep your strength up," he said around a mouthful of burger.

The wariness never left her eyes but she did sit back down at the table. With a small headshake she reached for a fry. And he didn't miss the way her eyes fell to half-mast as crispy potato and salty coating hit her tongue.

Good.

Hell, it was damn good. And getting some food into her was a step in the right direction.

He figured they might be out of the woods when she picked up her burger and took a bite.

"It's good, isn't it?"

She eyed him narrowly over the burger, before nodding. "Yeah, it is."

"Never underestimate the power of food."

"Is that a rule of the law?"

"No, it's a rule of my stepmother." He couldn't help but smile as he pictured Leanne Palmer Colton standing in the middle of the family kitchen. "She always says very little can't be helped by a bit of food and a good night's sleep."

"She's a wise woman."

"Yes, she is."

Leanne was amazing. She had come into their father's life, and by extension, his and Desiree's, before they even knew they needed her. But she found a way to reach them—all of them—through the nearly paralyzing grief of Amanda McMahon Colton's horrifying murder.

A big heart and love that overflowed from it had

been Leanne's secret. She'd fallen in love with all of them, she'd told Troy once, and knew that her life had become complete when he and his father and sister had come into hers.

It was a lesson he'd carried with him. That even in the midst of sadness and tragedy, something good and meaningful could flourish and grow. It never diminished the pain of losing his mother, but through Leanne's love, he had found a way through it. They all had.

Even now, she was the first to call him on the anniversary of his mother's death and she'd made sure that photos of Amanda and his father, Geoff, were in the family home, and on the mantel. They sat alongside photos of the family they'd raised together. Troy and Desiree, Geoff and Leanne's two biological daughters, Annalise and Grace, and their adoptive son, Palmer, had all grown up knowing they were loved.

They were a family, Troy thought with no small amount of happiness and deep-seated pride. One that had been born as much as made.

Through love.

His father was a good man and Troy had always known Geoff would do anything to keep him and Desiree safe. But finding Leanne had made all the difference. Her generosity of spirit was a gift and Troy knew that he was beyond fortunate for it. All his siblings were.

"You speak of her with such love. You're quite lucky. Not everyone speaks of a step-parent in that way."

"I am lucky. Desiree and I talk about that a lot. How we kind of hit the stepmom jackpot with Leanne."

His mother's murder was something that was well known around Grave Gulch, and he had no doubt that Evangeline knew the story. Yet Troy still felt compelled to add, "There are times I think my mother sent her straight to us. That somehow she knew we never would have survived without Leanne's love."

"That's a very beautiful way to look at it."

"I think it's true."

"I think you're right." Evangeline opened her mouth, then closed it again, as if she were hesitant to say something. Troy waited, giving her a moment, curious to see if she'd continue.

He was pleased when she started in on her story. "When I was little, my grandmother from the Philippines came to visit. She told me a story of a small bird that lived in her village growing up."

She stopped again, seeming to question herself, but Troy waved her on. "Please. I'd like to hear it."

"She said the bird was little but very beautiful, its feathers plumed in rich shades of blue and purple. And she often heard it singing."

Troy set his burger down and reached for a napkin to wipe his fingers. He sensed this conversation was important to her and felt that she needed his full attention.

"A rash of crows had come to the village and one morning she found the small bird on the ground, hurt and on the verge of death from an attack of the larger birds." Evangeline played with one of her fries, taking a small bite as she summoned the words of her story. "My grandmother took the bird in, terrified it would die but unable to leave it alone. She cared for it and nursed it back to health."

"That's very caring of her." And not a surprise based on what he knew of Evangeline. She was known for her strong preparation in the courtroom. She fought hard, but fairly and compassionately, seeking outcomes that would help someone find the road back to society, instead of away.

"It was caring, but in a lot of ways it wasn't enough. The bird grew strong again, but it wouldn't sing, and its feathers faded, their brilliance turning a mottled, grayish color.

"It was as if the attack had taken away its spirit. I remember being so sad when she told me that story. Because I could picture the bird in my mind and could feel his pain."

"It's part of life."

"I suppose it is, but I still thought it was sad. That even after being saved, the bird couldn't quite find its way." She took a deep breath. "But fortunately, that wasn't all. My grandmother cared for the bird for many months. She never heard it sing again, but she did see it was healing. And one day she was on her morning walk and found another bird, not nearly as broken as the colorful one, but still in need of help."

Although he had a sense of where the story was going, Troy was captivated, and wanted to hear to the end of her tale.

"She nursed the new bird, splinting its wing and giving it the proper time to heal. Through it all, she kept the two birds near each other in side-by-side cages. As days passed, the bird with the broken wing got better. And so did the colorful bird who needed to heal."

She leaned forward and laid a hand on his. "It's a gift, that sort of love. Companionship. Understanding. And the time to heal. So I believe you when you say that your mother sent Leanne."

"Thank you for that. And I agree with you."

Evangeline sat back in her chair, her eyes far away with a memory.

"Is your grandmother still alive?"

"No." She shook her head. "She died the year after that visit. My mother was devastated to lose her. Even more devastated when my father wouldn't allow her to go to the funeral."

"Why not?"

He saw it then. Despite the myriad of emotions, he'd seen cross Evangeline's face throughout the evening, that one was new.

And the sign to back off was crystal clear.

"Not everyone is fortunate to have an understanding companion like that colorful bird."

Although his mother's death was a painful subject, because it had happened when he was a toddler, he'd spent his entire life dealing with it and discussing it. Troy recognized in Evangeline's quiet the truth of her situation, as an adult living with the aftereffects of trauma. For her, there existed a desperate need to keep that suffering buried, because it lived much too close to the surface most of the time.

He was curious about her experience but respected her privacy all the same.

And wondered what had made her feel comfortable enough to tell him the story of the bird and her grand-mother's passing in the first place.

Although she'd intended to only eat a few bites, Evangeline stared down at her now-empty plate in wonder. She had no idea how he did it, but Troy had managed to get her talking, weaving from one subject to the next, and enjoying her meal throughout.

There were those few strained moments, when she'd spoken of her family. Why she'd even brought up her grandmother's death she had no idea. Grandmother's

passing had nothing to do with the story of the two healing birds, yet she'd blithely followed that story with another even more personal one.

Why?

Even as she mentally berated herself, she couldn't
deny his kindness in moving their conversation on to
something new after she'd so obviously shut down.
Her father's mercurial anger and unfair edicts over her
mother weren't something she discussed with anyone.
She didn't even discuss them with her mother any longer, the years of living with that unprompted rage having done their fair share of damage to Dora Whittaker's
nerves.

And to her own.

Yet something about sharing a meal with Troy and
the words seemed to spill out, almost of their own ac-
cord.

Was it because she felt a kindred spirit in him?

She knew the story of his mother's death. There were
few in Grave Gulch—and certainly no one around law
enforcement—who were unaware of the terrible tragedy. Not only was Amanda McMahon Colton murdered
when her two children were small, but her killer had
never been found. It was a reality that haunted the family and something she'd heard spoken of more than once.

Amanda's death had somehow galvanized the
Coltons. It was as if they all understood that justice
wasn't always served and it was essential to do everything you could to work for that outcome. As a result,
most of them had gone into law enforcement of some
sort. And still, despite every effort, there were cases
that remained open and cold, a frustrating reality for
the loved ones left behind.

"So Danny is enjoying being spoiled even more than

usual," Troy continued their thread of conversation, pulling Evangeline back from the wayward direction of her thoughts. "My father and Leanne do a darn fine job with their grandson, but now that Stavros is in his life he's a very happy toddler."

She knew Troy spoke of Stavros Makros, the ER doctor who was now engaged to his sister. He'd talked of the man throughout their dinner and it was easy to see Troy genuinely liked his sister's fiancé.

"And Uncle Troy doesn't spoil his nephew?" Evangeline said with a smile. She could only assume what a wonderful experience it was to have nieces and nephews. She didn't have any as she had no siblings, but the way people talked about the little ones in their lives had always made her wish for some tiny relatives of her own to spoil.

Or even children of her own. A fact she quickly shut down at the reality she had no partner to make a family with. Something she'd always hoped would change but, as of yet, hadn't.

"You found me out." He lifted his hands and shrugged his shoulders, the move enough to pull her from her dour thoughts. "I just can't resist that little guy."

"Although you and I have known each other through work for a long time, I can't say the same about your sister. Is she in law enforcement, too?"

"Desiree is an artist. She does some part-time sketch work for the GGPD. She was essential to catching the kidnapper last month who went after Danny."

"How so?"

"It was all in the eyes."

"Desiree was able to capture that in her sketch?"

Troy nodded. "Amazing, isn't it? But yes. Although

heated words, she had no idea. But in that moment
as so nice to simply be.

With him.

The quiet tension spun out, Troy's gaze never leaving
rs. And it was only as she was about to move away
at his hand came over her shoulder, pulling her close.
e bent his head, his lips finding hers on a quiet sigh.

The kiss was unexpected and lovely, that sigh feath-
ring over her lips on a warm exhale of breath. She
eaned into it, moving closer into his arms, surprised
at the immediate flare of desire that filled her. Yes,
she'd been attracted to him. For a long time she'd both
admired him and had a small crush on him. But this…

It was incendiary.

The immediate spark to flame of heat and need that
flowed effortlessly between them.

The feel of his large hands as they gripped her shoulders, pulling her even closer.

The touch of his tongue to her lips as he sought entrance to her mouth.

It was overwhelming and heady, a fantasy coming
to life.

And as she opened her lips against his, Evangeline
new this moment in time was everything.

Troy flowed with the waves of desire that battered
m, head to toe and back again. He felt their power in
e press of his lips against hers. The feel of her body
her lithe frame fit against him. The softness of her
n as his fingertips ran, featherlight, against her nape.
She was beautiful.

And, for the moment, every fantasy he'd ever had
ut Evangeline Whittaker was coming true. Right
e in the middle of her kitchen.

the woman had a face covering on, Desiree could see
her eyes before she tried to grab Danny in the park.
When it happened again, during an incident in the hospital, Desiree was close enough to capture the look in
her sketch."

"And that saved your nephew?"

"It was Stavros again. He recognized the instability
in the woman and understood they were dealing with
someone battling mental illness. It was scary, but his
medical training and his own personal experience ensured he knew the signs."

"His own experience?" It felt like an intrusive question, yet it also seemed right to ask. Natural, even, as
their conversation had unfolded throughout dinner.

"Stavros lost his own child several years ago. His ex-
wife was unstable, a situation made worse when Stavros was awarded full custody. She kidnapped their child
while in the middle of an episode, killing them both in
a car accident during a snowstorm."

"I am so sorry." Those words often felt so useless,
yet she meant every bit. "To live through that must have
been awful."

"I don't think anyone ever gets over that. But I think
the fact that he's moving on with his life—" Troy hesitated "—and living again…it matters."

"It does."

Before she even realized his intention, Troy stood,
dish in hand, and reached across the table to take hers.

"Oh, you don't have to do that."

"It's my pleasure. I haven't had such a lovely dinner companion in a long time. It's been nice to sit and
talk for a bit."

"I know what you mean. I've been—" She broke off,
not comfortable with how sad and lonely she sounded.

Or how sad and lonely she *would* sound if she expressed how desperately she'd craved conversation these past few weeks. So instead, Evangeline settled for polite platitudes. They were safe. Easy. And they didn't smack of those overtones of neediness that were about to come roaring out of her mouth once more. "It's nice to have a professional discussion that can also blend with the personal."

"I agree. And although I didn't want to spoil your dinner, I would like to get your take on Len Davison."

"You mean the psychopathic criminal I let go free?"

And there they were, right back to desperate and needy.

Troy had obviously keyed in on her words, his eyebrows slashing over that magnetic hazel gaze as he turned toward her after snapping the water on at the kitchen sink. "You didn't let him go free."

"I was the one who prosecuted him. Ineffectively. That rests on me."

"Actually, it rests on Randall Bowe. In the information he falsified. In the records he deliberately didn't keep."

"Then I should have dug deeper."

"On what? A man who had no history of criminal activity? One who also hadn't shown signs of nefarious behavior?"

He twisted the water off, his economical motions tense. "Tell me, Evangeline. Dug deeper how? You relied on the information that was given to you. Information from the GGPD you should have been able to trust."

"It's not enough. I hold myself to a higher standard."

"And you think I don't? You think the rest of the GGPD doesn't? You think Arielle Parks as the DA of Grave Gulch County doesn't?"

There it was again. That flash of ___ gested Troy Colton wasn't at all fine wit___ were going in his jurisdiction.

"I know you hold yourself to a very ___ My comments weren't about you, nor we___ to insult you."

"I know that, Evangeline. That's my poin___ up against an enemy we never expected. A___ got inside our garden. It's humbling and it's fi___ But that doesn't mean you stop fighting."

All the internal struggles she had battled sin___ on leave from her job had made her feel so lonel___ been dealing with those accusations of failure all___ struggling with the consequences of her legal dec___ and their impact on the community. And other th___ few conversations with Arielle, not once in all that tim___ had she experienced any kind of kinship with others. But here, now, talking to Troy, was different.

For the first time in quite a while she felt unders___ And that meant more than she could say.

"Thank you. I needed to hear that. And I ne___ perspective other than my own. More than I ___ realized."

She stared up at him, the two of them no___ ing side by side at her sink. He'd somehow m___ wash and rinse their dinner plates, all while___ the raw truth of what the entire police and l___ ment community was dealing with. It was___ handed him a towel from the counter, tu___ faced one another, that Evangeline real___ physically close they were.

She was a tall woman, but he was stil___ had to look up at him as their eyes met. ___ a trick of the light or the quiet tenor of ___

Whittaker right now, barreling through any and all red tape to get the answers I want."

"There she is. The fighter we all know and love." Troy headed for the door, satisfied they'd hit more even ground. "And I still promise to call tomorrow."

It was only when he stepped through her front door, waiting on the other side until he heard the snick of the lock, that Troy realized the words he'd used to reassure her. One big one in particular. *Love.*

As he got into his car and started the ignition, it continued to linger in his thoughts, keeping him company on the drive across town toward home.

Evangeline walked back to the kitchen, surprised to realize Troy's light scent still lingered in the air. Just as his kiss still lingered on her lips. The subtle hints of leather from his holster stood out, as did the remembrance of how warm his skin had felt through the material of his shirt beneath her fingers.

She'd kissed him.

The thought dazzled her as she put their now-clean dinner dishes back in the cabinet. Right there, in front of the sink. And it had been amazing. Yes, she'd been lonely when she'd headed out that night, but wonderfully enough, the kiss hadn't been about loneliness. Or sadness. Or any sense that she was failing at life.

Oh no, this kiss was about passion and interest and mutual need. And for the first time in more months than she could describe, she felt something other than fear or gloom or disappointment.

The cabinet door slipped from her fingers, hitting the frame with a thud. It was only when she heard an answering noise, much harder, from the back of her condo, that something dark and cold ran down her spine.

Even as her mind whispered, warning her to calm down, Evangeline fought it. She knew what she'd heard. And while she'd felt the lock in the front door turn beneath her own fingers mere moments before, she hadn't been anywhere near her back door.

As an owner on the bottom floor of the condo complex, she had two entrances to her home. The front door she normally used and a door that led to the grassy public area between buildings. Hadn't she locked it earlier?

She remembered checking it, but had she actually turned the lock in the door? Felt the hard snap of the dead bolt beneath her fingers?

As that fear kicked in again, knocking her heart against her chest with heavy thumps, she fought for a deep breath. It was an odd night wrapping up a tiring and difficult stretch of weeks. That was all. It was summertime and people enjoyed the common area of the complex long into the evening, barbecuing, or it could be neighbors sitting around talking. Maybe someone tried the wrong door heading back to their own home.

Yet even as she tried to talk herself out of what she'd heard, Evangeline reached for the sharp kitchen scissors in the small caddy she kept near the stove. With the handle-end wrapped tightly in her fist, she left the kitchen and headed for her back door. Even from this distance, she couldn't see any sign of entry. The door was closed firmly. She kept her gaze trained on the hallway and the small powder room that speared off near the back door.

Could someone be hiding in there?

Tightening her grip, Evangeline moved closer. Just shy of the bathroom she twisted so her free hand could swing around the doorframe and flip on the lights, even as her body remained physically protected by the wall.

Only no one was there as light flooded the small space.

The heavy thump of her heartbeat calmed slightly as she took in the area. The back door was closed and she could see from where she stood that the dead bolt was still thrown. No one was in the bathroom. There wasn't any other place to hide on the back side of the condo. And Troy had been with her for the past hour, walking through the front of her home.

They'd have both heard if anyone had gotten by.

Satisfied it was one more weird occurrence in a night full of them, Evangeline rechecked the dead bolt for her own comfort and walked back to the kitchen, dropping the scissors back into their rightful place.

"Skittish much, Whittaker?"

The sound of her voice did little to comfort the tangling, jangling nerves that still twisted beneath her skin, but she was determined to ignore it.

What was it Troy had said? Very little couldn't be helped by a bit of food and a good night's sleep.

She'd had the burger and now it was time for rest.

The lovely image Troy had painted of his stepmother's kind warmth and genuine caring kept her company as she walked into her bedroom. It was only as she hit the light switch and saw the book on her nightstand, propped up and facing her, that she screamed.

She had never purchased a travel book about the state of Michigan.

Nor had she left one in her room.

Chapter 5

Troy answered the call on the first ring, his in-dash Bluetooth lighting up with Evangeline's name.

"Hello?"

"Troy!" A hard sob muffled his name but nothing could hide the agony in her tone. "Someone's here! Or was here!"

He had just turned into his neighborhood and was already swinging around the nearest cul-de-sac as her frantic words continued spilling from the speakers. Something about her back door and a book and her bedroom, all running together in a rush of words.

"Evangeline." When she continued sobbing, he pushed harder. "Evangeline!"

"Yes?"

"Are you still in the house? Have you called nine-one-one?"

"No one—" She hiccupped. "No one is here. I checked."

She checked?

White hot anger filled him at the thought of her being in the house by herself, walking around looking for an intruder.

And what the hell was an intruder doing in her home in the first place? He was just there. Hell, he'd left less than ten minutes ago. And while he'd own being somewhat distracted, especially there at the end with their kiss, he'd have known if someone was in her condo.

Wouldn't he?

He might not have seen her entire place but he hadn't missed how the bedrooms had been tucked away off a hallway on the opposite side of the living room. The layout was well done, keeping the bedrooms separate from the kitchen to allow for privacy while entertaining. Would that have given someone time to get inside? Or more to the point, to get out while he and Evangeline had been enjoying dinner?

He raced through several lights leading into downtown, retracing the route he'd just driven.

He needed to get to her.

That lone thought accompanied him as he navigated through the last mile to her home. As the various landmarks that made up his hometown flew past, Troy considered all he knew.

Evangeline's initial 911 call earlier this evening. The strange, empty alley even CSI couldn't decipher. And now a possible intruder.

What was going on with this woman?

Did someone have an ax to grind? Or worse, was she targeted in some way? As an image of their latest case file on Len Davison came up, Troy's blood ran cold.

Was it possible Davison was changing pattern?

He wasn't that well versed in serial-killer behavior

but he'd had enough police training to understand the basics. The adherence to pattern. The odd comfort the killer found in repetitive actions, matching some internal motive only he or she understood. And the even more dangerous points of tension when that pattern escalated.

It was Len Davison's escalation that had put the GGPD in their current situation, facing off against the man's devious mind. But another change in that pattern? That would be akin to a bomb going off in the middle of Grave Gulch. They had some sense of what they were up against based on Davison's approach to his victims. Men of a certain age, out alone after dark. A kill every two months.

But if that pattern changed?

Then no one in Grave Gulch was safe.

Troy swung into Evangeline's parking lot, pulling into an empty space in front of her home. He raced for the door, his hand lifted to pound on the thick wood just as it swung open. She stood there, still in the outfit she'd worn through dinner. If he'd thought she looked peaked and scared when he met her on the street in Grave Gulch, it was nothing compared to the pallor that now filled her face.

"You're here." She said it on a breathy sob before throwing herself into his arms.

Troy held on tight, his gaze already roaming over her head and through the open door beyond. He couldn't see anything out of place but she'd sobbed into the phone about her bedroom and a book.

Pulling back, Troy stared down at her. Her dark eyes were wild in her face, the pupils blown wide with another burst of fear-pumping adrenaline. But in the midst of that panic, he saw something else.

Terror.

And the man who'd spent his life imagining his mother's last moments simply couldn't walk away.

"Let's go inside and I'll check everything out."

"I already did."

"I'll do it again. And then I want you to tell me what happened."

They walked back into the house, his arm around her shoulders. With deliberate motions, he turned and closed the door, flipping the lock as he did so. Pointing toward the sofa, he directed her there. "Why don't you take a seat for a minute and I'll check everything out?"

Evangeline nodded, taking the seat as he instructed. Her shoulders trembled and he walked back to her, grabbing a blanket off the back of the couch and settling it around her shoulders.

"It's the dead of summer."

"And you're shaking like it's February." Troy nestled the blanket around her shoulders. "Warm up a bit. I'll be right back."

He walked through the entire house, itching to pull his service piece out of its holster but holding back. Evangeline had already confirmed her own visual search and it felt like an unnecessary step that carried more risk of scaring her instead of protecting them. But he remained conscious of its heft and weight as he combed her house, room by room.

Enter, sweep, review.

He did the two bedrooms off the living room, checking closets, the en suite bathrooms and even under the bed, before moving on. The book she'd mentioned—what looked like a travel guide on her nightstand—was there and Troy eyed it but didn't touch it. He'd ask her about that after he cleared the rest of her home.

He glanced at her briefly as he moved back through the living room. Evangeline was still huddled on the same chair where he'd left her, the blanket wrapped around her. The haunted look still rode her dark gaze but he could see some color returning, erasing the pallor of her skin. Satisfied she was warming up, the fear of an intruder fading, Troy headed for the kitchen and then on down the small hallway to her back door.

That door wasn't as formal as her front entrance, but its thick wood was serviceable. He'd gotten a good sense of the layout of the condo complex, with front doors facing the parking lot and any back entrances to the homes facing a common area. He opened the door now, bending to search the locks and the area beyond. The dead bolt seemed sturdy enough and he saw no sign of scratches when he looked at it. Still, he'd like to check it in the light, as well, to look for anything that might be out of place.

Stepping through the door, he kept his gaze on the small spread of poured stone that made up her back patio, two overstuffed chairs set up around a wrought iron coffee table. The area was pretty, he noted. Simple but cozy, with the inviting chairs giving a place to curl up and enjoy a book on a summer afternoon. The nearby firepit ensured she could use the space well into the fall, even as the Michigan nights grew crisp.

Executing a full turn, Troy surveyed the space. Looking to his left and right, he could see matched patios spreading down in both directions, Evangeline's neighbors having various furniture setups of their own. Everyone had managed a sense of privacy, even without formal fencing separating each home. It was only as he gazed on past the patios to the shared lawn beyond that

Troy recognized how easy it would be to sneak around behind her building.

The furniture did provide a layer of cover and if no one was in the yard—or the reverse, if there were a lot of people milling around and enjoying the day—it wouldn't take much to walk up to the back entryway of any of the first-floor homes.

He headed back into the house, closing up and locking the door. He saw nothing to indicate an intruder had been in her condo or had used aggressive means to gain entry. A flag that was too close for comfort to the incident earlier in the alley.

A frantic call with no body.

Now a frantic call without any evidence of a break-in.

Troy stared down the hallway toward the living room.

It was time to talk to Evangeline.

Evangeline finally felt the warmth return to her limbs, the achy trembling that had suffused her body fading. Although the blanket had seemed silly overkill for June, she was grateful for Troy's quick thinking.

And his even quicker arrival.

She'd been tempted to follow him as he searched the house, but he seemed insistent that she wait in the living room. And the few quiet minutes gave her a chance to gather her thoughts.

What was someone doing in her home?

Over and over, she'd sought some sort of explanation but had none. That book wasn't hers. And even more jarring, other than going out this evening for a bit of a walk, she'd been home nearly nonstop for two weeks. She had gone out the day before to get some groceries while the cleaning woman was in, doing the house, but

Kathy hadn't reported anything odd when Evangeline had returned home.

Although she hadn't made much of a mess over the past few weeks, tidying to keep herself busy, Evangeline didn't have the heart to call Kathy off and not pay her for a service. Because the house was spotless, she had finished earlier than usual, heading out a few minutes after Evangeline had unpacked her groceries. They'd exchanged a few pleasantries before Kathy headed off to her next job.

No mention of anyone even knocking on the door. No delivery of a package. And while Kathy was an avid reader and could have left something behind as a pass along, her tastes trended toward popular fiction, not travel guides to the state where she had already lived a lifetime.

The book made no sense. And certainly not perched on her nightstand, the cover facing out.

"I've checked everything," Troy said, his large, competent form seeming to fill the living room by his very presence. "The house is secure and I can't find anything out of place."

The house is secure.

Not "no one is here," Evangeline thought.

Just a quick, clinical *The house is secure.*

Secure implied safe. And she felt neither.

"Thank you for checking. And for coming back."

Troy took a seat on the couch, facing her. "Why don't you take me through it? From the point I left until the point I got back here."

Evangeline considered the best way to start. The slamming of the door? The book? Or maybe she should just start by pleading with him to believe that she had her sanity firmly intact.

In the end, she did as he requested—at the beginning—and went straight through to the end. Troy never interrupted, but a whirl of emotions crossed his face, from anger to grim resolve, with a stop at fury along the way.

"Have you had any issues with your back door before? Anyone unwanted?"

"My neighbor made a mistake the first week she lived here. She'd gone down to sit out in the common area and tried the wrong door when she came back up, confusing which condo was hers. It was totally innocent and she apologized profusely. It also gave us a chance to meet each other."

"You've had no other problems since?"

"Troy, it was hardly a problem." She sat up, pushing the blanket off her shoulders. "That was a mistake."

"And I'm trying to understand if it was possible it could happen again."

"It wasn't like that."

"How was it different?"

Just like the series of questions earlier, she recognized his patience and appreciated it. Yet even as she knew his questions were fair, Evangeline couldn't fully fight the tense knot of embarrassment that kept screaming he didn't believe her.

"It was—" She hesitated, well aware how the next words would make her sound. She told herself to hold it back, but something pushed her forward. "It was different tonight. There was a sinister quality to it I can't explain. Just like I haven't been able to explain why I feel like I've been watched for the past few weeks, even though it's been there all the same."

"You what?" Troy leaned forward, his forearms

perching on the edge of his knees. "You've been watched?"

"I feel like I've been watched. I can't prove it."

Troy had been on high alert since racing up to her front door, but at the admission she'd felt watched, his entire demeanor changed. "Watched? Where?"

"Everywhere. It's been going on for a few weeks now. I felt it a few times before I went on leave from my job and now that I've been home it's happened more frequently. Even sometimes when I'm in the house."

That sense of someone looking at her through the window. Or the feeling of a *presence* on the few occasions she'd gone to sit on the back porch, trying to divert her mind with a book or magazine.

"When was the last time it happened?"

"Earlier. Tonight." The same fury she'd sensed earlier was back in full force, darkening his hazel eyes to a fiery amber. "When I was walking around downtown."

"And you didn't think to mention it?"

"I forgot. And when I thought about it again it didn't seem relevant to what I saw in the alley."

"It's all relevant, Evangeline. And when you add on that we've got a serial killer on the loose, ignoring your instincts is the worst thing you can do."

Without warning, a long-forgotten memory rose up to the forefront of her thoughts. It had been one of her biggest cases to date at the DA's office and she'd had to depose darn near half of the county in the process. A beloved, well-respected teacher had been embezzling from the district, siphoning money off over a span of nearly two decades. Administrators, fellow teachers and the PTA were all up in arms that they'd had no idea what had been happening just under their noses. But it was an older woman who worked in the administration office whose testimony about the guilty teacher had resonated.

Something was off from the day she started. I couldn't put my finger on it and I'd never have guessed she was doing this, but I knew something wasn't right with her.

That testimony had stuck with Evangeline through the years. The woman's absolute conviction something was wrong. And the reality that she'd been right all that time.

It felt stupid to say it out loud, with no obvious evidence to back her up, but she had felt off. The world around her had felt off. And her instincts had been clamoring at her for weeks now.

Maybe it was time to start paying attention. Real attention. The sort that caught criminals.

"I wasn't ignoring anything. Or more to the point, I wasn't trying to," Evangeline added. "It felt silly to admit it. To say it out loud."

"It's not silly and it's something you should be admitting. It's one more piece I need to look for. Anyone lurking around here that doesn't belong is a good place to start."

"Troy, you don't need to make this your problem. The GGPD is dealing with a whole lot worse right now."

"You are my problem. The moment I took the call to come help you tonight, you became my problem. You're also the prosecuting attorney directly tied to Len Davison's freedom. Which only further reinforces my point."

She wanted to be his partner, not his problem. That thought came on her swiftly, the memories of their kiss winging right back along, as well. The noise in the house and the scare from the book—about Michigan, of all things?—had erased their kiss from her immediate thoughts, but now that Troy was sitting here, looking like the very source of safety in his big, broad shoulders and large, capable hands, the memory was back.

Her lips still tingled from the feel of his. Her body was still warm in all the places that muscular form had pressed against her. And for the first time, Evangeline had to wonder if she was in real danger. She believed in the GGPD's ability to watch out for her and keep her safe.

But she had no idea how she was going to hide the very real feelings of attraction she had for Troy. Feelings she'd kept tamped down for so long, which she now had a glimmer of hope about.

Troy poured boiling water from the teakettle into two mugs. He hadn't gotten much more out of his discussion with Evangeline. Any questions he posed about her feelings of being watched were met with vague descriptions.

How did you use that? The reality was that you couldn't.

While he didn't disregard her feelings, the sensation of being watched was different than actually being able to describe someone. Height, build, possible weight. All of it was needed to go find a suspect.

Again, his thoughts swirled around the subject of Len Davison. Was the man escalating? Did he have Evangeline in his sights? His initial concern—that Davison was breaking pattern—was still there, but Troy knew it wasn't the only answer. If Davison had put his focus on Evangeline, it could also be out of a desire to remove an obstacle from his path.

Yes, she'd been instrumental to ensuring Davison stayed out of jail, but now that she knew the truth, she was a voice for putting him away. It could be enough to break pattern.

And what about Bowe?

Troy nearly bobbled the mug, as his hand tightened on the handle, his anger at Randall Bowe a living thing. Damn, but the man had done damage. Terrible damage that had cost people their lives.

Righting both mugs in his hands, Troy walked back to the living room. That peaked look had left her features, but Evangeline still appeared wrung out from the day's events, her legs curled under her on the large oversize chair that sat offset from her couch. Had it only been a matter of hours since she put that 911 call into the precinct?

Yes, he thought with no small measure of surprise, it had.

In that time, he had been forced to question her motives more than once, and yet still managed to kiss her. An act that was so far out of line he was still upbraiding himself for the personal slip.

"Here's your tea." He set one of the mugs down on the small coffee table before taking his own seat on the couch.

"Can I ask you a question?"

"Of course," Troy said.

"Do you believe me?"

"I believe you believe what you're telling me."

As answers went, he knew it was unsatisfactory, but he had nothing else to give her and he wasn't going to prevaricate on an answer to make her feel better. The reality was, this was an active investigation barely six hours old.

"I guess that's something." Her tone was flat as she stared into her mug.

"It *is* something, Evangeline." Troy leaned forward, setting his mug on the coffee table. He wanted her to understand his perspective, even if it wasn't what she wanted to hear. "I'm not going to lie to you. And I'm not going to give you information that is untrue. But just as I told you before, I can't tell you everything. And I take my job seriously enough to do it the right and proper way."

Even if I did kiss you.

It continued to haunt him. He'd *kissed* her. Really kissed her, the sort that had mouths and breaths and bodies mingling as they joined. And it had been all he had ever imagined. All he'd hoped, really.

It was funny, Troy realized, that all this time he'd admired her from afar, keeping his professional distance, he'd known deep down that he had feelings for her. Feelings that, if he were to give in to them, could be so much more.

Only now, the timing was off. He needed to protect her, not romance her. And wasn't that the real surprise?

"I'm not lying to you, Troy. I'm not making this up."

Grateful for the distraction from his errant thoughts, Troy keyed back into Evangeline's plea. "That's why I said I believe you."

"But if I'm being fair, I can also understand why you think the way you do. I realize there isn't any evidence. I know how outlandish it sounds to tell you things happened, when there's no proof that they did. All I can tell you is that I know what I saw earlier in that alley. I know what I heard in my own home. I know for a fact that book on my dresser is not mine."

At her mention of the book, Troy stood. "I left the book where it was when I swept the house, but I'd like to look at it again. I'd like to understand what it was about this particular book that upset you."

As if pleased there was something to do, Evangeline stood, those dark eyes a little bit brighter. "It was the book itself, as well as where it was placed. Standing up, face out, so that I wouldn't miss it."

She made a good point, especially the fact the book was standing. Even if the travel guide was her own, some forgotten impulse purchase, no one left books standing up face out.

He followed her into the bedroom, the entire experience much more intimate than when he had done the sweep of her home earlier. This was where she slept. He felt surrounded by her scent in here, the light swirl of mint and jasmine a sensual feast.

Determined to ignore that thought, and the hints of impropriety it smacked of, Troy followed her to the nightstand. "A travel guide to Michigan?"

"Yes. I don't have a book like this. Nor do I have any interest in owning a book like this, so it's not like I forgot that I purchased it at some point."

"Is it possible anyone left it behind?"

"I thought about that, earlier. Other than the woman who cleans my home, no one has been here. And she's hardly diving into books about Michigan travel, either, or leaving them as a present for me to read."

He considered saving the book for prints, but knew it was a bit frivolous, based on CSI's already overworked caseload. Still, it was worth keeping, especially with his suspicions about Davison.

He snagged a tissue from the box on the corner of the nightstand, gingerly lifting the book but not putting his own fingerprints on it. With careful movements, he turned it over to read the back.

Thoughts of Davison filled his mind once again. Was this some sort of clue? So far, they believed all of the man's crimes had been concentrated in Michigan. Was this meant to be some sort of taunt? A sign that he would strike again? Or more, a sign that he could do his deeds anywhere across the state and not just in Grave Gulch County?

"Have you prosecuted any cases that could be tied to this?"

"Not that I can think of. Nothing I've done, or the crimes I've handled, have screamed 'travelogue.'"

Gingerly, Troy set the book back down, leaving the tissue lying on top of the cover. He would come back in with a plastic bag and take it in for evidence. CSI may not be able to prioritize the fingerprints, but at least they would have the book in evidence. They couldn't afford to overlook any and all things that might relate to the Davison case.

If there was something nefarious afoot, processing the book would need to be prioritized on CSI's exhaustive caseload.

Hadn't this evening suggested as much? He was well aware he couldn't divert his focus from the problems currently plaguing Grave Gulch. But as he stared down at that book, Troy knew he was in this now.

Evangeline Whittaker needed help. And he'd be damned sure she was going to get whatever she needed.

"I'd like to stay here tonight. I'll take the couch or your spare room, but I don't want you here alone."

"You don't have to do that. Especially because I'm starting to feel really silly sobbing into your ear over a travel book."

He saw the false bravado and couldn't stop the impulse to reach out and brush a wayward lock of hair that had fallen over her cheek. Tucking it gently behind her ear, Troy insisted, "You weren't silly and you need to stop saying that."

"It was silly."

"You were scared. And I'd like to take a look at that lock in the fresh light of morning anyway."

"It's silly and—" She broke off on a deep exhale before turning to face him fully. "And I'd really appreciate having you here as backup."

Chapter 6

Troy took another big sip of coffee and navigated his way through the seemingly ever-present protesters outside the police station. He respected and admired the right to peacefully assemble but it was getting increasingly difficult to hear the shouting reverberating throughout the precinct. He was as frustrated as the protesters with the current situation in Grave Gulch and their waving signs felt like a visual reminder of the GGPD's failure to protect them.

The added pressure of a sleepless night, his proximity to Evangeline more challenging than he would've anticipated, had him feeling like a tired grizzly bear this morning.

And of course, he had Melissa's staff meeting first thing.

Heading into the precinct, he waved at the team on the front desk with the second cup of coffee he had in hand for Brett. "Is Detective Shea in yet?"

The earnest young man riding the front desk nodded his head, Mary Suzuki's Sunday shift earning her a day off. "Yes, sir. Detective Shea has been in for about an hour."

"Thank you." Troy avoided the inwardly disparaging thoughts that threatened, well aware he was entitled to an evening off, even if Brett had stayed. And it was not like his time with Evangeline was a date. Her involvement in the Davison case meant her situation needed to be watched and monitored. Evaluated.

Evaluation that includes kissing? his inner voice piped up.

Ignoring the mental taunts, Troy headed straight for Brett's office, not even stopping at his own to drop his workbag off.

"You look like you had a night," Brett greeted him with a hearty smile as he looked up from his desk.

"Then I'm keeping the extra coffee I picked up for you all to myself."

"Gimme." Brett held out a hand as Ember perked up from her large pillowed perch beside the desk.

"I'm sorry, girl, I didn't bring anything for you." Troy said to the pretty, black Lab, who thumped her tail in response.

"Don't worry," Brett said. "She's got her after-practice bone coming her way in another hour or so."

"It's a full-time job, isn't it?"

"Ember's training?" Brett looked up from his coffee at the question. "It is, but it's time we both enjoy."

"Is there any chance that training could've overlooked something in the alley last night?"

As questions went it was certainly loaded, and more than a little fraught with hope. But he had to ask anyway.

"I'd like to tell you no, but unfortunately I don't think

I can. And if it just rested on her training, I wouldn't be so confident. But the CSI report was pretty clear."

"Damn it, I know. I read through it this morning before heading in."

He had done a quick scan first for the basics and then a second time through to get all the nuances. The report was clear and irrefutable. No sign of any violent activity or blood.

"Look, you know you've got backup on this," Brett said. "I saw that woman's face last night when we arrived on scene, and I don't think the sheer terror that paled her skin was made up."

"Thank you for that. I appreciate it. And the support."

"I only have one question for you in return."

"What's that?" Troy replied.

"Are you prepared if the answer doesn't come back in her favor?"

It was a fair question, and one that he'd asked himself more than once through the long hours in Evangeline's spare bedroom until dawn. He believed her and thought that she was telling the truth as she knew it. Yet even with that confidence in her, he couldn't deny that there were doubts. In the lack of CSI evidence as well as any trace a K-9 could pick up.

Both sat at the top of his list.

"I'll do what needs to be done. You can count on that," Troy assured his partner.

"All I need to hear."

Brett stood at that, Ember coming to immediate attention at his side. "It's time to head into the chief's meeting."

When Troy and Brett walked into the main conference room, Melissa was already putting together her notes at the head of the table. She turned to look at both men as they entered. "Sounds like you two had quite an evening last night."

"One more frustrating dead end in a year that's been full of them," Troy said, hearing the ready annoyance in his own voice.

"Is that all?"

Troy loved his cousin Melissa and had absolute respect for her as their chief of police, but it was never very comfortable to be on the receiving end of her questions, especially the ones that ended in raised eyebrows. "I think so. The investigation is open and active, even if initial results are inconclusive."

"Can you have the full report to me by this afternoon?" she asked.

"Yes, absolutely." Troy would have it done by lunch, unwilling to let the situation with Evangeline rest. They had too much riding on this, both for Evangeline's own safety as well as the potential connections to Len Davison and Randall Bowe. "I'm also happy to give an update during the meeting, as to what I know so far."

Melissa nodded. "See that you do."

Troy took a seat and settled in. He enjoyed their staff meetings. He'd come to look forward to the camaraderie and partnership he felt inside that conference room.

While their collective sense of team spirit had never been higher, their work had become more challenging of late. Grave Gulch wasn't small, per se, but its share of violent crime had always been at manageable levels. Unlike their counterparts in Grand Rapids or even larger metropolitan areas like Detroit, they'd always found overall crime here to be somewhat subdued.

Until the start of this year.

The things that had happened since January—his

nephew's kidnapping at Mary's wedding almost a catalyst of sorts—had been on the extreme end of what law enforcement would experience in an average year.

And nothing about this year had been average so far.

It was like he'd said to Evangeline the night before. Things just felt *off.* And while that was hardly a term he'd use with his colleagues, it was one that fit.

Within minutes, the rest of the squad had taken seats around the room and Melissa called the meeting to order. They would hit the high points of their ongoing investigations, but Melissa usually started by asking about any late-breaking or important details they needed to know.

This morning was no different.

"We have an update on Davison." Melissa broke her typical pattern by launching into their most pressing case herself.

Troy opened his mouth, before snapping it shut at the dark look from Melissa.

"Saturday, Davison broke into the home of an elderly couple here in Grave Gulch. They are thankfully unharmed, but terribly scared. He tied them up while he went through their home, used their shower, stole their food and ultimately cleaned them out of all money and valuables inside the house."

"Son of a bitch," Brett muttered under his breath.

"That he is, Detective Shea." Melissa eyed him from where she stood at the front of the room, her comment both the signal that she had heard him regardless of how quietly he spoke, and that she agreed with her newest detective wholeheartedly.

"He is armed and dangerous, proof from the fact that he held that couple tied up and at gunpoint for almost thirty-six hours. And while we remain pleased that he didn't take the situation any further, and both the husband and wife have been checked out and released at this point with a clean bill of health, Davison continues to prove himself a dangerous criminal."

Troy considered the timeline, as he listened to the rest of Melissa's overview. Work had already begun to notify any pawnshops who might get some of the jewelry described by the couple, and additional K-9 resources were being brought in to comb the area around the couple's home. "Detective Shea," Melissa continued, "we need you and Ember over there with the rest of the team today."

"Of course." Brett nodded, shooting the dog a quick glance over his shoulder where she rested behind his chair.

"Melissa? When did Davison gain entry into the home?" Troy asked.

"Sometime Saturday, best the couple can tell. They were out earlier in the day and he was there in the afternoon once they had come back in from running errands. He departed late last night. The couple finally worked themselves free from the ropes he'd used to tie them up around three this morning. They immediately called for help."

Troy backed his way through the timeline. Davison had been in Grave Gulch for at least thirty-six hours as he held the couple hostage. Possibly longer since there was no telling exactly how early he'd gotten into their home while they were out. But if the man had been in Grave Gulch throughout the weekend, it was very possible he could have also orchestrated the situation Evangeline saw the alley. Especially if he was on the run and fighting with some sort of female helper.

It could fit.

Yet even as he considered it, Troy knew the scenario rang false. The timing was a possible match but little else. Davison was a suspected lone wolf. From all they'd learned, the man continued to bear the grief of losing his wife to cancer after more than thirty years of marriage and it was that spark—the death of his wife—that pushed him into killing.

Additionally, Evangeline might not have clearly seen the man at the end of the alley, but based on her description of his height, weight and overall physical heft, the assailant she observed wasn't a match for Davison.

Which meant it was very possible they were dealing with someone else altogether.

A reality that didn't sit any better on his shoulders.

He meant his promise to Brett. He would do whatever needed to be done. He'd never let his partner, his chief or his department down like that.

But he'd do what needed to be done for Evangeline, too.

He just hoped like hell those promises weren't at odds with one another.

Evangeline finally quit roaming around the house about an hour after Troy left. She'd already taken a walk around the condo complex, talking for a while with her upstairs neighbor, Ella, and trying to clear her mind of the cobwebs that seemed to have settled there. She was restless and anxious, despite the exercise, but enough was enough. It was only when she'd settled on the idea to sit down with a legal pad that she'd finally felt a bit like her old self.

With a pen and paper in hand, she was the problem solver. The strategist. And the woman who knew how to take charge and use the legal system to its full benefit. A woman who made lists, reviewed evidence, wrote briefs and understood that the truth didn't come in waves, but as a series of revelations and approaches that got you to a successful outcome. It was how she'd argued cases for years and it was time to apply that same logic to her own life.

With renewed energy coursing through her veins, she wrote down her first question. What did she know?

Randall Bowe had falsified evidence in numerous cases. A situation Arielle's office had been combing through, trying to determine where falsely imprisoned individuals needed their cases reviewed.

She knew the DA's side but needed Troy's additional details there through a cop's eyes. Best they currently understood, the disgraced CSI leader had tampered with evidence for reasons only he seemed to know and, once discovered, gone on the run. He wasn't a killer but he'd enabled one in Len Davison.

Which brought her to her second note. Len Davison was responsible for the murder she'd prosecuted; thanks to Bowe's tampering with the evidence, he'd been acquitted. He'd gone on to kill again, his pattern focused on men in their fifties, out alone, walking dogs in the park. Each victim had died with a single gunshot to the chest. He'd struck three times and while Troy hadn't said much the night before, she knew enough legal psychology to know that the third murder meant Davison had graduated to serial killer.

Interestingly, the dogs hadn't been harmed. Evangeline tapped the back of her pen to the paper, considering the angle. Did it mean something?

She got up and padded to her spare room to retrieve her laptop from the small desk she maintained in there. It was only as she entered the room that she stilled. The bed was neatly made, no sign that Troy had ever been there. Unless you counted the lingering scent of him and the knowledge that his head had lain on the very pillows now propped on the bedframe. Something warm filled her stomach, suffusing out to her limbs, and she couldn't hold back the smile.

He'd been the soul of propriety last night, but he'd also insisted on staying. It had been sweet of him and incredibly caring. And it added one more dimension to their kiss. Was it possible he cared?

She'd always been attracted to him, and she knew many women in the county's legal system felt the same. Troy Colton was an attractive man, his broad shoulders and slim hips always sure to garner attention. But when you added on the competence in his work and the innate kindness in his eyes, that attraction had nowhere to go but up.

Unwilling to let her thoughts move too closely toward her quietly held fantasies, Evangeline snagged the laptop quickly off the desk and left the room. And if those hints of sandalwood and fresh summer sunlight still lingered in the room—scents she had reveled in as she'd kissed Troy—well, she needed to shut that part of herself off.

He'd come to help her, not date her. She'd do well to remember that.

Back in front of her legal pad, she opened the laptop and tapped in the details of the Davison murders into a search bar. Just as she'd already known, news reports confirmed he'd killed three times, the pattern the same. All men in their fifties, all out walking dogs in the park. And in each case the pet was unharmed.

A positive situation to be sure, but it seemed significant somehow. As if the dog was the conduit to get to the man in the park but not the object of the attack.

She enjoyed a good thriller as much as the next person and recognized her serial-killer knowledge was heavily steeped in the books she'd read or the movies she'd watched. But there was something about animals… Many future killers escalated over time, having hurt animals as their initial targets.

Yet Davison hadn't touched the dogs. The beloved pets of his victims. That meant something.

With that as her focus, she added more questions to her notepad.

What was his motive? Why these men? And why now, after what seemed like a crime-free life? What had driven Davison to his actions?

Hadn't that been one of the things that made her legal argument seem so clear? Davison didn't have a history of violence and had been considered a good, upstanding citizen. At the time of his trial, she'd had no reason to think the evidence had been tampered with because the man on trial hadn't exhibited any bad behavior— and they hadn't yet known of Bowe's crimes. It didn't excuse her role in his trial, but it was one more item in the "it doesn't add up" column on her notepad.

Nor did it really explain what she was personally dealing with.

Davison might be unstable and increasingly violent, but he had a pattern. One that didn't at all match what was happening to her.

The ongoing sensation of being watched.

The events that had unfolded at work.

Even the incidents the night before felt off.

She knew what she saw, yet there was no evidence to suggest it had ever happened. Crimes just didn't work that way. Humans left forensic trails, no matter how hard they tried to suppress them. So did guns and ammunition. Yet despite what she'd seen, a trained K-9 and a well-honed team of CSI experts had found nothing in that alley.

It just seemed…impossible.

Which only led to more questions.

Was she overtired and hallucinating? She'd slept terribly over the past few months, the situation at work all-consuming. While she took deep pride in her work ethic and willingness to give her job her all, including late nights and long weekends if necessary, was it possible she'd imagined her fears into existence?

A dark shudder ran the length of her spine and Evangeline stood, heading to the kitchen for a glass of water. She needed to shake this off. This negative thinking that suggested she didn't know her own mind.

Wasn't that the root of her parents' difficult marriage for so many years? Her father had issues controlling his rage, so he'd lash out at the most minimal of offenses or situations. Her mother would cower and cry and he'd apologize later, telling her that his behavior wasn't nearly as out of proportion as her reaction suggested.

A constant game of push-pull on her mother's emotions, suggesting she didn't know her own mind or understand what she'd experienced. That she somehow didn't understand Cecil Whittaker's rage issues and their serious consequences.

For years, Evangeline had observed the problem, helpless to make it change. Her mother protected her as best as she could, bearing the brunt of the emotional abuse and demanding Evangeline stay out of it.

But how did you stay out of it, even as a child?

a dropped into Troy's guest chair, her strong,
houlders deflating. "I know you know. That's
tough here."

ust like that, he saw the Melissa he'd grown
sitting before him across the desk. "I'm run-
of answers here, Troy. The man's in his mid-
and until his first murder is so squeaky clean
ely rated a speeding ticket. How does the death
ouse—even if she was so beloved—make some-
this? To change course so badly? And worse,
e he isn't a criminal and presumably has never
those circles, how has he managed to get away
all for this long?"

on't know, Mel. I really don't."

wasn't that the worst part of it all? They knew
who they were up against. They'd discovered his
ne assistance he'd gotten from Bowe, and they'd
uilt a relationship with Len's daughter, Tatiana.
pite all that progress, they were no closer to get-
e man in custody.

w's Tatiana holding up?" Troy asked. Although
initially questioned how Davison's daughter
ave been unaware of her father's actions, they'd
learn that she was as shocked and hurt by the
s the families of the man's victims.

r cousin Travis had had a fling with Tatiana, his
O. They'd soon fallen in love while both were
g at Colton Plastics, but her surprise pregnancy
ome public around the same time she was being
ned by the police about her father.

s an extraordinary set of circumstances, but the
family had quickly closed ranks around Len's
er, unwilling to paint her with the same brush
did her father.

It wasn't a situation that could be ignored. The roiling anger that seethed beneath the surface in her home had been a steady companion throughout her childhood. It was only once Evangeline was out of the house, off to college, that Dora Whittaker had finally made a change. Had finally left, satisfied that her daughter could no longer be a pawn in a divorce settlement.

Or worse, have to face the same consequences if she were to spend time with her father in a shared custody agreement.

It was no way to live. And while she was grateful her mother had finally gotten out—that they both had—it didn't change the lingering damage her first eighteen years had done.

She took another sip of water, willing the cool liquid to ease her suddenly tight throat. The memories of her parents' marriage always upset her and nothing good ever came of reliving that time in her life. The helpless feelings. The anger at her father, even as she continued to love him as her parent.

It was hurtful and confusing and had left an incredibly dark mark on her life.

The heavy knock on the door pulled her from her musings and Evangeline was grateful for the distraction. She'd go answer it and then make some lunch. She had some of her mother's *sinigang* in the fridge and it would make a soothing antidote to the painful memories. The tamarind soup had always been a favorite and she was already anticipating the rich flavors that had only grown stronger as it spent a few days as a leftover in her fridge.

The knock came again and Evangeline headed more quickly down the hall. She had no idea why whoever was out there hadn't rung the bell but disregarded it as she swung the door open.

And looked down to find a bloody white shirt on her front entryway.

Troy scrolled through the notes he'd jotted down on his phone, confirming he'd included everything in his report for Melissa. He'd already added in the notes he'd taken down in the conference room the day before as Evangeline walked him through the events she witnessed in the alley and now sat back to reread through the report one final time.

He'd nearly finished his read-through when the knock came at his door. "Melissa." He sat back, not surprised his cousin had found her way to his office. "Come in."

"I wanted to discuss the Whittaker case."

He'd figured as much but didn't say it, giving her time to settle in instead. Melissa was a good chief because she innately understood the places that required more of her attention versus the cases that her team had well in hand. She shifted her attention as it was needed and was able to pivot quickly, taking in new information and feeding back theories to her team that they might not have considered yet.

She was also engaged and planning a wedding *and* dealing with the department's troubles. It was that reality that Troy couldn't disregard. The sheer pressure on her shoulders, upholding justice for the citizens of Grave Gulch, all while trying to keep her large, extended family safe.

"Come on in and sit down."

Melissa came fully into his office but she remained standing, her hands clasped behind her back as she

stood in front of his desk. "Y... conference room. I got the ve... share all you knew."

"I did share all I knew. My r...

"But?" She left the word har... moment she was 100 percent his... last name and family connection... her hunt for information.

"But nothing. Detective Shea... a nine-one-one call last evening. ... scene and were unable to find a bod... there'd been a violent incident."

"And you questioned the witness...

"Extensively. Her story remained... what she reported to the nine-one-on... her initial feedback on site to Brett a...

"She's been put on leave from work... lissa's vivid blue gaze was direct as sh... adding to the undertones in her comm...

"A point Ms. Whittaker and I discu...

"You don't think that's suspicious?...

"Suspicious how? It has no bearin... a crime."

"What crime? There's no body a... Troy."

It was the reality he kept slammin... how much he wanted to ignore it.

"Tell me you understand that," Mel...

"Of course I understand it."

"Good. Because I can't afford to hav... off the Davison case. He's struck twic... and based on his pattern, we need to... he hits again soon."

"I know what we're up against."

Meliss...
capable s...
what's s...
And ...
up with...
ning ou...
sixties ...
he's ba...
of a sp...
one d...
becaus...
run in...
with i...
"I ...
Ar...
exact...
guilt...
even...
Yet ...
ting ...
"F...
they'...
coul...
come...
news...
T...
co-C...
work...
had ...
ques...
It ...
Colt...
daug...
as th...

"As good as can be expected," Melissa said. "Travis keeps a close eye and the two of them are busy with Colton Plastics and planning for the baby's arrival. It's keeping her occupied, which has to be good in this situation."

"Does she know this latest news? About the home invasion?"

Melissa nodded. "I called her myself this morning. She handled it. She didn't ask a lot of questions, but she held it together. And Travis has been a rock for her."

Troy thought about what his cousin and his fiancée had dealt with over the past several months and was glad they had each other. He'd always believed he could handle whatever life threw at him—and had little interest in dragging a romantic partner into the risks that came with his work—but he also recognized the power of love.

Although he'd lost his mother when he was barely old enough to remember her, his father had always talked of the great love he shared with Amanda Colton. Geoff also spoke of how lucky he was to find a deep and lasting love with Leanne, long after he'd believed he would never find that sort of companionship and affection again. Lightening had struck twice, as it were. A special circumstance few were fortunate to experience.

"It's good they're together." Troy nearly expanded on the point when his phone went off. Evangeline's name registered on the readout. "I'm sorry, Mel, I need to take this."

She waved him on, even as her gaze narrowed.

"Evangeline. What's—"

"Troy! Someone was here. Outside. The shirt!"

Just like the night before, deep panic vibrated

through the phone like a living, writhing entity. "What shirt?"

"The white shirt. It's a bloody mess on my front step."

Chapter 7

Evangeline huddled on the same living room chair as last night, the air conditioning blowing through the room making it feel like a tomb. She wanted to act—wanted to do *something*—but no matter how often she told herself to move, all she could do was huddle on the chair.

What was wrong with her?

That question frittered and flowed through her mind, at moments an insistent banging and at others quiet and meandering. It was the only one she could seem to conjure, even as fragments of thought kept telling her she should wait outside or at least stand near the window, keeping an eye on that shirt.

But the blood. It was so red. So real. And so…vicious.

The killer must have left it on her front door, a taunting tease that not only reinforced the fear of last night, but ensured something else.

He *knew* where she lived—and had been in her home, too.

The urgent sound of sirens suddenly filled the room. Troy had come.

He was close. He was here. And that meant she was safe.

It was the only thing that could get her moving, she realized, as she stood and walked to the door. The sound of sirens was nearly overpowering as police cars pulled into the parking lot of her building. It was only when Evangeline heard the shouts through the door—and Troy's reassuring voice—that she finally felt ready to open it again.

The door handle was heavy in her hand and she needed to grip it with both hands to turn it. Slowly, slowly it turned and she pulled on the door.

Only to find Troy standing across the threshold, a line of officers behind him.

"Evangeline!" His voice sounded far away as she stared down at the front stoop of her home.

The concrete was empty, no sign of anything even having been there. Frantically, her gaze shifted to the lawn that stretched out to either side. Had the shirt blown away? The summer air felt still around her, not a breeze in sight, but it wouldn't take much to move a shirt, right?

Wind could have blown it from the front porch.

Only, as her gaze roamed the lawn on either side of her and further down the length of her condo building, Evangeline had to accept the truth.

There was no shirt.

No blood.

And no evidence it had ever existed.

* * *

The man watched from across the parking lot, a casual observer of what was taking place through his windshield. To anyone who saw him, including the rash of cops, he knew he'd just look like another guy waiting for someone in his car. The book in his lap would be a handy excuse should anyone knock on the window and question what he was doing there. Not that he was planning on sticking around.

But oh, how he'd wanted to see her face.

He'd been hiding down the yard when she opened the door to find the shirt and hadn't had a chance to enjoy the stark shock that would have covered those angelic features.

But he heard the scream.

Loud and pure, it practically reverberated off the bricks of her condo building. And damn, was it a fitting punishment for all she'd failed to do. Because it turned out the angel had a pair of broken wings. And she deserved what she got.

A fact he was more than happy to prove to her by removing the shirt after she'd slammed the door on the evidence. Again, more proof that she couldn't be trusted with the truth.

If she were a good lawyer working for the citizens of Grave Gulch County, she'd never have run in fear like that. She'd have picked up the shirt, no matter how much it bothered her, and brought it inside until her precious cop showed up.

But no.

She did just what he expected her to do. Slam the door on the truth. Just like she'd believed all the evidence from that phony, Randall Bowe.

Oh yeah, he thought as he slowly pulled out of his

spot, circling the back of the parking lot to steer clear of the cops. Those wings were mighty broken. And she deserved every single thing that was coming her way.

Troy felt the hard, unyielding gazes of his chief and two fellow cops as he watched Evangeline, stare sightlessly from the chair in her living room. The scene felt way too much like the night before and he was struggling to find any sense of equilibrium as he considered the shuddering woman in the chair.

How did he reconcile her with the strong, competent lawyer he knew?

And what in the hell was going on with her?

She hadn't faked the dread in her voice when she'd called him, nor was she faking the situation now. He'd bet his badge on it.

But still, something remained overwhelmingly off. How was it possible she'd had three panic-inducing scares in a matter of twenty-four hours, yet there was no evidence any of them had taken place? They would get the security footage of the building and several uniforms were already fanning out to canvas the property for witnesses, but the lack of a bloody shirt was a problem.

He'd been so focused on thinking Davison was responsible, but was it possible Randall Bowe had targeted her somehow?

"Troy. Can I speak with you?" Melissa's question was really a request and Troy shot a look at one of the deputies who'd arrived on scene, their silent exchange an order to keep watch on Evangeline.

Melissa waited at the front door of Evangeline's condo and gestured Troy outside. The midday sun was high in the sky, summer making its presence known in the sticky heat. "You want to tell me what's going on here?"

"She called me in distress, Mel."

"I can see that. And you responded in kind." His cousin spread her hand wide to take in the four police cars and scattering of cops milling around the small yard and parking area that made up the exterior of the condo complex. "What I can't see is any sign of evidence."

"I have an idea about that. Is it possible Bowe's trying to exact some revenge? Planting evidence on her, then taking it away."

"Troy—"

"He could do it. He's already proven he knows how to tamper with evidence, and he's enjoyed making taunts when he can. Wouldn't this be an escalation?"

"Troy!" Her voice was clipped and any sign of the family member and friend he knew and loved had vanished. Right now, she was fully his boss. "Are you listening to yourself? You're making up reasons which, while fair, remove any and all responsibility off Ms. Whittaker."

"But she's scared, Mel."

"And also currently on leave from a high-stress job. A leave that was directly related to letting a very guilty man go. A man who has murdered two more times in a serial fashion since her legal arguments got him released from our custody."

"You're blaming that on her?"

"Some of it, yes," she admitted.

"Because she used evidence our department improperly handled?"

"Where are your loyalties, Troy?"

"Where are yours?"

In all the years he and Melissa had worked together, Troy couldn't ever remember a harsher disagreement between the two of them. In addition to their familial bond, they had a close working relationship and had always been compatible.

But on this he simply couldn't agree with her. He'd seen Evangeline's face. Had watched her tremble in fear. Hell, he'd held her himself, and felt that bone-deep anxiety ripple through her.

He just couldn't walk away from this.

"This isn't about loyalty. This is about doing the job," he said.

"Doing what job? Running at the drop of a hat to placate a hysterical woman?"

"That's not fair."

"The truth isn't always fair." Melissa shook her head before extending a hand in frustration. "Look at it out here. I've got damn near a third of the department stomping around this condo complex while a serial killer roams loose."

"Other crimes haven't stopped because Davison is out free. The Coltons know that better than most." Troy saw the moment he might have gotten through to her. "Drew Orr tried to kill you in January, at the same time we were discovering the depth of Randall Bowe's deception."

"I know that. I lived it." She had had to shoot the man dead herself when he attempted to kill her and her now-fiancé, Antonio.

"Clarke and Everleigh, too," Troy pressed. "Everleigh was nearly killed by her ex-husband's lover, the woman was so hell-bent on revenge."

"You going to give me the whole list of Colton cousins, Troy? Because Travis and Tatiana are still reeling from that creep at Colton Plastics who had his twisted eye on her for far too long. Stanton and Dominique helped us uncover a drug ring operating right here in Grave Gulch County. And Desiree is finally able to sleep at night thanks to getting Danny back and living with the security and protection of Stavros's love. You think I haven't understood the pain my family has gone through these past months?"

"I know you have."

"Then why are you tossing it in my face?"

"Because we Coltons know it better than most. We can't ignore an upstanding citizen right here in Grave Gulch who needs our help."

"What if she's making it up?"

And there it was. The one piece of the puzzle he didn't have an argument for. Because in each of his family's experiences, there had been a clear problem. Escalating violence. Kidnappings. Serious threats.

Where was that here?

Other than what Evangeline claimed to have witnessed, there was nothing he could go on as tangible proof. And unlike his family situations where those terrible incidents had still somehow led to his family finding love, he and Evangeline weren't a couple. Nor did interfering in her life as if he had a right to be there meet his personal standards as a member of the Grave Gulch PD.

In the end, all he could go on was his gut. And the continued feeling that something was going very, very wrong around Evangeline Whittaker.

"What if she isn't?" Troy finally asked Melissa. "Can you honestly say we would have done our job serving and protecting this community if we ignore her?"

Melissa's steady gaze finally dropped, that brilliant

blue going cloudy when she lifted her eyes to him once more. "No. That's not what I want."

It was why Melissa was a good cop and an even better chief. She always did what was right and put the health and safety of her constituents above everything else.

"Let me ask you one thing, though."

Troy nodded, already anticipating the warning.

"We've worked long and hard to have a good relationship between our precinct and the DA's office. Randall Bowe's actions have put a serious dent in that relationship."

"Has anyone said anything to you? Has Arielle called you?"

Arielle Parks had a stellar reputation as Grave Gulch County's district attorney but the pressure she'd been under could get to anyone.

"Arielle and I talk regularly about any number of things. We respect each other and also respect the offices we each represent. We've each taken our collective ownership for the damage Bowe has done."

"Why do I sense a *but* in there?"

"I'm giving in on this a bit because Evangeline is one of Arielle's best and most well-respected ADAs. And I trust Arielle's opinion." Melissa glanced around once more. Troy's gaze followed and he couldn't deny the way his fellow officers appeared to be done with work, the lack of evidence leaving them with little to do. "But I also can't allow resources to be used this way."

"I understand."

"Why don't you go talk to Evangeline? See if you can't figure out what's happening. She doesn't have a door camera, which would have been a huge help in this situation."

put on the word *you* was pointed. But what that empha-sis meant was more than a little scary.

Pushing that away and unwilling to have him dis-suade her from doing the right thing, she dismissed his concern. "I'll be fine."

"With bloodied clothes on your front porch and strangers somehow sneaking into your house?"

"Who can even say that happened?"

"You can! You say it happened."

"What if—" She broke off on a hard, unexpected sob. The truth was too horrible to even say. But it haunted her, the idea that her mind could be playing tricks on her like this. "What if I'm wrong?"

Troy pulled her into his arms and as those tight, warm bands wrapped around her, Evangeline allowed herself to give in. She wanted to be strong. More, she believed it was required of her, to stand on her own two feet and handle whatever life threw her way.

But this was too much.

The anger and self-recrimination she'd carried for months now, over the case that let Len Davison go, had weighed heavy. The families who now suffered because he'd taken a beloved father, husband or brother away, haunted her.

What could she have done differently?

There hadn't been any answers. Not since the day Arielle had called Evangeline into her office to tell her the news. The mishandling of evidence that had allowed a guilty man to go free had become public, and with it, the reality of what they'd contributed to the situation by not conclusively proving Davison's guilt.

Despite her desire to stay on the job, she'd accepted the enforced leave. Had understood it as her due, a time to stop and reflect on her work and understand where she'd made missteps.

If that was all she'd had to live with, she'd have accepted it. A legal career was fraught with the cases that haunted you. Evangeline accepted that reality as part of the job. Even when it felt bad.

But all that had come since?

It was terrifying and maddening, all at once.

She clung to Troy, grateful for both the physical support as well as the emotional. He had been such a surprise in all this, almost as if he had come to her rescue. The idea of a rescuer wasn't language or imagery she particularly cared for, especially with the way she had grown up, yet she couldn't quite shake the image, either.

Troy Colton had, literally, come to her aid. He had shown up after the 911 call when she believed she had seen a murder. He had come here to her home, taking care of her with food, understanding and protection. It was humbling, to know someone could care that much. Would give of themselves that freely.

"Are you doing okay?"

She lifted her head, unable to look away from his deep hazel gaze. "Not yet, but I'm trying."

"For starters, you need to stop doubting yourself."

"How can I do that? The things that keep happening, they're impossible."

"They can't be impossible. Which means they have to have a reason. A possibility, if you will, for why they're happening."

"They have a possibility. It's that I'm hallucinating."

His eyes darkened at that, his mouth dropping into a deep frown. "Don't say that."

"What if it's true?" she argued back, the idea taking root. "If there has to be a reason, that is as good as any other one."

"Okay." He tilted his head, considering. "Let's play that idea out. Have you ever hallucinated before?"

"No."

"Not once?"

"No, not that I'm aware of."

"So why did you suddenly start now?"

She let out a frustrated breath, perked up by his reasoning even if she still questioned her own mind. "For people who experience hallucinations, they have to have one for the first time."

"Yes, that's true. But what would be the reason you suddenly have one? One day, randomly walking to get some dinner, in the middle of downtown Grave Gulch."

"Stress. The situation with my job. A serial killer on the loose. Take your pick." The reasons were endless. He had to know that as a law enforcement professional. Heck, he lived with stress every day. Lived with the consequences of criminals that got away with crimes they perpetrated, no matter how well-intentioned the police.

"Fine, let's play that out, too. You've been under stress at other times in your life. Law school's pretty tough and works you intentionally hard to make sure you've got the mental fortitude for the job. The difficulty keeps up as no sooner do you graduate then you have to study for the bar. And now, working your professional career in the DA's office. Is that a piece of cake?"

"No."

And it wasn't easy. She and her fellow ADAs handled a caseload that would fell most people. But it was the life of someone in the district attorney's office. Too few lawyers for far too many cases.

But as she contemplated the picture Troy painted

and weighed the truth of his words, Evangeline did feel some of that oppressive load of fear recede a bit. The Davison case might be on a level no one in the county had seen or experienced, but she had lived with stress. Professionally, absolutely.

And if she also considered how she'd grown up—in a highly emotional atmosphere with her father's behavior—she could add additional stressful situations to the tally of examples Troy had provided.

Yet in every one of those situations, hallucinations had never been a part of how she handled things. With any of it. Instead, she just put one foot in front of the other and tried to work through the answers.

"You've been coping with everything, Evangeline. There's no reason to think otherwise."

Troy's kind words—and the sudden realization she was still in his arms—had her pressing her hands against his chest. It felt so good to stand here with him, surrounded by his gentle strength. But there was no way she could come to depend on this. She'd already taken up far too much of his time.

And he was increasingly taking up too much space in her thoughts.

"Thank you."

She knew she should back away. It was the right thing to do, here in the midst of an emotional meltdown. Yet as she stood there, feeling both safe and confident for the first time in weeks, Evangeline found she couldn't move away.

Instead, she lifted her head as her gaze never left his. And when her mouth met his, she found that same quiet strength in the press of his lips to hers.

Chapter 8

He needed to walk away. Troy knew that. Felt it down to his marrow. Yet as Evangeline's lips met his, soft and warm, he could no sooner move away from her than he could stop drawing breath or force his heartbeat to still.

He wanted her.

It was the wrong time in the wrong place, but he couldn't quite find it in himself to care.

Where their kiss the night before had been tentative movements and a dive into the forbidden, this time it was different. This time, he knew how good she'd taste and how badly he'd wanted to kiss her again.

To hold her in his arms.

Even if he shouldn't.

Actions that should have been motivated solely by a protective urge had turned on him. He knew she needed comfort and he'd believed himself capable of giving it. Only now, he knew a hunger he couldn't deny.

Yes, he wanted her safe. And increasingly, he believed himself the only one who could keep her that way.

But he also wanted her.

Mouths merged, a soft sigh—his? hers?—mingling between them. Troy trailed his fingers down her spine before settling at the enticing curve of her lower back. Pleased with the way his hand fit there, nestled in the arch, he found his need turning wanton, and in seconds he'd fisted the material of her blouse in his hand.

Had he wanted like this before?

And how had he waited this long to taste her? To feel her?

Could he have known how neatly they'd fit together, her tall, lithe figure pressed to his? She was strong. He could feel that in the long lines of her body, in the firm sweep of muscle down the back of her arm, in the play of subtle strength beneath her shoulder blades.

He wanted.

In the end, it was really that simple.

And in the simplicity of that knowledge, Troy knew he needed to stop. To step away from Evangeline and the increasingly desperate desire to be near her.

Lifting his head, he stared down at her. Her thick eyelashes swept up from lids that were half-closed, the irises underneath dark with desire. "Troy?"

"I'm sorry. I've come into your home—" he glanced around "—your kitchen no less, and taken what I shouldn't have." He held onto her shoulders to keep her from swaying, but took a firm step back. "I'm sorry."

"For kissing me?"

"For taking advantage when you're vulnerable and scared."

"I'm fine."

He kept his gaze on hers, sharing the only truth he had. "I'm not."

"Oh."

She stepped back and he let his hands drop, satisfied she had her footing. He sensed that a wholly unnecessary apology sat on her tongue before she seemed to think better of it. "I'm going to go check if the remaining cops are still outside."

"I'll do it. And then I'd like to talk about something. I had an idea earlier, talking to Melissa. I wanted to run it by you."

It wasn't an out-and-out lie, exactly, but it was a slight prevarication. One that, while a bit spur-of-the-moment, increasingly made sense as Troy turned it over in his mind. He followed Evangeline to the living room, then moved to look out the front windows toward the parking lot.

"Is anyone there?"

"No. They're all gone." He let the curtain fall back in place in front of the large window framing her living room.

"Good. I can't begin to imagine what my neighbors must think."

"Let them think. Maybe it'll get them to pay attention a bit more, too."

Her head tilted, a soft waterfall of black hair skimming down over her shoulder. "I hadn't considered that."

"Maybe it's time to. The challenge of living in a complex like you do is that it's not quite as easy to notice strangers. But the benefits are that there are a lot more eyes, all focused on the same places. Someone lurking around your home should get noticed if they do it too often."

He hated using scare words like *lurk* and *stranger*,

but there was no help for it. And more to the point, he wanted to stress those things so Evangeline would understand she wasn't alone. The quicker she understood that and recognized it, the better off she would be. She lived in a crowded housing complex and it was time to try and use that to their advantage. Especially since the threat to her seemed so ephemeral.

"What was your idea?"

"Before, when I was talking to Melissa, we talked about my cousins."

"What does your family have to do with today?"

"I might have mentioned it yesterday, but my sister, as well as various Colton cousins, have had some strange experiences so far this year. Run-ins that have necessitated law enforcement involvement."

"We do have crime here, Troy. I see the caseload that regularly comes into the DA's office and while we're not rolling in it, we're hardly crime-free."

Her quick assessment was a good sign that her earlier fear had receded and Troy was pleased to see how deftly Evangeline questioned his points. It was a far cry from the shaken woman he and Melissa had found less than an hour ago.

"It's disappointing," she continued, "but we live in a big enough jurisdiction with a big enough population that we deal with our fair share of bad things happening."

She sat down, clearly engaged in their discussion, and Troy took his first easy breath since their kiss. While he would like nothing more than to keep kissing her, he knew they needed to stop. More, he knew he needed some physical distance from her. The easiest way to get back on common ground was to talk about a subject they could both wrap their heads around.

A subject that her legal brain would quickly assess in a way he might be more likely to miss.

"I heard about Melissa. When something happens to the chief of police, that's big news. She and Arielle are friendly, as well, so my boss shared some of the details as she knew them, too."

"The stalker that went after Melissa was pretty big news." News that still shook Troy down to the marrow. It wasn't something he liked to dwell on, but knowing his cousin had experienced that situation had lit a fire under him to catch Len Davison. "And a cop discharging their weapon, even in self-defense, is even more news. Ever since, the Davison case has consumed us all. It's also given her the head space to work through her act of self-defense with a bit of distance."

"That's good. I'm sure it helps that she's planning a wedding, too."

"You do have a pulse on the Grave Gulch grapevine."

A light blush colored her cheeks. "Like I said, Melissa and Arielle are friendly. And there's little a group of women love to talk about more than wedding plans. With Antonio Ruiz owning the Grave Gulch Hotel, well, it's hot gossip."

"Well, if we're talking weddings, personally, I'm a tulle guy."

The joke was enough to get a quick laugh before her smile faded. "That's not news to me about Melissa but you said 'cousins' as in plural. What else has happened?"

In careful detail, Troy walked her through all his family had experienced. Other than the few details intersecting with the ongoing Davison investigation, which he skipped, he gave her the unvarnished truth.

"How is your family holding up?"

"We're managing. We're Coltons and when bad things happen, we tend to close ranks and watch each other's backs. They did that years ago for my father after my mother was killed. And the next generation is committed to doing the same."

"Her death impacted all of you."

"It did."

"I don't mean that in an offhanded way, either. Obviously, losing your mother at any age is hard. What you and your sister had to endure is unimaginable."

He'd lived with it for most of his life: the knowledge that a stranger—one who had never been caught—murdered his mom. He had coping mechanisms and the love of his father, sister, half siblings and stepmother, as well as his extended family, to manage the grief. But until that moment, Troy hadn't realized how much it meant for someone who was basically a stranger to simply acknowledge his mother.

Her value.

Her worth.

Even her death.

"Troy, I'm sorry. I said the wrong thing."

"No, actually you didn't. You said the exact right thing. Thank you."

Her direct gaze was as skeptical as Melissa's had been earlier. "The right thing? Really?"

"Yes, really. My sister and I have talked about this through the years. People don't typically know what to say when you tell them that your mother has passed. That is only more real and more acute when the reason for death is murder. It's out of the ordinary and people don't know how to handle it."

"She was a person, Troy. She mattered. She doesn't deserve to be erased."

"No, she doesn't."

To the Colton family, Amanda McMahon Colton had never been erased. Her memory and the desire to seek justice for others drove all of them. But that still didn't mean that others outside the family understood it.

But Evangeline did.

The ever-present knot of grief that was usually tied so tightly around his heart eased at that revelation. And for an impossible moment, he was able to sit with another person and celebrate his mother's memory fully, instead of simply trying to erase the pain.

Evangeline still wondered if she'd said the wrong thing about Troy's mother, but couldn't find any hint of anger in his face. She knew how to read anger. She'd gotten good—very good—at reading her father's anger cues until she could pinpoint what would put him into a rage.

But Troy seemed calmer, somehow. As if talking about the horrible death of a loved one could calm instead of enrage.

It made little sense and she still mentally braced for some blowback, but as their conversation shifted once more, this time as Troy spoke of his sister and her wedding plans, Evangeline began to suspect he wasn't upset at all.

Although she had listened to everything Troy said, that clamoring sense of the threat faded. As it did, she keyed in more closely to what he was saying, only to be surprised once more when he stood up, crossing the room in two long strides. "I don't know how I missed this. Why I didn't think of it sooner."

Before she could even ask what he had missed, Troy had his phone in hand. "Dez, it's me."

Evangeline listened to Troy's side of the discussion, but it wasn't hard to piece together his sister's responses.

"I need you to do a sketch for me." He paused as he got some answer before adding, "Can we come over?"

We? Come over? Troy wanted her to come to his sister's house?

"Me and Evangeline Whittaker." He nodded, adding, "Yes, from the DA's office." She heard the hard laugh as well as a more distant one through the phone before he pressed on. "Yes and yes. I will bring dinner. See you at six."

Yes to what? Dinner was one yes, but what was the other?

Troy shoved the phone into his pocket, the rapid-fire call obviously at an end. "We're going to my sister's for dinner."

"We can't. I mean, I can't. I mean, why?"

"She's a sketch artist. I don't know why I didn't think of this sooner but I want you to work with her to sketch out the man you saw in the alley."

"But I didn't see him. I have impressions of him, but I never saw his face."

"That's Desiree's job. She'll pull out of you what she needs for the sketch."

"But we're intruding." Evangeline looked at her watch, frantic for some excuse that would keep her from meeting the no-doubt practiced—and discerning eye—of Troy's sister. "And it's four already. She wasn't expecting company."

"She is now."

"But she's got a little one. And a new fiancé. She doesn't need a stranger intruding on her personal time."

"It's fine."

"But I can't. What if I don't remember anything?"

*What if that makes you think I'm an even bigger phony
than you already do?*

The fear was irrational—it had to be. But the idea
of sitting with someone and trying to scrape her brain
for any memory of a man whose face she'd never seen
anyway felt tantamount to losing any and all credibility.

Troy had already dropped back onto the couch, his
pose relaxed. Confident, even. And why wouldn't it be?
He had nothing to lose.

"This isn't going to work."

"It will work."

"But I didn't see his face."

"But you saw something. Likely more than you realize, actually. Desiree is trained to do this. She has a
way of bringing an image to life. You just have to trust
the process."

Trust it? How?

The sense of looming disaster didn't fade, but
strangely, as she and Troy walked up the front walk-
way of Desiree Colton's home, it wasn't getting worse.
Maybe, Evangeline thought, it was the small scattering
of toys on the front lawn that calmed her. Or perhaps
the warm, welcoming smile on the face of the woman
who held the door open for them.

"Troy." Desiree Colton held out her hands to her
brother, enfolding him in a tight hug before turning
to face Evangeline. "I'm Desiree. It's wonderful to finally meet you."

Evangeline took the proffered hand, and Desiree's
slim fingers—what Evangeline thought of as artist's
fingers—clasped hers. "I'm glad you're here. I'm sure
my brother railroaded you into this seeing as how we

only spoke a few hours ago. So come on in, we'll have a glass of wine and some dinner and relax a bit."

"I'm on the clock, Dez," Troy said as they followed her into her home, his hands full of the tray of lasagna they'd picked up in town.

Without skipping a beat, Desiree tossed a look over her shoulder for her brother. "No wine for you, then." She reached out and gave Evangeline's hand another squeeze. "More for us, then."

In a matter of minutes, Desiree had taken the hot tray into the kitchen, poured two glasses of wine and a seltzer for Troy and settled them all in the living room. Evangeline had no idea how the woman had done it, but everything moved seamlessly. Effortlessly, really.

And Desiree managed this all while looking picture-perfect at the end of a long day and keeping up with a toddler.

One whose toys were all over the room but who was nowhere in sight.

Before she could ask, Troy beat her to it. "Where are Danny and Stavros?"

"Danny had a late nap and if we don't wear him out a bit he'll be up until midnight. Stavros ran him down to the park for a bit to run out the wiggles."

Evangeline could only assume she'd given Desiree a blank stare, because the woman smiled and added, "Also known as some serious two-year-old energy."

"Ah." Evangeline nodded, the picture in her head of an energetic child suddenly making much more sense.

"I'm also not above admitting I had another motive, as well."

"Subtle, Dez," Troy said, glancing at his sister from where he sat beside her on the couch.

"Subtlety went out the window with this whole year."

Desiree leaned forward, her expression eager. "Troy mentioned some of the things that you've been dealing with. I'd like to help however I can."

"I appreciate that." While she had initially said the words as a platitude, as they came out, Evangeline quickly realized they were completely true. She did appreciate the help. More, she appreciated the idea that someone besides Troy might believe her. Especially since her own doubts had begun to waver since that afternoon with the incident on her front porch. "You need me to tell you everything that's happened?"

"Yes, that will help. I'd like to get a sense of what you're dealing with. It will also help you later, when we try to work through the images."

Evangeline took a sip of her wine, Desiree's kind eyes and steady manner more of a relief than she ever could have imagined. "I've only ever been on the other side of it, looking at police sketches after they've been generated. But Troy said that you'll be able to pull images from me, even if I can't remember what the man I saw looks like."

Desiree nodded. "That's mostly true. The mind is fascinating in the way that we capture and snag fragments of images. My job to take those fragments and put them together into a complete picture."

The process as Desiree described it made sense and Evangeline was surprised to realize how excited she was to get started. "That's an interesting way to describe it. I never thought of what you do in that way, but I can see how a picture could come together, piece by piece."

"It feels like it shouldn't work, but it does. I've done hundreds and hundreds of sketches through the years, and I'm always amazed to see how a face comes to light on the page."

"Dez is one of the best," Troy said with pride. It was clear the siblings were close—Evangeline saw that from the moment they'd arrived—but it was equally nice to see how he supported her.

Yet one more experience she'd never had as an only child. Nor had she seen much pride in her parents' eyes. Especially her father's. Oh, sure, he was proud the day she graduated from law school, but that emotion never seemed to last. Never seemed to overcome the anger and disillusionment he carried around for life.

Shaking the bitter memories off, Evangeline focused on Troy and Desiree. She wasn't here to be maudlin and it was actually nice to be out for an evening talking with other people. "How long have you worked for the GGPD?"

"Almost ten years." Desiree took a sip of her wine, considering. "I've been an artist my whole life, and I got interested in all things police procedural as part of processing the loss of my mother. Doing the police sketches seemed like a natural fit."

"It's a tremendous way to use your talents."

Once again, the discussion she had with Troy about his mother filled her thoughts. How sad that both Troy and Desiree had often felt they couldn't celebrate their mother's memory. She was a person. One that they loved. There was nothing about those memories that should be erased or diminished.

"Thank you. I like to think it makes Mom proud."

"I've no doubt it does."

Before Evangeline could say anything else, a delighted giggle filtered in from outside. She heard a deeper laugh and then another chuckle and saw Desiree's eyes alight with excitement. "My boys are home."

The next half hour flew by in a blur. Evangeline

hadn't spent a lot of time with small children. She'd babysat when she was younger, but since becoming an adult, kids hadn't been a big part of her life. And in a matter of minutes, little Danny had her wrapped around his finger. Or, she thought with a rueful smile, his chubby little fist.

Although he took a few minutes to warm up, by the time Evangeline took a seat next to him on the floor, nodding to his mix of words and baby babble as he showed her his toys, he had become her chattering little best friend.

"Vange. Lean. Here—" He held out his hands, full of a fuzzy teddy bear. "Bear."

Evangeline's heart melted a little at the way he said her name. *Vange. Lean.* It had a sweet little ring to it coming from the mouth of a two-year-old. "What is your bear's name?"

"Mike."

"His favorite character from his favorite movie," Desiree was quick to add as she joined them with a seat on the floor. She shot Stavros a saucy smile as she did. "A movie that has quickly become Stavros's favorite, too."

Stavros shrugged, his smile equally cheeky and even more smitten than Desiree's. "I like little green sidekicks, what can I say?"

Evangeline had warmed to Stavros as quickly as she did to Desiree and Danny. The handsome ER doctor had an easy way about him, confident and competent, yet still warm and approachable. He'd extended his hand as soon as he walked in the door, introducing himself around a wiggling armful of toddler, and immediately putting her at ease. She imagined it was the skill that came in handy as he dealt with people in some of their most challenging personal moments.

The warm welcome made her glad she had come. Or, more to the point, glad Troy had suggested they visit with his sister and her family. She was still a little spooked at the idea of doing the police sketch, but had enough confidence that Desiree knew what she was doing that it would be a worthwhile experience.

It was only as she glanced up from her careful perusal of Mike's fur and button nose that she caught Troy's steady gaze. That sensual hazel had turned golden in the late afternoon light filtering into the living room and, for an unguarded moment, she felt herself caught up in it. Caught up in him.

She was captivated.

And while her life might be upside down at the moment, going wrong at every turn, it was increasingly difficult to think of Troy Colton as anything but absolutely right.

Chapter 9

"You most certainly did walk past her house every day for a solid month," Desiree shot back across the table, tossing her wadded-up napkin for good measure. "Little Lisa Baker. I remember it like it was yesterday."

Troy felt the heat creeping up his neck but made one, final valiant effort to redeem himself. "You make me sound like some sort of hopeless fool."

"You *were* a hopeless fool!" Desiree cackled, her glee at his expense more than evident. "A sixth grader in love with an eighth grader. Like that ever works."

"That's some serious pining," Evangeline added.

Troy turned to her, deliberately ignoring his sister's eye roll. "You're picking on me, too?"

Evangeline shrugged, her smile wide. "If the shoe fits."

Although his overt intention had been to bring Evangeline to Desiree's to do the police sketch, as the evening wore on, he couldn't deny how helpful the time had been to simply allow her to relax.

He could watch it happening, too. Her smile came easier, and the haunted look he had seen in her eyes had vanished around the same time she got on the floor to play with Danny.

What was funny was how neatly she and his sister turned the tables on him. Desiree's love of telling embarrassing stories—most often with him as their subject—had rung true this evening. But those stories had delivered the added benefit of putting Evangeline at ease. Maybe at his expense, but it was wonderful to see her smile all the same.

Which was the exact opposite reaction he should be having. He'd brought her here to get his sister's professional help. Not to notice the easing stress in Evangeline's shoulders or her smile. Even if that smile was beautiful.

He'd battled those wayward thoughts all evening. Even on the drive over here, as they stopped to pick up dinner, he had to force himself not to think of the evening as a date. Yes, he was bringing a woman to his sister's home. And yes, he had an interest in her that went well beyond the platonic. But this wasn't a date.

So why did it feel like one?

Embarrassing sixth grade stories aside, it amazed Troy to realize how comfortable he felt. On most dates, he worried about what to say or how the evening was going or how the evening might wrap up. But right now, sitting here with Evangeline and his family, he was at ease.

And he reminded himself as he reached for his glass of seltzer, this wasn't a date.

Was. Not. A. Date.

Without warning, Evangeline's comments about his mother filtered back into his thoughts. He meant what he had said to her earlier. Most people found it hard to talk about Amanda Colton and the way she had died.

Only Evangeline hadn't shied away from it. Instead, she had shown compassion as well as a willingness to speak of the dead. It was so simple. For something so complex as grief and loss and all the ways you coped with childhood trauma well into adulthood, the simplicity of just speaking of his mother was humbling.

And somewhere deep inside, he was grateful.

"Do you think it might be time to get started?" Evangeline asked the question of Desiree, but her gaze quickly shifted to Troy.

"I'm ready if you are," his sister agreed, her tone easy and warm.

Desiree had excused herself about a half hour before to put Danny to bed. After returning, she had sat back down at the table and continued with the discussion as if she'd never left. Troy was pleased to see how she quietly allowed Evangeline to pick the time instead of interrupting their after-dinner conversation.

It was one more thing about his sibling that he admired. Not just her compassion, but her ability to acknowledge where someone else was coming from. Desiree hadn't missed Evangeline's wide eyes and nervous demeanor when they had arrived earlier at the house. But in her own inimitable fashion, his sister had looked past it all and brick by brick, helped Evangeline take down the emotional wall that had locked her in. It was a skill, and one he didn't compliment her for often enough.

"Troy and I will take dish duty," Stavros said with a big smile, standing and picking up plates.

"I say we take it and run, Evangeline," Desiree said. She stood and gave Stavros a smacking kiss before turning back to Evangeline with a wink.

At ease with the lighthearted moment, Evangeline smiled and nodded. "I think you're right."

In moments, the women had disappeared to Desiree's studio, leaving Troy and Stavros alone in the kitchen.

"She's going through a tough time." Stavros started right in while setting the dishes in the sink.

"She is. I hope Dez can help her with the sketch."

"If anyone can, it's your sister. That woman does the most amazing things with a pencil and paper. I'm lucky if I can draw a stick figure and even then, it's never in proportion to a house or a tree."

"I feel like I'm violating some sort of important brotherly responsibility," Troy said as dumped the rest of the plates in the sink before slapping Stavros on the back. "But you really love my sister. It makes me happy."

"More than my own life. I don't know how it happened, and as fast as it did, too. But yes, I love her. And I love Danny. And I love the life we're making. It's nothing I thought would ever happen for me. Especially not after losing Sammy."

It was sort of amazing how Desiree and Danny had come into Stavros's life, just as Leanne had come into his father's so many years ago. A blessing, long after it seemed there wasn't any good left to experience or feel.

Stavros had lost his baby daughter in such a horrible way. He'd thrown himself into his work and found a way forward, but he'd done it all alone.

Troy could still remember Desiree's concerns as she'd spoken of her growing feelings for the doctor.

How she cared for him but wasn't sure if Stavros could find it in his heart to love again.

To live again.

Yet he had. They'd found their way and would continue to find their way. Together.

"You've got an eye for the pretty lawyer."

Stavros's quiet words hit him like a shot to the chest and Troy nearly bobbled the rinsed plate he was loading into the dishwasher. "It's not like that. She's in trouble. And I've known her for a long time. And she's—"

He broke off as Stavros grinned. "In trouble. Yeah. I get it. Doesn't mean she isn't pretty and pretty great, all at the same time."

"She is those things, but this isn't like that. I'm helping her. Protecting her."

"You can help her and protect her and still think she's pretty great."

"It's just not like that."

Stavros handed him a dish, his stare direct. "But maybe it could be."

"Was the man taller than the woman or shorter?"

"Taller. Much taller."

"Taller, like he loomed over her?"

Desiree's question stopped her and Evangeline closed her eyes, replaying the memory in her mind's eye. She'd believed the man a lot taller than the woman but now that she thought about it, had he been?

Her eyes popped open, even as the memory still lingered in her thoughts. "Well, maybe he wasn't as tall as I think. It was more that he had a big, hulking body to him. He had height on her, yes, but it was also the breadth and heft of his frame."

"Good. That's good," Desiree said as she sketched.

Evangeline waited as Desiree made some changes to the paper in front of her, using her pencil and eraser in equal measure. The whole process had been interesting, and far more methodical than she could have imagined. Each of Desiree's questions built on the one before, and many were things Evangeline wouldn't have immediately thought of.

The man's height was an example. Yes, he was tall. Definitely taller than the woman. She had seen that clearly while they struggled at the end of the alley. But now, being forced to think about it, she realized that some of that feeling of height was also tied to his solid form. It wasn't like there was a foot's difference between him and the woman. Instead, his physical bulk had given her the perception he was so much bigger.

Height hadn't been the only revelation, either. The man had worn a hat and Evangeline had struggled to see his eyes. But with Desiree's questions, she realized she had gotten a solid look at his chin and neck. When pressed, she could bring that image back in her mind's eye. The rounded chin, and the fleshy throat beneath it. He had a heavy, bulldog-like look that now took real shape in her mind. Like it had been there all along, but she just needed to think about his face in pieces instead of as a single memory.

Desiree continued making tweaks to the paper and Evangeline used the lull in questions to look around the room. Desiree's studio was just a converted bedroom within the house, but it had her artist's stamp on it in every way.

While the artistic components were expected, she hadn't counted on the pin-neat desk or the state-of-the-art computer mounted on the surface. Desiree had excitedly showed her the sketch program she'd use later, after the initial session, to work and refine the images Evangeline had provided. The tool was brand new, an investment the GGPD had made in expanding its capabilities, and Desiree was like a kid at Christmas, she was so excited to use it.

For her part, Evangeline was amazed by the entire process. The computer program was just the icing on the cake. It was a fascinating blend of art meeting science and she'd marveled at how truly functional Desiree had made her talent.

Not that it diminished anything from her art. There were several pencil sketches framed on the walls, some of them of Danny. She could see his progression, from infant, to baby, to the toddler he was now. Although each image was beautiful, it was the love that came through so clearly that truly captured Evangeline.

"There are times I can't believe he was so little," Desiree said, her gaze skipping over the various prints.

"He's still pretty little, but I do see what you mean."

"He's my miracle."

Evangeline briefly weighed not bringing up the kidnapping, but it had come up a few times during dinner and Desiree seemed able to handle discussing it. "I'm so glad he's unharmed and doing so well."

"Thank you. It's been a difficult time, but so much good has come out of it, too. Every time I wake up in a cold sweat, I try to remind myself of that."

Evangeline knew that Desiree meant finding Stavros, when she referred to the good that had come about, and she was happy that things had worked out so well. "It always amazes me how things come into our lives when we least expect them."

"Well, since you brought it up—" Desiree let the

comment hang there, before she continued. "I'm glad that you're spending time with my brother."

"Oh no, no. It's not like that."

"Are you sure?"

"He's been so kind to me. Looking out for me as he works this case. That's all it is. Really."

Was that all?

If the situation was different and she wasn't afraid because of the weird, violent happenings in her life, would she consider Troy differently? Think about a relationship with him? Yet it was exactly *because* of what was happening in her life that he'd walked into it.

"Maybe it's like you said. Good things come into our lives in unexpected ways." Desiree's tone was casual but it was impossible to miss the woman's point underneath. And the belief that there could be something going on between her and Troy.

Which was why she had to keep pressing against that fantasy. It was wonderful that Desiree and Stavros had fallen in love, especially in such an extremely tense and challenging time in her life. But that didn't work for everyone. And Evangeline had no reason to assume she and Troy would have the same sort of outcome.

"It's a difficult time for the GGPD and for Grave Gulch overall. I feel like I'm only adding to the problem, with whatever it is that's happening to me." She shook her head. "If there even is anything happening to me."

"Of course something happened to you."

"But that's the problem. What if nothing *did*?"

She hated saying the words, especially to this woman, who had done nothing but open her home and offer her kindness. But no matter how hard she tried, Evangeline could not shake the continued feeling that the things she thought were happening somehow *weren't*. That phantom killers in alleyways and invisible intruders who left travel books behind didn't exist.

"You don't really believe that." Desiree set her sketchbook down, her gaze as direct as her brother's. "What happened to you is real. You saw something in that alley."

"But the police didn't find anything. CSI hasn't found anything. Even a K-9 tracker came up with nothing."

"Then there has to be different reason. But you saw something. What you just shared with me, when you walked me through your images of the man in the alley? That's real."

Desiree's conviction went a long way toward making her feel better, even if it couldn't quite erase the lingering doubt.

"Here. I'll show you how real." Desiree picked up the sketchbook, turning it around so that the image was facing outward.

On a hard gasp, Evangeline leaned forward in her chair, reaching out to touch the edge of the paper. As promised, the man she'd seen struggling with that woman in the white shirt was facing her from Desiree's sketchbook. Her disparate memories of his features had somehow, some way, coalesced into the image of a person.

A real person.

One who'd murdered a woman while she stood and watched.

Troy continued to mull over his conversation with Stavros long after the two men had settled back in the living room. Danny's toys had been moved into a neat pile in the corner and there was once again room to sit.

It was surprising, on some level, to have his feelings

read so easily. He didn't date much, but he had been in relationships off and on throughout his adult life. Never before had his sister keyed in so quickly on a woman he was interested in. And while Stavros was a recent entry into the family, it was equally unsettling to have another man pinpoint the feelings Troy was working so hard to deny.

Although he probably shouldn't be surprised. Stavros and Desiree had only recently gotten together, and the lingering pain of losing his child had colored Stavros's world for many years. Love and relationships weren't a part of that. Maybe Stavros was having an easier time recognizing attraction because he was still in the early stages of it himself, relatively speaking.

"Desiree didn't have a chance to tell me much, but it sounds like Evangeline has been having a difficult time coming to terms with this crime she witnessed."

Grateful for the break from his thoughts—and any and all musings that suggested he was talking about feelings with Stavros—Troy grasped for the conversational lifeline. "She has. We all have. Detective Shea and I arrived on scene last night to investigate her nine-one-one call, and all signs of a crime scene had vanished."

Stavros frowned at that. "What you mean vanished? Humans shed far too much DNA in day-to-day life, let alone in a violent situation, for it to simply vanish."

"That's the problem. We didn't get anything from a visual review of the scene, but CSI hasn't gotten anything on a molecular level, either."

"It's just not possible."

"Evangeline is doubting herself because of it."

Stavros quieted, glancing in the direction of Desiree's studio. It was only when he seemed satisfied that the women couldn't hear them, that he spoke. "Is it possible she's having hallucinations of some sort? A mental impulse could make a situation seem real, even if it isn't."

It was the same question Evangeline had brought up and he had been quick to dismiss it. To tell her was impossible. But now, to have the same question come from a doctor? Maybe it was time to consider it.

"Is that possible, especially if she's never had any sort of struggle like that before?"

"Anything is possible. She's been under a tremendous amount of stress with work and we never know exactly what it is that can cause a lapse of that sort in the mind."

"It still doesn't make a lot of sense. I recognize she has been under stress with her job, but her record is impeccable. And being an ADA isn't easy in normal times. Wouldn't there be some sort of decline? Something that would've been recognizable, before a strong hallucination that lasted for several minutes?"

As Stavros considered the counter argument, Troy forced himself to reflect honestly on the man's points. Since his time in the GGPD, he'd experienced plenty of situations with individuals who had some mental or emotional break with reality. Mental illness or extreme stress brought on by life-changing situations or those times when life was simply too much. He'd learned to think more favorably of others in those moments, recognizing that he'd want—and more important, *need*—the same compassion in return if the situation were reversed.

And even with that understanding, he still chafed at the idea that Evangeline was experiencing some sort of emotional break with reality. Especially when it seemed like everything happening to her centered on some phantom threat.

A phantom threat that kept executing real, tangible actions.

Tangible actions that vanished the moment someone else showed up...

Was it possible? Troy mused.

He hadn't had many in his career, but he had seen people, often women, the victim of gaslighting. A sort of slow, steady drip of behavior from a hidden foe, making them believe there was a danger, then hiding it.

Was that happening here?

"I don't think you're wrong," Stavros finally said. "But I do think you need to be open to all possibilities."

Troy's mind still churned with the possibilities, even as Stavros's kind words gave him one more avenue to consider.

One more thread in what was becoming an increasingly complex knot.

Brett and Melissa had all shared similar warnings and it would be foolish to disregard a consistent theme from others he respected.

But he also respected Evangeline.

They might not have exchanged much in the past beyond the occasional hello, but he'd observed her plenty in the courtroom. Even now, he remembered a small incident she likely had no memory of.

She'd been prosecuting a hit-and-run case. Additional challenges had arisen when it was discovered a child was in the car that had fled the scene. The driver was eventually apprehended, and through the course of the deliberations, the man's daughter had been brought to court. Troy had been convinced at the time the child was being used as a prop for sympathy, but he knew his role and avoided editorializing when he gave his testimony. Even as he vowed to himself that he was going to look into his suspicions of abuse.

It was only during a recess, when the child and her mother were in the hallway outside the courtroom, that he'd overheard Evangeline. She wasn't supposed to approach the other side, the potential for judicial action against her a real possibility if she was discovered. But Troy had heard her all the same, telling the wife quietly that she and her daughter could get away from the woman's husband and get help. That Evangeline could find them a safe place.

He'd been even more surprised when Evangeline had reached into her bag to produce a card and, along with it, a small stuffed animal she'd handed over to the girl. It wasn't much bigger than her fist, the sort that was sold in the stationery and gift shop on the corner next to the courthouse, but the little girl had wrapped the plush cat in her arms as if it were a lifeline.

She hadn't seen him. Troy was sure of it, the spot he'd stood observing the exchange hidden behind a large pamphlet rack. But as the woman rushed away, leaving Evangeline alone in the corridor, he'd seen Evangeline drop her head and brush away a tear.

He'd always respected her and he'd thought her beautiful from the first moment he'd laid eyes on her. But in that moment, he'd seen the genuine care and concern in her actions and he'd never been able to shake that memory.

Or that quick rush of tears she'd brushed away before anyone could notice.

Evangeline stared at the parked cars underneath the lights in her condo's parking lot and tried desperately to ignore the wash of fear that suddenly roiled through her stomach. It had been a good night. A great night, actually. She'd spent the evening with nice people. She'd laughed, talked and had even played with a small child who reminded her that all the work they did, from law enforcement to the entire legal process, was worth it.

And she'd spent the evening with Troy.

For all the fear and confusion of the past few days, he had been a bright beacon of calm, caring and concern.

She was also becoming far too comfortable having him near.

"Thanks for this evening. I had no idea how badly I needed a night out and the company of other people. Your sister and her family are wonderful."

"Dez and Danny were great all by themselves. But I'm happy to see her have a new love in Stavros."

It was so simple. That he could accept others so easily. No frustration or anger at the disruption in his life by someone new. No distrust that someone had come along and captured his sister's heart.

"Who are you, Troy Colton?"

The question was out, weird and silly, and now hanging between them in the car as he pulled up in front of her door.

Troy put the car in Park and turned to face her. The light that filtered in from the overheads painted everything with a stark fluorescent glow, yet even in the neon haze of the illumination she could see the warmth in his eyes. "I'm just me, Evangeline. I'm a cop. A brother. A son. An uncle. A cousin. And maybe someday soon, a brother-in-law."

Although she heard no censure in his tone, something compelled her to keep going.

"But your family is so open. So welcoming. Your

sister has a new love and just like that, you and he get along famously. Your cousins seem to number the stars and you have a relationship with all of them. You might think your nephew has you wrapped around his finger but you've got him equally wrapped around yours." She took a deep breath. "It's not anything I'm used to. And I just wanted to tell you how special it is."

"Thank you."

She saw the question before he asked it. It filled his gaze, his brow furrowing as he obviously weighed whether or not he was going to say something.

"I mean that thank-you. We never really know how our family situations look on the outside. I'm lucky to have mine and it's nice to hear that the affection we have for each other is obvious."

"Of course."

"But it does make me curious. Was your family different?" he asked. "Because you don't seem to just be observing my relationships—you seem surprised that they exist."

"My family wasn't at all like yours. I'm an only child, for starters."

His grin was quick and immediate, and Evangeline felt it blow through her with all the force of a hurricane. "That's not a problem in the Colton family." That smile soon faded. "But your questions aren't just because you're an only child. Are they?"

"I've never seen anything like it. A bond like that. I know anger and rage and then silence. But not easy laughter at the table and welcoming visitors into your home with open arms."

Later, she'd likely tell herself she shared all those things because she was tired and her guard was down and the sketch work with Desiree had forced her to draw on her last reserves of emotional strength.

But right now, she said the words because she needed to say them.

Troy nodded, that furrowed brow as serious as before. Only before he said anything, an electrifying series of pops lit the air. Quick, heavy bursts of sound suddenly bombarding them from all sides.

And then the lights above the car went out, plunging them into darkness.

Chapter 10

Troy immediately reached for Evangeline, pressing his hand to the crown of her head and forcing her down in the seat to take cover. The noises continued but as his initial burst of adrenaline wore off to the point he could think over simply reacting, he realized the sound remained outside. There were no shot-out windows. No broken glass, even. Just that continued loud popping and bursting.

And then it stopped.

"Troy?" Evangeline unfurled from where she'd slunk down in her seat.

"Stay there," he ordered, his phone already in hand to call for backup.

He needed to wait to get out of the car but people from her condo complex were already opening their doors, lights appearing at the same time on some of the floors above.

In clipped tones, he relayed to dispatch what had

happened and what little he knew of the scene before giving the warning that never failed to make his skin crawl. "Possible active shooter."

He got quick reassurance that several patrol cars nearby were already on their way.

"An active shooter?" Evangeline asked. "At us?"

"We can't know."

"Those were gunshots?" Evangeline glanced around frantically, twisting in the small space of the front seat. "What are all these people doing outside?"

"I'm going to go ask everyone to go back inside their homes. Stay here."

"You can't—"

He cut her off. "Stay here. Patrol is en route and we can assess once they're here. I'm a trained officer and I can handle this."

The quick nod was all he got but it had to be enough, especially as more lights went on behind darkened windows and a few more neighbors stepped out their front doors.

Troy got out and pushed as much authority into his tone as he could.

"Grave Gulch Police! I need everyone to go back in their homes until we know what's going on."

Various shouts rang out from the people who'd come outside or who'd lifted their windows to take in the scene.

What right do you have?

This is my house.

What's going on?

"I repeat! Grave Gulch PD." He ran through the particulars again and by the time he'd finished, the sound of sirens was already audible, flashing blue lights visible shortly after.

The sensation of being an open target refused to leave him. His gaze kept darting through the now-darkened parking lot as he sought to narrow in on anything suspicious or out of place. He kept his back to Evangeline's building and his body angled toward the ground, hoping to minimize himself in a shooter's vision.

Although that wait dragged on, he knew by the sound of sirens that he and Evangeline had only been waiting a few minutes at most. In another thirty seconds he had police cars filling the parking lot, cops milling around the area.

A strange sense of relief filled him when Brett jumped out of one of the cars, Ember on his heels. Brett assessed the situation, his gaze as careful as Troy's had been as he dissected the parking lot in quadrants. Satisfied he saw no one out in the open, Brett gave the all clear to the surrounding officers and then they swarmed through the parking lot and on into the grass.

Troy eyed Evangeline through the windshield and gestured for her to stay down, despite the clearance. He still wasn't comfortable, nor did he feel it was safe for her yet out in the open. When he saw her subtle nod in return, he shifted his attention to Brett.

"Fancy meeting you here," Brett said, his grim smile and active gaze that continued to scan the area around them proof that this wasn't a social call.

"I hear you. This is getting to be a bit of a habit."

"Evangeline?" Brett was discreet and never even tilted his gaze toward the car, but Troy knew the detective was aware of Evangeline's presence.

"Yeah. I took her over to my sister's so Desiree could do a police sketch tonight. We just got back and then this happened."

"Want to walk me through it?"

Troy gave Brett the details, explaining how they had parked and were finishing up a discussion covering the evening's events. He avoided all mention she'd made of her family, recognizing that was personal and not relevant to the discussion anyway. He then detailed the punching noise that had broken through the evening stillness before the lights went out.

"But you don't think it's gunshots?" Brett asked.

"No. I don't see anything. There aren't any casings on the ground, and we weren't hit with any bullet holes in the car windows. Not even a scrape on the paint."

Brett tilted his head back and stared up at the structures that kept the condo's parking lot well lit for residents and visitors. He tilted his head once more, obviously trying to get a clear gaze at the light directly over Troy's car. "Do you have a flashlight in your glove box?"

Before Troy could go get it, one of the patrol officers handed over a flashlight from his belt. "Here you are, Detective."

Brett shined the narrow beam upward onto the oval shape of the light. "Isn't this interesting?"

Troy stepped closer and stared up, following the line of Brett's gaze.

"Light's been shot out, Buddy. Right over Evangeline's passenger side door."

"But there aren't any shell casings on the ground." A quick glance showed the other lights all continued to glow, a fact he was already cursing himself for not noticing.

The assembled officers all had their flashlights in hand, and began inspecting the ground, but nothing else glittered.

What the hell was going on?

The light had obviously been blown out, and those pops had echoed like gunshots, loud and persistent and much too close to the car.

"Detectives! Over here."

Troy and Brett walked over to where a young rookie pointed at the ground. Troy recognized her, one of their fresh-faced new recruits who had joined the GGPD in the last couple of months. "What did you find, officer?"

"It looks like a string of firecrackers. Look here." She pointed where small, seemingly innocuous poppers had exploded off of their pasteboard holders. "Is it possible this is what you heard?"

It was entirely possible. And as Troy reconsidered that quick burst of noise, he realized that small firecrackers made sense.

"You think someone's playing a prank?" Brett dropped to his knee and lifted one of the discarded paper casings.

"A prank? This close to Evangeline's house?" Troy pushed back. "No way."

"Troy, come on. It's June already. And it's summertime. Everybody starts getting excited for fireworks this time of year."

"Detective, sir?" Grace Colton, Troy's sister and one of the newest rookies on the force, stepped forward. She was diligent about treating him with the respect of his rank, and while he appreciated it, it always made him feel a bit awkward when she went into formal mode. "Is it possible some kids were here playing? And when they realized it upset you, they ran."

Although Troy had been focused on Evangeline when they pulled into the parking lot, and even more so once he cut the ignition and turned to face her, he didn't recall seeing anyone milling around the lawn. He might be into her, but he certainly would have recognized a group of kids. Even if they hadn't been making mischief, he would've seen them and carefully navigated so that he didn't come too close to one or potentially run over a bike. Children were careless in summer when they had their freedom from school and he always paid extra attention when he saw one anywhere in close proximity.

Plus, it was after 11 p.m. Would they still be out playing, summer vacation or not?

And why so close to her home and nowhere else?

"I suppose anything is possible, Grace. But it feels like a long shot."

Brett didn't respond and Troy heard a world of information in that lack of answer.

"Long shot? What makes you think that?"

Once again, Brett proved himself the consummate partner, and pulled Troy to the side, out of the way of anyone who might hear them. "Come on, man, you really think this is anything?"

"Do you think it isn't? She's been under attack for almost thirty-six hours."

"Under attack? If it's even that, it's an attack by things no one can see but her."

"Because the threat is hiding out of view."

Brett stared up at the darkened light again before returning his gaze fully to Troy's. "I'm not saying it's not strange, but I don't think it's a problem that necessitates half the GGPD out here. And for the second time today."

Troy knew that resources were stretched to the bone. The Davison case as well as all the other things Randall Bowe had deliberately blown up needed every bit of the precinct's focus. But he simply couldn't stand down on this one. "Something is happening to her, Brett. I know it. I feel it. This can't be a coincidence."

"Look, I get it. Instincts are a huge part of this job. But are you sure your instincts are right on this one?"

It was because of both the respect he heard in Brett's voice and the seriousness that he saw on the man's face the Troy was willing to end the conversation right there.

But it was the first clue that he might be up against more than a few doubts. First Melissa's that afternoon, and now Brett's.

If his closest allies had questions, it was only natural to assume that the GGPD did not believe that Evangeline Whitaker was in danger.

Yet however he spun it, Troy couldn't conceive of any way that she wasn't.

Watching the body language of the cops from her safe perch in the car, Evangeline wanted to scream with the frustration of it all.

They didn't believe her.

It hadn't taken much in the way of intuition to read the skepticism painted across the various officers' faces. Nor did she need clairvoyance to understand what Detective Shea was saying to Troy.

It was one more problem laid at her feet.

And she hadn't even called this one in to the GGPD.

But there are still a dozen police officers swarming your home.

As that thought filled her mind, the urge to sink lower in the car expanded in her lungs until she nearly burst with it. Which was the exact reason she sat up straight and opened the door. She'd worked too damn long and hard to overcome the frustrations of her childhood to sit and cower. Digging her keys out of her purse as she crossed toward her door, she had them in the lock before Troy caught up to her.

"Hey. I want you to stay in there."

"And I want to be in my home."

"But it's not safe."

Evangeline blew out a hard breath and turned to face him before flinging out a hand toward the flashlight-illuminated officers. "I've got a dozen cops on my lawn. I think I'm fine."

"Let me at least do a sweep of the house first."

"I'm *fine*, Troy."

The words spewed out, harsh and bitter, but try as she might, she couldn't pull them back. They were the culmination of more than a day's worth of fear and exhaustion, layered on top of months' worth of the same. Twisting hard on the key, she shoved on the door and pushed into the house. She had no interest in being the center of gossip in her condo complex, nor did she have any interest in seeing the mix of what was sure to be pity and censure in Brett Shea's eyes. Hell, his dog would probably wear the same expression at this point.

"Let me." Troy followed her into the house, flipping on lights as he went. "I'll do a sweep of the house."

"I've got this."

He stilled at that, laying a hand on her forearm. She expected him to say something but when he remained silent, she finally looked up.

"Please let me do this."

The emotional fire that had carried her inside suddenly sputtered out and all she could do was nod. "Okay."

Although she refused to huddle on a chair underneath a blanket this time, she did remain in the living room as he did the same sweep as the night before. Onward toward the back door, flipping on lights and opening closet doors. Then back down the hall and on into her two bedrooms. He finished the search in a matter of minutes. "All clear."

"Good."

"Thank you for letting me check."

"No, thank you. I'm sorry I was so petulant and ill-behaved."

Something flashed across his features. It was quick—if she'd looked away from him for even a moment, she'd have missed it.

But in that flash, Evangeline thought it looked a lot like anger.

Petulant and ill-behaved?

Troy was still rolling those treasures around on his tongue a half hour later as he went back outside to wave Brett and Ember off and out of the condo parking lot. They were the last to leave, the other officers on scene all having dispersed already, after getting all clears from Troy or Brett.

Troy had requested they take in the firecracker casings, and the officer who'd discovered them had quickly complied, securing them in evidence bags. Brett might have his doubts but Troy wanted those casings in to CSI and he knew his cousin Jillian would make them a priority. She might only be in her first year on CSI but she was good and she was motivated to succeed. A fact that had only grown exponentially when Randall Bowe tried to pin his criminal evidence techniques on her.

It had been a bad time, Troy thought, as he headed back toward his partner. Jillian had struggled for quite a while as Bowe's transgressions came to light. Each and every time, their CSI head tried to pin the faults on his junior investigator, even though Jillian's work was impeccable.

Her work ethic even more so.

Yet Bowe had still managed to make her doubt herself.

Which brought him back to his own problem. He'd only worked with Brett for a few months, but he trusted the man implicitly. Melissa had partnered them up on the Davison case and they'd shown great promise as a working pair. Yet here he was, arguing with Brett's instincts and forcing his own.

"I'm sorry about before."

Brett glanced briefly away toward Evangeline's front door. "Look, I get it. She's in some sort of trouble. Too much is going on to think this incident is totally innocent. I'm just not so sure it's as sinister as you believe it is, either."

"I can see that."

"Sleep on it and we'll put fresh eyes to it in the morning?"

Troy took the proffered hand that came with the offer and shook it, satisfied he and his working partner were absolutely finding common ground. "I'll be in before eight. Coffee's on me."

Brett called for Ember and the two loped off to his car. The urgency with which they'd arrived had faded and Troy didn't miss the weight that rode Brett's shoulders as he watched him cross the parking lot beneath the working lights.

Wasn't he feeling the same?

That endless weight that had settled over the entire GGPD when Len Davison and Randall Bowe's crimes were discovered?

One that seemed to have Evangeline in its grips, as well.

I'm sorry I was so petulant and ill-behaved.

There it was again. That odd apology that suggested Evangeline believed she'd acted like a child. She was a woman in danger and that was all she could come up with? Some apology for it all?

I know anger and rage and then silence. But not easy laughter at the table and welcoming visitors into your home with open arms.

Things had happened so fast in the car that Troy hadn't had a lot of time to process her last comment. But now that he did, he considered what she'd said. And all that lay beneath those words that spoke of fear and tension and a volatility that shaped the way she thought of families.

How she believed they acted.

He'd been a cop for a long time and he wasn't a stranger to the more terrible things people did to one another. That was as true of how family members treated one another as it was in the crimes he saw committed month in and month out, year after year.

What he hadn't expected was that Evangeline might have lived with that in her own life.

The strong, competent attorney he'd observed for years was a grown woman apparently still processing the sins of her upbringing.

He took a deep breath on that knowledge, not quite ready to head back into her house yet. He was determined to stay another night, not comfortable with leaving her alone. A feeling that had only grown stronger with the reality that the large light closest her home was out. She had a front door light but its radius offered limited protection, and as far as he was concerned, it wasn't enough.

So he'd stay. He'd argue the point if he needed to or sleep out front in his car, but he'd stay. But before he did either, he needed the soothing quality of the evening air and a few minutes with his racing, roiling thoughts.

With nothing more than observation in mind, Troy walked the perimeter of the parking lot. He took stock of the way cars were stationed in front of the building—which he assumed was meant for the residents. And then there were additional spots that spread out as a paved parking lot, providing additional spaces for guests.

He counted the number of overhead lights, similar to the one in front of Evangeline's door. And as he looked up at each one, the bulbs were bright and shining.

Coincidence?

"What are you looking at?"

Troy turned to see a woman, likely no more than twenty-two or twenty-three, staring up in the same direction.

"Nothing. Just curious that the light's out."

"I heard all that noise earlier." She shrugged. "My boyfriend told me to ignore it. 'Ella,' he said, 'why are you always so nosy about what the neighbors are doing?'"

Troy wasn't so certain it was nosy, but he took full advantage of the young woman's curiosity. "It's good to keep an eye on your surroundings."

"That's what I said!" she said and brightened at Troy's ready agreement. "I want to know what's happening where I live."

"And what did you find?" Troy asked.

"Nothing." Ella kicked the grass at her feet. "Probably just a bunch of kids playing around with fireworks."

Her boyfriend hollered down from a window above and she glanced up before backing away. "I've been out here a while. I'll see you later."

Troy took a solid look at the boyfriend. Although Ella

seemed awfully quick to do his bidding, Troy didn't see much in the man's gaze other than annoyance his girl-friend was traipsing around the parking lot at midnight.

The interlude hadn't taken long, but as Troy reconsid-ered the lamps, he went back to his original frustration.

There was no way the lights going out over Evange-line's door was a coincidence.

Everything in him fought back at that idea. If she hadn't had the panic over the bloody shirt earlier, he might have said it was possible. But now? Two incidents within a few feet of her home?

No way.

As he continued working his way around, he ended up at the end of her particular building. It was one of four that made up the overall condominium complex. The front door of the first unit was painted just like hers, a color scheme that was repeated all the way down the building. There were two other overhead lights, spaced at equal intervals from the one that was now dark.

If he hadn't been looking, he'd likely have missed it. But now, as he stared up at the second light, the one closer to Evangeline's, he saw it. A thin thread that connected that lamp to the one in front of her building. Curious, he turned to gauge the same distance between the middle lamp and the one at the opposite end of the building, but nothing was visible.

That strange thread was much too high to reach, the oval of the lamp at least as high as the second story of condos, but it was visible all the same. Hastening back, he ran to his car to get his flashlight.

Cursing the oversight, he snagged the flashlight out of his glove box. There had been a dozen cops here, and every one of them had missed it. It irritated him, even as he acknowledged they were all on edge and stretched far too thin. Especially when it had become evident the cause of the lamp going out had been a firecracker.

Crossing back to the lamps, he positioned the beam directly on the thread. As he'd originally suspected, a thin wire was strung between the two lights, ending at the now-empty socket. He pulled out his phone and snapped off a few photos. Was it a fuse of some sort?

It was more plausible than whatever else they'd come up with. But it also meant that whoever set it off had still been relatively close to the car as he and Evangeline talked. Had Troy been that oblivious to his surroundings when he was with her?

Troy moved back to the light still lit and snapped a few more photos for good measure before shoving his phone in his pocket.

He'd send Jillian a text tonight and have her meet him here first thing in the morning. They'd need a ladder anyway, so he'd have her bring the big investigation truck the CSI team brought out to sites.

That lamp going out practically over his and Evangeline's heads wasn't a coincidence. And they were going to get the evidence to prove it.

He waited until the cop was gone, irritated that some dumbass punk kid had steered him wrong about the fireworks. He'd asked, hadn't he? How to set a fuse that would light the poppers from a distance?

And he'd been given minute details on how to make the thin braided fuse do the work.

Only it hadn't incinerated like he'd believed it would. And now there was a link from where he lit it and where it detonated.

That damned, persistent cop had seen it.

All his plans would go to hell if he left any evidence behind. The goal was to make the lawyer look like she was making things up so no one believed her. But if the cops started finding evidence, his entire plan would fall apart.

There was no way he was letting that happen.

He'd lain low down by the end of the condo building, waiting for the melee to die down. He couldn't risk going to his car with all the cops around, especially for the second time that day. And he wasn't walking back to downtown, either.

He'd intended to get in his car and leave once the cops were gone. It had only been the last-minute urge to count to a thousand and let the scene lie a bit longer that gave him what he needed. If he'd left a few minutes before or after he'd have missed the cop's late-night investigation altogether.

But now that he'd seen it, he had to do something.

The setup earlier that day had been easy. He'd played local handyman and had even changed the light bulbs for good measure. No one had even noticed him up there on a ladder *or* before he'd left that doctored shirt on her doorstep.

Did anyone ever notice anything?

Wasn't that why he was in this damn mess? Tampered evidence no one bothered to notice. A problem the damn DA's office couldn't even see? How was that justice?

It wasn't.

The rising anger that always burned in his stomach like battery acid welled up again and he savored it. Used it.

That damn lawyer was why he was in this position. His business was nearly bankrupt and he owed more people than a bookie after a game upset. And to hell with it all, he wasn't going down without a fight.

The cop took a few more pictures with his camera before heading back inside the lawyer's fancy digs. He'd give it another minute or two and then he was pulling down what was left of the fuse. The damn cop might have pictures but he wasn't going to have any evidence.

And like the lawyer's shoddy prosecution had shown him, evidence was the only thing that mattered.

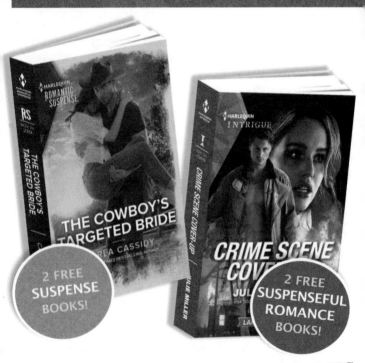

YOU pick your books – WE pay for everything.

You get up to FOUR New Books and TWO Mystery Gifts...absolutely FREE

Dear Reader,

I am writing to announce the launch of a huge **FREE BOOKS GIVEAWAY**... and to let you know that YOU are entitled to choose up to FOUR fantastic books that WE pay for.

Try **Harlequin® Romantic Suspense** books featuring heart-racing page-turners with unexpected plot twists and irresistible chemistry that will keep you guessing to the very end.

Try **Harlequin Intrigue® Larger-Print** books featuring action-packed stories that will keep you on the edge of your seat. Solve the crime and deliver justice at all costs. family and community unite.

Or **TRY BOTH!**

In return, we ask just one favor: Would you please participate in our brief Reader Survey? We'd love to hear from you.

This FREE BOOKS GIVEAWAY means that we pay for everything! We'll even cover the shipping, and no purchase is necessary, now or later. So please return your survey today.

You'll get **Two Free Books** and **Two Mystery Gifts** from each series to try, altogether worth over **$20!**

Sincerely

Pam Powers

Pam Powers
For Harlequin Reader Service

Complete the survey below and return it today to receive up to 4 FREE BOOKS and FREE GIFTS guaranteed!

FREE BOOKS GIVEAWAY
Reader Survey

1
Do you prefer stories with suspensful storylines?

○ YES   ○ NO

2
Do you share your favorite books with friends?

○ YES   ○ NO

3
Do you often choose to read instead of watching TV?

○ YES   ○ NO

YES! Please send me my Free Rewards, consisting of **2 Free Books from each series I select** and **Free Mystery Gifts**. I understand that I am under no obligation to buy anything, as explained on the back of this card.

❏ Harlequin® Romantic Suspense (240/340 HDL GQ56)
❏ Harlequin Intrigue® Larger-Print (199/399 HDL GQ56)
❏ Try Both (240/340 & 199/399 HDL GQ6J)

FIRST NAME	LAST NAME

ADDRESS

APT.#	CITY

STATE/PROV.	ZIP/POSTAL CODE

EMAIL ❏ Please check this box if you would like to receive newsletters and promotional emails from Harlequin Enterprises ULC and its affiliates. You can unsubscribe anytime.

HARLEQUIN® Reader Service — Here's how it works:

Chapter 11

Evangeline listened to Troy's recounting of what he'd observed outside and shuddered at the idea of more deliberate action against her. "You think someone did that on purpose?"

"Yes."

"Against me?"

"As one more way to make you frightened, at minimum. It's also the personal nature of doing it at your home. I don't like it and that's why I'm staying again tonight."

"You don't have to do that."

"Consider yourself in possession of a roommate for the foreseeable future. I won't make a mess and you'll barely know I'm here."

She wanted to argue with him. Realistically, she knew how to take care of herself. She had been active in strength training and various forms of self-defense her entire life.

But she'd be lying if she didn't admit that having a cop with a gun in her home went a long way toward making her feel safer.

Which was the exact opposite reaction of her hormones. Because there was nothing safe about Troy Colton's effect on her. She realized that now, after spending a few days with him, as well as seeing him with his sister and her family.

But even if she found him attractive, Evangeline knew she had to manage her expectations. He was here to help her. Yes, they'd kissed and exchanged some lingering glances, but it wasn't enough. And it certainly wasn't something she needed to explore here in the midst of whatever was going on against her.

Or, more to the point, to her.

"Tell me more about this string between the lights."

"I don't know exactly, but it's strange. To be fair, it could be nothing more than a string that's been there for quite a while. Did your complex ever have any decorations up there? Or any sort of sign that the sales office might've put up?"

"No, not that I remember. But I was one of the last residents to buy a unit here. I suppose it could have been placed up there, welcoming people to the condominium complex and encouraging them to look at the model units."

And to be fair, it could have been. She had been in her condo for a few years now, but the complex overall was relatively new. Although, would string like that have lasted that long?

"It's suspicious—that's all I need to know. If I had a ladder, I'd get up there myself right now to take it down and log it in as evidence. But I already got a text back from my cousin Jillian. She'll be here first thing tomorrow morning, with a ladder."

"Jillian's the one in CSI?"

"Yes. And as Randall Bowe tried to make her his scapegoat, she's got an ax to grind and a willingness to review any and all evidence, no matter how remote it might seem."

"His crimes were endless, weren't they? I mean, Davison is scary all on his own and his crimes are horrifying. But the way Bowe did it? Operating behind the scenes. It's diabolical, really."

"A lot of his motives came to light as we were investigating Everleigh Emerson."

"The woman who was accused of murdering her ex-husband?" When Troy nodded, Evangeline added, "I wasn't involved with that case, one of my coworkers was. But it was a strange case from the beginning."

"What makes you say that?"

"Well, Ms. Emerson got a divorce from the ex. By all accounts, that suggested she'd moved on. Yet somehow she's suddenly a suspect in her ex-husband's murder? Obviously, we were following the evidence prosecuting the case, but I remember when we discussed it in a team meeting thinking how odd it was."

"You don't think a marriage gone bad can be a reason for murder?"

"I've done this long enough to realize anything can be a motive, regardless of how irrational it seems to anyone else. But in this particular case, there was just something about it all that never quite fit. Here is a young woman who found a way to move on from a bad time in her life, yet suddenly she comes back?" Evangeline shrugged. "It just always rang false to me."

"It did for my cousin Clarke, too. He took on her case. Now they're a couple and planning their future."

She shook her head, smiling as Desiree's words from earlier sank in. "Your sister made a comment, and in this instance it's very clearly true. Sometimes the things in our life that are unpleasant or difficult lead us to something wonderful on the other side."

"Dez said that?"

"She did. Or my paraphrased version of it."

He quieted, the light smile fading from his lips. "Your opinion on Everleigh's case, and some of the things that you said earlier...in the car... Does that all have anything to do with your perspective on your own family?"

That sudden feeling of exposure hit fast and hard. Why had she said those things in the car? Yes, her guard was down a bit from the pleasant evening they'd shared with Desiree, Stavros and Danny. And in the darkened interior of the car, it had felt safe somehow. A quiet place where she could share her thoughts.

"I was just a bit surprised, I guess. Your family is special."

"Is that all?"

She should have expected he wouldn't take a simple answer or platitude in place of the truth. Although that *was* the truth. His family was special. Despite the trauma of losing his mother in the way that he had, he and his sister clearly had a deep and special bond. And the way he described his stepmother, Leanne, the day before was further proof of that.

So how did you explain those feelings of envy and confusion when confronted with someone whose experience had been so different from your own? More, how did you reconcile that with your own experiences growing up?

Maybe you didn't.

And in the quiet acceptance in Troy's golden gaze, Evangeline tried to explain. "My parents had a volatile marriage. I spent my childhood living with that. But there are times, when I observe other people's lives or hear other people's experiences, that I realize we aren't all the same. That not everyone grew up the way I did."

"Was there violence?"

"Physical, you mean? No." She shook her head, the idea of her father exacting his rage with that sort of violence as off-kilter as thinking he could ever remain silent on any subject.

He'd prided himself, in fact, that he was above "those men who use their fists to make a point." Hadn't she heard that over and over?

Yet hadn't that "self-control" he prized vanished with the swift lash of his tongue, over and over?

"My father had issues managing his emotions. Presumably he still has that problem but neither my mother nor I live under his roof any longer. Anything and everything could set him off, but once unleashed, he'd rage and rage."

"Lashing out emotionally is a form of violence, as well, Evangeline."

"Yes, it is." While she wouldn't have believed that as a child, she'd worked through the slow journey toward understanding it now. Both through her own therapy and through her casework, she'd come to understand that emotional abuse was real and could do damage, just like a fist.

"He refused to accept any of his own faults or any responsibility for his choices. If my mother ever dared to complain, he'd verbally strike out, claiming she was anything from a harpy to a madwoman for her thoughts."

"Are they still together?"

"Thankfully, no. They divorced when I was in college."

Her mother had stayed in her loveless, emotionally troubled marriage for far longer than she should have. Evangeline had always known it was because she'd feared leaving her only child to battle those forces alone. And still, it bothered Evangeline that her mother had felt the need to do that. That she'd given up her own happiness for so long.

"I'm glad you and your mother are out of that."

"I am, too. But it still can't change the fact that I'd rather have a real, functioning relationship with my father. Instead, we have cool and distant conversations once a month."

It was a situation that had come to suit them well and she had long ago stopped crying about it. Yes, it chafed every so often, a wound that never fully healed. But she'd moved on.

And had determined to live a better life for herself.

"Is it at all possible the altercation you saw in the alley yesterday was triggered by your experiences?"

It was a fair question. She knew that and understood it. As a prosecutor, it would be a question she'd ask herself if she'd evaluated this case through a legal lens. Most of all, based on the time she had spent in Troy's company, she recognized he meant it in a collaborative way.

Despite all those things, she couldn't help but feel the sharp point of his doubt.

"You think I made it up? That because my father

couldn't control himself, suddenly I'm seeing women murdered in alleyways because of it?"

"I didn't say that."

"Are you sure? Because that's exactly what I heard."

"That's not what I said."

"Right. Because I tell you about a piece of my past that I don't discuss with anyone and suddenly it's the reason I'm seeing women murdered in Grave Gulch. I sat in that car out there, Troy." She pointed in the direction of the door. "I saw the doubt in everyone's eyes."

"I'm not doubting you, Evangeline."

"That's exactly what you're doing. I've seen enough of it for the past two days to know that I'm right."

"Are you including me in that number?" Troy struggled against the rising ire, the bile nearly overriding his quiet tone. But even in his frustration, he recognized yelling wasn't the answer.

By her own admission, she'd lived with enough of that growing up.

When she said nothing, he pressed on. "This isn't about doubt. This is about understanding what is happening to you."

"What's happening to me is that I saw a woman murdered in an alley. I saw the blood spread across her white shirt. I didn't make that up. Especially since said shirt showed up on my front doorstep."

Only it hadn't stayed there.

He'd raced over here at top speed, several officers in pursuit behind him, and they'd arrived to find nothing. No shirt, no blood and no remnant of either existed, let alone proof that it had been placed in front of her home.

"I know what's being said about me," she finally said.

"Not by me."

"But you've thought it. Come on, Troy. How couldn't you?"

"It's not about what I think. It's about understanding what's happening to you."

"PTSD over my father isn't what's happening here." She shook her head and stood. "I need some water."

As he watched her walk out of the living room, Troy had to admit that he wasn't being entirely honest with her. He believed her...to an extent. Almost like that belief was just out of reach, in view but not quite in his grasp.

He knew how he wanted to feel, but what was in his heart kept warring with the facts as he knew them.

And much as he struggled to admit it, between Melissa, Brett and then, this evening, Stavros, he did have doubts. Legitimate ones. The sort of doubts a detective was supposed to have when working on a case.

It was the man who was attracted to her who didn't have them.

And wasn't that the whole problem?

He followed Evangeline into the kitchen, and found her with her back against the counter, a cold bottle of water in her hand.

"I'm sorry I can't be the person you need me to be," he said. "I'm sorry that my job keeps getting in the way. But I need to keep my focus on the Davison case."

"I get it."

"Do you?" He moved in closer, his hands planting against the counter on either side of her waist. "Do you really?"

"You're in a difficult position. We both are."

He was enamored by the way her pulse tapped there, in the hollow of her throat. He saw the slight flutter and had the overwhelming urge to press his lips to her flesh.

Because she wasn't unaffected.

He lifted his gaze from temptation, his voice dropping to a lower register. "What are you going to do about it?"

"For starters, I think you need some distance from this case. I appreciate the help you've given me, more than you can ever know. But I think you should get back to work and quit worrying about me."

"I don't think I can do that."

Her pulse continued to pound, a fact that must have finally caught up to her when her voice trembled, breathless. "Why not?"

"Because all I can think about is doing this."

Temptation roared back in and he recognized fully that he was past the ability to resist. Bending his head, he pressed his lips against her throat, trailing his tongue over that throbbing pulse. Her light moan filled his ears and provided all the encouragement he needed to keep going.

His lips traveled the tender skin of her throat, nipping beneath her chin, before he took her mouth with his. Those light moans became deeper, more urgent, as she opened her lips beneath his. And as his tongue swept in and met with hers, Troy finally acknowledged to himself the problem all along.

As a detective, he needed objectivity.

But as a man, he had none.

Evangeline felt the water bottle slip from her grip and was abstractly happy she had remembered to put the cap back on. Not that a backsplash of cold water would hurt her right now.

He was so hot.

Like a furnace. He was pressed against her now, with

the most delicious sort of heat. With her hands now free, she gripped the shirt at his waistband, the fistfuls of material soft to the touch. As his lips moved over hers, more of that delicious heat branded her, as their glorious kiss spun on and on and on.

Bolder, her hand shifted from his waist to drift over his back. He was so solid, the strength beneath her fingertips an impressive testament to the way that he kept his body in top shape.

His hands shifted over her body, as well, stroking and coaxing the most delicious responses. When one large hand closed over her breast, his thumb rubbing against her nipple, Evangeline's knees went weak. Pleasure, an impossible thought over the past few months, was suddenly present, ripe with possibility.

She wanted him.

And while she knew it made no sense, nor was it something they could indulge in at this point in time, the opportunity to steal a few moments in his arms was priceless.

With that thought foremost in her mind, she took. She took all that pleasure and sweet need and drank in as much as she could. Tomorrow would come soon enough. The events swirling around her that made no sense, the ones that were as real and tangible as the man holding her in his arms, would still be there.

So for now, she took.

And when he lifted his head to stare down at her, his hazel eyes drugged with desire and his lips still wet from their kiss, she smiled.

No, he wasn't unaffected at all.

"What do you do to me?" she whispered.

His question, voiced in that husky whisper, was a surprise, and her smile faded at the confused look that painted his face in harsh lines. "Inconvenient attraction?"

"Really?" That was how he saw this? What was between them.

"How is it anything else?"

Or more to the point, how *could* it be anything else? She wanted to be angry. And some small part of her was hurt. Bruised feelings, really. But if she were honest, she also recognized what he was saying. Because it was nearly impossible to think that this could be real. That this fire between them could be a product of something deeper, instead of the tense, fraught situation she found herself in.

"I don't know. I honestly don't know." He sighed. "But I've never been tempted like this before. I know my job and I know my responsibilities. That is as clear to me as my own name. As the love I have for my family. As the next breath I'm going to take. Yet with you, I question my responsibilities."

"You're a good cop, Troy. You're well respected, and you know how to do the job. Whatever has happened to me over the past few days, you can't doubt your work. The value you bring to the badge, that's important."

"I know it is. That's the problem, isn't it? The badge *is* important. For a long time, it was everything. But see, these past few days, I've realized something."

"What?" It almost hurt to ask the question, but she had to know.

"You, Evangeline. You're important, too. And it scares the hell out of me."

Randall Bowe picked up the burner phone, one of several in his possession, and dialed the number he knew by heart. The line rang, and rang some more, each peal a resounding endorsement of his wife's betrayal.

Probably out with someone, he thought. Screwing around again, just like she had before their separation. His heart slammed in his chest with the anger and injustice of it all, just like the day he'd discovered her infidelity.

"Hello?"

Her answer was a surprise, but now that he had her on the line he couldn't keep quiet. "You mean you aren't out right now cheating and defiling yourself with someone else?"

"Randall." That was all she said, his name coming out on a strangled breath.

"Yeah, it's me. Who'd you think it would be?"

"You shouldn't be calling me. You know I'm going to have to call this in to the police."

"Like I care." And like it mattered. They'd never trace the call anyway.

"Randall, what are you doing? Where are you?"

That familiar anger churned, low in his gut. It was so dark, so deep.

So overwhelming.

Until he'd finally figured out how to use it. How to mold it and shape it, really, so that it became something more than grief and anger. So that it became useful. Like a tool he could wield to derive justice.

She'd done him wrong, and someone had to pay. And since she hadn't seemed particularly contrite, or particularly interested in being the one to pay, he'd channeled all that anger toward others.

He ignored her question about where he was. He missed her to a degree that bordered on stupidity, but even he wasn't that dumb. "It's not what I've done. It's about what *you've* done."

"I've done nothing."

"You call cheating on me nothing?"

She sighed, but it was nothing like the way her sighs had sounded when they were first together. The sweet, delicate ones she'd make when he pulled her close, into his arms.

"I'm sorry that I didn't wait until I found a way to talk to you about my unhappiness, but you have to know we both needed to move on."

"No!" The shout tore from his lips. "*You* needed to move on. I thought we were perfectly happy."

"Happy? I've thought about it a lot these past months. We were miserable, Randall. All the time. You have to remember it, too."

Lies.

Lies she told herself, no doubt to make herself feel better about the cheating. Because if she could make herself out to be a victim, claiming their marriage was a dead end, then she could walk away from it all without any guilt.

Damn it, it didn't work that way. She *was* guilty. And now, anyone else who behaved like her was guilty, too.

And he could make it public.

He had that power. Or he did, until the damn Everleigh Emerson case blew it all to hell.

"We made a vow. A commitment."

"No, Randall, we made a mistake."

"How convenient of you to think that now. But it's because of you I'm in this situation."

"The one where you lied at your job, falsified information and helped a serial killer go free?" Her voice rose on each point, a slamming indictment of him and how she thought of him. "That situation?"

"Davison was an upstanding citizen for years. He was *faithful* to his wife." He deliberately emphasized the word "faithful," well aware his own wife was unable to grasp that concept. "And after nursing her through cancer, then losing her, he couldn't deal with it."

"So it drove him to become a killer? Grief doesn't work that way."

"He deserves his revenge, too."

"Stop this. You're talking nonsense."

He might have believed her. Once, he really might have. But now, after seeing what it was to have your marriage dissolve—not because of a virulent disease, but from your spouse's innate desire to walk away from you—he knew better.

"No, sweetheart, it's not nonsense at all. It's justice."

Chapter 12

Evangeline lay in bed and stared at the bright sunlight that streamed in through the curtains. She'd had a restless night and the sun seemed like a particularly sharp insult as it hit her bleary eyes.

Was it a sleepless night because Troy lay in the bed down the hall? Or was it because she couldn't get her thoughts to still, no matter how hard she tried. Their kiss had played out every time she tried to close her eyes, like a movie running on the backs of her eyelids.

A sensual movie. One that had been full of action and very little conversation.

After their honest admittances to one another in the kitchen, they'd both made quick excuses to head to bed. He still needed to check email, he'd claimed, to make sure his cousin Jillian would be over in the morning.

And she'd needed to escape.

It was still hard to believe she had told him about her

father. The stories of her childhood were things that she kept to herself and it was odd now to think that someone else knew. Someone outside of her own family. Yet at the same time, she trusted Troy implicitly. The situation she currently found herself in was far from normal, but she did trust that he would keep her confidence.

Sitting up, she rubbed the grit out of her eyes and reached for a hair tie on the end table. Pulling up her hair into a loose knot, she swung out of bed and hunted for clothes. Attraction or not, Troy had stayed to watch out for her last night and she at least owed him some hot coffee. Maybe even a frozen waffle. She thought she had those in the freezer.

Padding down to the kitchen a few minutes later, she got the coffeepot set up and went hunting for the waffles.

And let out a small yelp when she turned to find Troy sitting at the kitchen table, his phone in hand.

"I'm sorry, I didn't mean to scare you."

Realizing she must look like a Gothic heroine, with her hand pressed against her chest, Evangeline dropped it. "I'm not sure how I missed you sitting there."

"You seem sort of focused on your task." He smiled, the look a sweet cross between sheepish and amused. "And for the record, I would've put the coffee on. I only beat you here by about two minutes. I just wanted to check my email first."

"It's fine. You are a guest. You shouldn't be expected to start your own coffee."

"Jillian should be here soon. She was swinging by the precinct to trade her car for the CSI vehicle, so she'd have the materials she needed. Namely a ladder."

"Okay."

His cousin's impending arrival was a swift reminder of what they'd dealt with last night.

And of the danger that still lurked outside her door.

"Are you hungry?"

"I can get something on my way to work."

"I have frozen waffles." She busied herself with opening the freezer, tossing back suggestions that she peered inside. "I also have some raisin bread I can defrost. Or some chicken tenders, if you prefer protein."

"I'm okay. But fix yourself something if you're hungry."

She closed the freezer door without pulling anything out. What was wrong with her? Chicken tenders? For breakfast?

Willing the awkward thoughts away, she focused on action. "Is there anything I need to do? For Jillian?"

"No, she'll take care of everything. I'll stick around to help her quickly with the ladder and gathering the sample and then we'll get back to the precinct so she can take everything to the lab."

"That's great."

And it was great. That wire was the first real evidence they had toward finding out what was going on around her. And while it could be nothing more than a string that held up a sign or some sort of lingering condominium project, it felt like something.

Something tangible.

Which had been woefully lacking to this point.

"Look, I was thinking about it. And while I appreciate all of your help, you don't need to come back later."

Troy looked up at her from his seat. Setting his phone facedown on the table, he stood up at her words. "What's this about?"

"You have a life. You have an active caseload. And

there's a killer on the loose. Your attention is needed there."

"My attention is needed where there's a problem. You've been having a problem, Evangeline."

Again, that ready willingness to help her meant more than she could describe. But his cousin would be here soon and would be collecting the wire as evidence. That should get her case moving in the right direction, and they could get things figured out. He didn't need to be wasting his time with her.

"It'll just be easier that way. You don't need to keep checking up on me like I'm your responsibility."

"Where is this coming from? You need help right now. Not only that, but we have an active and open case dealing with what happened in that alley the other night. I'm here to help you."

"By moving in?"

"I hardly think sleeping in your spare room for two nights qualifies as moving in."

Why was he being so calm and collected about this? She was trying to make a point, damn it. But either he didn't hear her, or he refused to listen.

"Look, I just don't think you need to put all this time in on my behalf. You got me connected with Desiree and now there's a police sketch. I'm sure that'll be enough."

Before he could respond, a heavy knock came at her front door. He walked toward the exit of the kitchen but stopped to fully face her. "I'm sure that's Jillian. I'm going to get set up with her outside. But we're not done talking about this."

And then he was gone.

As the coffee maker made its last gurgle, Evangeline fixed herself a cup. What was she going to do with him?

While she might have exaggerated a bit, Troy had sort of moved in over the past couple of days. His scent lingered in the air, and even though he made the bed neat as a pin, she still knew he had been there. In her home.

Add on the fact that the GGPD was clearly questioning his judgment about helping her and she knew they needed to put some distance in place.

And then there was the kissing. And the sleepless night she'd experienced because of the kissing.

She couldn't do too many more of those. That acute sense of nonfulfillment because she knew how good it could be between them.

It wasn't possible to keep on the way they were. And it was even worse to think about having him so close but not be able to progress things between them.

She considered one of those frozen waffles once again and crossed to the fridge to pull one out of the freezer. She barely had the door open when a shout came from the front of her condo.

"Evangeline! Get out here."

"I'm sorry, Troy, I don't see anything." Jillian Colton stared down from her perch high up on her ladder, near the dome of the streetlamp that stood sentinel in front of Evangeline's door.

"There's nothing there?" Evangeline had joined them outside and stood on the other side of the ladder, helping him hold it in place.

Troy looked up toward his cousin, squinting into the early morning sunlight. "You're honestly telling me it's disappeared?"

"I'm telling you, there's no wire. There's nothing hanging between the two lamps."

"Jill, I saw it last night. I took pictures of it."

Jillian stared down at him, her gaze direct. "You want to come up here, then?"

"Damn it." He shook his head. He'd had trouble seeing the thin wire connecting the two lamps this morning but had assumed it was a function of the bright, early morning sunlight. But if there was nothing strung between the two lamps that meant someone had removed it. He'd stood here less than eight hours ago and laid eyes on it himself. "Come on down."

"What's going on?" Evangeline asked.

"I can only assume whoever put what looked like a wire up there was actually stringing the fuse to the firecrackers."

"And?"

"And they're the same person who pulled it back down."

"Right outside my door?"

"Yeah." Right outside her door. All while he was inside, kissing her, completely distracted from his surroundings. He let out a quiet curse, before reaching for Jillian's hand to help her down the last few ladder steps.

Jillian squeezed his hand gently. "I'm sorry, Troy. I just don't see anything."

"Because it's gone." Troy had already shown her the photos on his phone, but he flipped to them again, handing the device over to Jillian. He was disgusted, but also knew they were on to something.

Finally.

"Based on what you described, that had to be the fuse," Jillian scrolled through the digital photos. "Because at this point, if it was just some innocuous leftover from another event, it would still be hanging there."

He couldn't deny how good it felt to have Jillian's

support on this as she handed him back his phone. "That's what I'm afraid of."

"Help me move this ladder over to the other light. I do want to take some scrapings from up there and see if we can get a handle on the firecrackers that were used. It's a long shot, especially now that it's summer and they're being sold in about a million places, but it's a place to start."

Grateful for something to do, he folded the ladder and moved it to the lamp closest to Evangeline's door. He didn't miss the way she'd gone quiet, giving them space to do the work. Nor did he did miss the rising fear, evidenced by her thinned lips and clasped hands. Even with her fear, she did step forward as Jillian began the climb back up, holding her side of the ladder and ensuring Jillian had a solid space to work.

His cousin was thorough, and it didn't take her long to get what she needed. She wore a utility apron tied around her waist, and pulled out any number of tweezers, plastic bags and evidence labels as she worked.

"She's good and very prepared," Evangeline said.

"She is. She's one of the best CSI team members we have. Just one more reason to be monumentally pissed off at Randall Bowe."

"Because he didn't appreciate her?"

"Because he tried to pin his misdeeds on her."

The fear he had observed so recently shifted and changed as Evangeline's black eyes lit with fury. "That bastard. Is there anyone's career in Grave Gulch he didn't try to mess with or ruin outright?"

"At this point, I'm afraid not many."

Evangeline quieted, and he could see that fury shift and take on a new dimension, almost as if she channeled it. "Is it possible he did this?"

"Set the fuse?"

"The firecrackers, placing and removing the fuse. If he knows how to tamper with evidence, presumably he knows how to set it, too."

"That's an interesting take. The latest intel we have suggests he left Grave Gulch, but it's entirely possible he hasn't."

"If this is his home base, why would he?"

It was a good point and something he would add to his ongoing list of all things Randall Bowe. He had been working on Bowe's background, looking for any information he could find, including a brother the man was reported to have. Part of the hunt for the brother was to get information on Randall, but to also see if he had provided a hidey-hole.

It had seemed like the most likely choice, but Troy was grateful for the fresh perspective. A chance to bounce his working theories off someone was priceless. "True, but why would he stay? He can't go out. We're hunting for him to take him in and prosecute him for his crimes. If he's stayed close, he's got to have some sort of system set up to keep himself fed and off the radar."

All the more reason Bowe's brother, Baldwin, made sense as a probable hide out. Melissa had already been in consistent contact with Randall's estranged wife, Muriel, and the woman swore up and down she'd had no contact with him. She swore even more vehemently she wouldn't harbor him if he did show up and ask for help, and her protests hadn't been all that hard to believe. While anything was possible when dealing with people and emotions, he'd gotten the solid sense the man's estranged wife would likely be the last person to step up and help him.

"It's all about the revenge quotient," Jillian added as she climbed back down the ladder.

"How do you mean?" Evangeline asked.

"He's mad at the world. His wife, most of all."

That was interesting. Everything they'd understood so far was that infidelity had been the reason Bowe made the decisions he did. He manipulated evidence to incriminate anyone he believed to have cheated on their spouses or partners. "You think his marriage was in trouble?"

"Oh, yeah. He was in love but he didn't act like someone in love. Instead, he was jealous of her and always sabotaging them in some way." Jillian stopped and glanced at Evangeline. "I'm sorry. I don't normally talk about other people this way but he did a number on me. And, well, you know. I've got eyes."

Evangeline nodded, her expression free of judgment or censure. "You don't owe me an explanation. Besides, what you observed is important. Understanding someone's situation is essential to figuring out their motive."

Jillian smiled at that, her grin wide. "So I'm not coming off like a vindictive bitch?"

Evangeline smiled back, her first easy smile since they were at Desiree's house the evening before. "Nope. Not at all. I think you sound eminently reasonable."

"I like her."

Because they left Evangeline's condo at the same time, he and Jillian had arrived back at the precinct within moments of each other. Troy had already walked around to the back of the CSI van to help his cousin with the bags she needed to take back inside to the lab.

"Evangeline, I mean," Jillian added, as if the statement required clarification.

"I know. And I agree. She's great."

"Something's going on for her, too. Even if I'm desperate to catch Randall Jerk Face Bowe and it's my fondest wish we nab him as quickly as possible, I do recognize this particular situation might not be his work. But that doesn't change the fact that she's still dealing with a problem."

"You believe it?"

"I know it. She's scared and you don't make that up or fake it."

"Why are you mentioning faking it?"

Jillian stared him down, her gaze far more worldly than her twenty-seven years might suggest. "Come on, Troy. I get it, and I've even been there recently. You're getting blowback from everyone saying that she's making it up for sympathy. That she was responsible for the mess-up in the DA's office."

"Not exactly."

Jillian lifted one perfectly arched brow. "In any way?"

"Okay. Yeah, a bit. It's like this phantom argument sitting under the caution to be careful and to watch my back."

"Right. And all the while you are the one who can see exactly what's happening and know there's a problem."

He knew his cousin had experienced a rough go at the start of the year. Randall has used Jillian's status as one of the newest members of CSI to make her a scapegoat. She'd ultimately proven herself and pointed toward the work that was actually at his hands, but she'd been in a bad place.

"I'm sorry if I wasn't as understanding as I should have been when you were going through that."

"You stood by me. The whole family did."

"Yeah, but you still needed support. I hope you know we're always there for you."

"I know that." She stepped up and pulled him close for a hug. "We're Coltons. It's what we do."

"We are." Troy tightened his hold once more before letting her go. "And yes, it's what we do."

"We're also involved with one another and up in each other's business. You all know me which is why you stood up for me when Bowe was gaslighting me over the evidence. Now someone else needs help."

There it was again.

Gaslighting a person to make them feel off-kilter. Or worse, to scare them into thinking they are the problem.

It was the same thought he'd had the prior night and it was odd how neatly it meshed with Jillian's experience.

Before he could press her, Jillian kept on with her train of thought. "From one Colton to another, I am going to use my familial privilege to poke a bit more."

Despite the gleam in her eyes, Troy was still blindsided at what came next.

"You have feelings for Evangeline and I think she has them for you in return. Don't let this strange situation circling around you both keep you from recognizing that."

"It's not like that."

"Oh no?" Her lone, lifted eyebrow suggested just how much she believed him, but her next words proved it. "You're crazy about her, that much is obvious."

"She's part of an active investigation. That's all."

"Keep telling yourself that, cousin." Jillian reached down and hefted one of her bags of evidence. "Just keep telling yourself that."

When she took off in the direction of the precinct, all Troy could do was follow, her words trailing him the entire way.

Less than an hour later, Troy cursed Jillian for her perceptiveness: And for the endorsement she'd given for him to pursue Evangeline.

You have feelings for Evangeline and I think she has them for you in return. Don't let this strange situation circling around you both keep you from recognizing that.

Entirely inappropriate feelings, he amended.

He was a cop and a good one. He knew how to keep his head and he knew how to assess danger. Yet despite his attention and oversight, this case had moved from bizarre to sinister in the span of a heartbeat. A shift that had happened while he was kissing her in her kitchen, brainless from the *feelings* coursing through him.

That length of fuse, strung between lampposts, was the proof he needed that something was going on outside of Evangeline's imagination. But just like everything else she'd experienced so far, the evidence of wrongdoing had disappeared. And he'd been too distracted to keep an eye on the evidence before it disappeared.

Settling in at his desk, he pulled up his files. He'd promised Brett coffee and then he'd had to text him early that morning that he was waiting for Jillian instead. His partner had taken it in stride, wishing him luck.

And now here Troy was, with nothing to show for it anyway.

Which had done nothing for his mood. There had to be something he'd overlooked. Tapping in his password, he waited as his files booted up. As he did, he considered Jillian's theory on Randall Bowe.

Troy had been working on running down the brother, Baldwin Bowe, but hadn't found the man yet. He knew the two were estranged—or at least had been, based on last intel on either of them. But estranged or not, familial bonds could get someone to act on behalf of a sibling or parent.

If Randall was hanging around Grave Gulch, it gave a bit less credence to the idea he'd holed up with his brother. Troy wasn't quite ready to close the line of inquiry, but it was something to think about.

"One unsugared coffee, piping hot." Brett strolled in and set the to-go cup on Troy's desk. "Or more aptly named, why bother?"

"I call it high-test and I could say the same about your chocolate and sugar-laden coffee that doesn't deserve to carry the name."

"It's called energy, my friend." Brett pointed toward the computer. "And you look like you need it. What happened with Jillian this morning?"

Troy caught Brett up over coffee, the two of them bouncing theories back and forth.

"You've got photos of the fuse?"

"Yep." Troy called up the photos on his phone, handing them over. "It's thin but you can see it. And I got it from a few angles."

"And then it was gone this morning?" As Troy nodded, Brett pressed on. "I owe you an apology, then."

Troy considered Brett across the desk. They'd paired up well and worked well together and he knew Melissa was leaning that way. He wanted a partner who would be honest with him and who could call him on his bs.

That sense had always been true for him. It was even

more true now, as the GGPD faced one of its biggest challenges in the history of the department.

"No, you don't. Not for doing your job and asking the right questions."

"Yeah, but you also trusted your gut. And now you've got proof."

"It all depends on what Jillian finds in the lab. She took some evidence from the blown-out streetlamp. We'll see what she turns up from that."

Brett took a sip of his coffee, considering. "Your angle on Bowe is still a good one. We've been pursuing the idea he's outside of Grave Gulch. I know we haven't ignored the idea he's stayed local, but maybe we need to put a bit more focus there."

"He can't access his files. It's seemed more likely he'd cut and run."

"But he's got enough spite and anger to stick around. You know what I mean?" Brett added.

Troy did know what he meant and that assessment fit Bowe to a T. He was about to say as much when Melissa filled his doorway.

"Good. The two people I wanted to talk to." She came in and stood before them.

"What's going on?" Brett stood to greet Melissa.

"Randall Bowe."

"Yeah?" Troy asked. "Funny enough, we were just talking about him."

"I just got off the phone with his very frightened, still-estranged wife. He called her last night. Acted like an ass and accused her of a lot of things with respect to their marriage."

"You think we can get a trace?" Brett asked, sitting forward on his chair.

"Ellie's already on it."

Their tech guru, Ellie, had already been invaluable in this case. She'd been the one to recover Bowe's stolen files while the whole case broke open and had been working on tracking him since.

"Did Bowe give her any sense of where he was?"

"No," Melissa replied, before adding, "and she admitted it was a mistake on her part not to try and get more information. He caught her off guard and she's pretty shaken up. We've already started the paperwork to put her into protective custody."

"Good." Troy nodded. "That's good. What time did he call?"

"A little after eleven."

Troy did the quick math. Although it wasn't impossible, if Bowe was calling and picking a fight with his wife at that time, it was increasingly unlikely he was also at Evangeline's property, setting off fireworks and later drawing down evidence.

Which put them right back at square one.

No theories and some faceless threat lurking around Evangeline's home.

Troy quickly caught Melissa up on that detail as well as the news that Desiree had already sent through a police sketch for the file.

As he'd known she would, Melissa assessed the situation quickly and succinctly, cutting straight to the chase. "A fuse? So the job was done remotely? Or out of sight from where you were parked?"

Troy nodded. "It was quick and clean and I saw no one out of place by the time I got out of the car and did a visual inspection of the grounds."

"Is Evangeline all right?" his cousin asked.

"She is. Shaken, but okay."

Melissa took the seat beside Brett, dropping hard into the chair. "Maybe we've been looking at this all wrong."

It briefly crossed his mind to suggest Brett and Melissa *had* been looking at the situation all wrong, but Troy held his tongue. They were all under pressure, and reminding his colleagues—who were also friends and, in Mel's case, family *and* his boss—of that felt petty. Instead, he opted for "How so?"

"Based on the time of Evangeline's nine-one-one call and the report from the couple whose home he invaded, the would-be killer she observed wasn't Len Davison." Troy tapped his chin. "But what if Len is inspiring others?"

Brett took a sip of his coffee, thoughtful. "A sort of copycat?"

"She described a gunshot. That's Len's MO, too."

"But he's killing men," Troy argued. "A copycat would likely do the same, right?"

"Would he? Or might he use the killings as inspiration?"

There was hardly anything inspiring about Len Davison's actions. But Melissa's point still held.

Was it that hard to believe that all this recent confusion had turned husband against wife? Neighbor against neighbor? Friend against friend?

Or worse, had inspired the sort of mad fantasies better left alone?

Chapter 13

Evangeline peeked through the curtains once more, consoling herself that she was playing neighborhood watchdog and not indulging in mindless, paranoid behavior.

Yeah, right. If the shoe fits, Whittaker.

What she was doing was talking to herself and going slowly bonkers here in her living room all alone. Even her precious lists hadn't done a good enough job of quelling the mix of fear and anxiety that had been her constant companions since Troy had left that morning, and the legal pad she'd stared at determinedly for the past half hour was still blank.

And yes, while she might have encouraged him to go back to the precinct to handle his work and not worry about her, now left to her own quiet home, she had to admit that the push was rather shortsighted.

Had someone really lit a fuse on a bunch of firecrackers to blow out the light in front of her door? It seemed like an odd way to scare someone, yet it made a strange sort of sense, too. It was summer and firecrackers were a ready part of people's recreation in the evenings. No one would notice them going off. Nor would it look immediately suspicious as a scare tactic.

Heck, if she hadn't already witnessed the violence in the alley and experienced the scare of someone being in her home, she'd have ignored them completely, thinking them a prank gone slightly destructive.

The heavy ring of her phone pulled her out of her musings. When she saw it was her mother calling, she dived for it like a drowning woman going after a tossed lifeline. "Mom. Hi. How are you?"

"Sweetheart, I didn't expect you to answer. I expected you'd be working and I was just going to leave you a quick message to call me later."

Although she hated the fact that she'd kept her enforced leave quiet, she hadn't had the heart to tell her mother, either. While her mother knew about the outcome of the Davison case—who didn't?—Evangeline hadn't wanted to share more information. It felt too much like a failure.

"I've got a few days off."

"Oh, good. I hope you're making the most of them."

Right. Huddled in my house.

The urge to say just that—to have the words spill out so she could tell her mother everything—was nearly overwhelming. Instead, she forced a bright smile on her face and hoped it translated to her voice. "Well, it's lucky I can talk now, then. What's up?"

"I had some news I wanted to share with you." She heard her mother's quick inhale of breath before she pressed on. "Well, I've been seeing someone. Dating him, actually. He's a lovely man. His name's Bill."

"Oh." Realizing how that must have sounded, Evangeline quickly added, "Oh, Mom, that's wonderful!"

"I can't wait for you to meet him. And, well, it's a strange time right now, with all that's going on in Grave Gulch. But we met and it seems right. We're being careful and I won't let him walk in the park, even if he's with me."

Although she suspected Bill was a bit older than the men who'd been targeted by Len Davison, Evangeline was glad for her mother's caution. For the mysterious Bill and for her mom's own safety. "That's wise. We have to all hope this situation will clear up soon but until then I'm glad you're being so careful."

"You have to be. Even the protests downtown have me concerned. I respect the right of peaceful assembly, but it seems like a crowd like that could hide a person attempting to do harm, too."

Although their discussion was about a scary and dangerous topic, she could still hear the joy that floated beneath her mother's words. It was something she'd missed for a long time and it was only now, as she heard her mother's voice, that she understood what that sound was.

Hope.

"You sound really happy, Mom. I know you weren't for many years and, well, I'm glad you are now."

"Thank you for saying it. And it wasn't that bad."

Evangeline started to protest but her mother pressed on.

"What I mean is that it was bad, but I'd do it all over again to keep you safe."

"That wasn't a reason to stay in such a bad situation."

"Oh, sweetie. That's every reason and it's the only reason, all rolled into one."

Once more, that desperate urge to tell her mother all that was going on swelled deep in her chest but Evangeline held back. She'd never heard her mother this happy and there was no way she wanted to ruin that or dim it in any way with worrisome news.

News that was still too amorphous for comfort.

She could picture the conversation now. *So, Mom. I saw someone shot in an alley but there's no body, no blood and no sign that it ever happened. There was a mysterious book showing up in my house and someone's lurking outside my front door.*

Nope. No way. Not when her mother had finally found so much joy of her own.

Instead, she opted for a different tact. "When can I meet this Bill? Check him out myself."

"He's visiting his children this weekend down in Kalamazoo, but maybe next weekend?"

"I'd like that."

They spoke for a few more minutes and Evangeline promised to call later in the week to set some time for the following weekend. It was only when she hung up that the tears tightened her throat and the oppression of what she'd been living with for the past few weeks finally came crashing down.

An oppression she faced all alone, unable to even tell her mother.

She kept her gaze on the blank legal pad in front of her, the thin blue lines quickly going blurry with her tears.

Melissa Colton had no problem doing her job. Whatever was needed in her role as chief of the Grave Gulch

Police Department, she was willing to do. That included seeing difficult cases all the way through to conclusion, investigating disturbing crime scenes and testifying against worthless weasels when they finally got their day in court.

But as a woman, she avoided poking into other women's business like the very plague.

Which made her visit to Evangeline Whittaker's condo as out of place in her day's agenda as if she'd decided to take half a day off and go skinny-dipping in a nearby watering hole with her attractive fiancé.

Actually…she thought as she shut off car, that last one wasn't a bad idea. And with Antonio in the forefront of her thoughts, she quickly dialed his number.

"I was just thinking about you." His greeting brought a smile to her face and she marveled at how easy that had become since Antonio Ruiz had come into her life.

"Fancy that, since I was thinking about you." She gave herself thirty seconds to indulge in what she'd mentally dubbed the kissy-kissy aspects of their relationship before shifting gears. "I have an idea brewing and I wanted to see if you could reserve a private table in a private corner of the hotel's restaurant."

"For us?"

"Not us this evening but my cousin. Troy's been putting in quite a lot of overtime and I'm ordering some R and R. My treat."

"Our treat, darling. And a private table suggests that the R and R is with someone."

"That's my plan."

Antonio's laughter came rolling through the phone. "I'm not going to bet against you on that one."

Melissa indulged in fifteen more seconds of the kissy-kissy stuff before ending the call. With her smile still humming as she walked up to Evangeline's front door, she stared up at the parking lot lamps that had caused such a stir this morning. She'd looked at Troy's photos from the night before and there was clearly something strung between the two lights. But now, as she looked at them, it was obvious it had been removed.

Which meant she not only owed Evangeline an apology, but she also owed Troy a bit more of her attention on this case. The situation downtown was still puzzling, with a K-9 as well as the CSI team finding nothing that suggested a murder or any sort of gunshot wound.

But harassment at home was another layer that wouldn't be ignored.

Melissa knocked on the door, brisk and efficient, even as a small voice inside began to waver. The cop part was easy to handle. The woman part, not so much. What was she doing here? And would her overture be received in the way she'd meant?

Or maybe a better question, what did she possibly hope to accomplish?

The question vanished as she came face-to-face with Evangeline. And as she took in that tear-stained face, it was easy to see she'd shown up at just the right time. "May I come in?"

"Of…of course."

Evangeline waved her in, keeping her face turned slightly away. "Would you mind giving me a minute?"

She nodded, moving more fully into the condo while Evangeline disappeared into what looked like the master bedroom. Melissa looked around, unwilling to hide her curiosity or her perusal of the home. The ground floor unit made it more readily accessible off the bat, with two entrances in the front and back of the home.

The first-floor windows also offered someone intent on doing harm an easy view into the layout of the house.

A unique choice for an ADA. While Melissa firmly believed a woman should do what she wanted—and that included her choice of home—her cop's mind recognized the increased risk in selecting this unit.

"I'm sorry." Evangeline came back into the room. Although her eyes were still red, she must have splashed cold water on her face because the lingering vestiges of tears had vanished. "Thanks for giving me a few minutes."

Melissa took a seat on one of the pretty red chairs that flanked the couch, the color complementing its abstract print. "Nothing to worry about. And it's me who should be saying sorry."

Evangeline took a seat on the couch, her shoulders heavy. "You don't need to. I've used far too many resources from your department over the past few days and I can't tell you how sorry I am for it."

"You've used the resources afforded to you as a resident of Grave Gulch. There's nothing to apologize for and if I gave you that impression it's equally on me to correct it."

Those shoulders drooped a bit farther and Melissa considered what she knew about Evangeline Whittaker. They'd worked in the same community for over a decade and since they managed opposite ends of a case, from open to closed, their separate jobs ensured they spent minimal time together. Melissa came to court when needed and Evangeline had deposed her on a few occasions, but that was where it ended. A general awareness of one another instead of any real friendship or professional acquaintance.

Despite all that, she knew Evangeline to be a strong

prosecutor. She'd worked for Grave Gulch County for years and until the Len Davison case, her reputation had been impeccable.

As a woman who prided herself on her reputation, and who knew the pressure the GGPD was dealing with that hit her directly, Melissa had a deep sense of how it would feel to see that vanish in a matter of days.

"But more important, I owe you an apology for not believing you."

Those red-rimmed eyes widened, but Evangeline's tone was measured when she finally spoke. "I know what's happened the past few days has been unusual. The lack of evidence is hard to understand, no matter how I twist it around or think through what I *know* I saw. But it's also on top of the past few weeks that have had me professionally upside down. My leave of absence has been kept quiet, but it's not exactly a secret. I can see where that would add suspicion in anyone's eyes that I'm making this up."

It wasn't a secret but Melissa believed that the lack of gossip surrounding Evangeline's leave was a sign of respect for the ADA. She had a strong reputation. Yes, that reputation had taken a hit with the Davison case, but it didn't change all that had come before.

Nor should it.

"The Davison mess has us all upside down. A serial killer is unusual, despite what modern entertainment wants us to believe. But that, coupled with Randall Bowe's betrayal of the GGPD, has put the entire law and legal communities on edge. That doesn't mean you aren't being subjected to some sort of problem right now."

"Thank you for that."

The apology seemed to go a long way toward relaxing Evangeline, the stiff lines of her body softening. "Your cousin Jillian was here this morning. Whatever else you can say about Randall Bowe, his behavior has lit a fire under her. Troy mentioned how determined she is to prove herself and to catch him in the process."

"I know I might sound biased because she's family, but Jillian has an amazing future in CSI. She's only been in the role for about a year, but she's proven herself incredibly dedicated to the work."

"That's great to hear. We need more professionals like her. And especially after going through the experience she did with Bowe's behavior, I'm glad it hasn't turned her off the profession."

Melissa considered the genuine praise from Evangeline and added one more check in the "yes" column for all the reasons why she'd come here today. "I am here to apologize. You deserve that and it's important that you know that. But there is something else I'd like to discuss."

"Oh. Of course."

"What you've been dealing with over the last few days has put you in close proximity with Troy. He's a good man and he's dedicated to his work."

"That's so easy to see. The way he's handled my case, but even before that, I've recognized that quality about him. Anytime I've seen him in court, he's always incredibly well prepared and quite passionate about his job."

That was one way to describe it, Melissa thought. Workaholic tendencies without taking any time for himself could be another. "He is. Sometimes to the distraction of everything else."

"It's a big job. And it's been an extraordinarily difficult year."

"It has been, for everyone at the GGPD. And if I'm being honest, for the Colton family, as well. But I also know that Troy has borne the brunt of it. The search for Randall Bowe and all the work to expose the depth of his cover-ups. The ongoing hunt for Len Davison. And the continued frustration that both remain at large. It can be overwhelming sometimes."

Although Evangeline's red-rimmed eyes had calmed from their obvious crying jag, an unmistakable sheen filled them once more. "That it can be. I keep telling myself I should try to relax a little bit and enjoy this leave of absence. I haven't had personal time like this in quite a while." She held up her hands, gave a rueful smile. "But it's hard to relax when the time off isn't by choice."

"When it's time off it feels like an indulgence. When it's forced, it feels like punishment."

"Yes!" Her eyes lit up at that, the thin sheen of tears fading. "That's exactly how it feels."

"I was put on desk duty earlier this year. I earned it fair and square and it's a policy I require for my team, so I expect to follow it, too. But it was still hard."

"This was the Orr case?"

Melissa nodded, surprised at how fresh it all still felt. She'd believed herself past it yet couldn't deny that there were times when it reached up and grabbed her hard around the throat. Drew Orr had faced a jail sentence, but that hadn't been good enough and he'd tried to kill her, thinking somehow he'd get away with it. She didn't regret firing her weapon, but she also believed that if she didn't feel the impact of taking a life, no matter how depraved, she didn't deserve to wear the badge.

She thanked the heavens every day she had found Antonio. Finding him and falling in love had upended her world, in the best way possible. And in the months since she'd shot Orr, Antonio's deep, endless support had meant more to her than she could have ever imagined.

It meant everything.

Which was why she wanted the same for her cousin Troy. It was slightly presumptuous of her to be here and to press the issue, but if Troy didn't pick his head up once in a while and try living, there was going to come a day when he no longer could.

She'd nearly been there herself, before Antonio, and had no interest in seeing a beloved family member make the same mistake.

Especially when his interest in Evangeline Whittaker was so clear.

"I'm fortunate that the case is behind me and while I regret the loss of life, I would do the same again if my feet were held to the same fire."

"Orr faced a life in prison and instead of paying for his crime he tried to kill you." Evangeline stared down at her hands before looking back up. "And even with that truth I have to imagine it's still an impossible decision."

"It feels like that some days. Which is why Antonio is such a miracle. I don't have to face those days alone any longer." Melissa waited a beat before laying down her cards. "It's why I worry about Troy and his future."

"He's committed to his job. And his family, too," Evangeline added.

"A lovely thing, to be sure, but he needs more. Which is why there's a table with your name and his on it this evening at the restaurant in the Grave Gulch Hotel."

"Oh no, I couldn't. I mean, *we* couldn't. I mean, it's not like that."

"I know." *But it could be.*

Melissa kept that last piece to herself and kept on pressing. "It's a dinner, nothing more. A quiet evening for two people to relax and put the world around them in the rearview mirror for a bit."

"It's a lovely gesture, but—"

"It's already done. Antonio has it all set up."

"And Troy said yes?"

Spoken like a lawyer, Melissa thought.

But since she'd come this far, there was no way she wasn't going to see this through. "He will."

"What if he has plans?"

"He's spent nearly every day working late at the precinct for the past two months. He's entitled to a night off."

"But—"

Melissa leaned forward. "Please, Evangeline. Let me do this. As both an apology to you and as a much-needed evening off for my cousin."

"I don't know what to say."

"Say yes. It's an all-expenses-paid evening and I can personally vouch that the shrimp scampi is the best I've ever had."

Melissa saw Evangeline wavering and gave it her final push. She wasn't above playing dirty and if it meant she could try out her Cupid skills all at the same time, then she'd take it. "He needs a change of scenery and a break from the Davison case. The two of you get along well and I know you've been under a lot of stress from the same. It's a dinner. Enjoy the evening and forget about life for a few hours."

It's just dinner.

That thought had gone through her mind, over and

over, since Melissa Colton had walked out of her home an hour ago. She'd gone from restless and upset to restless, upset and—oddly—in possession of a date.

Even though it wasn't an official date.

But it was a dinner at one of the nicest restaurants in Grave Gulch with Troy Colton.

Evangeline had already gotten a text from him that he was looking forward to dinner and would be by to pick her up at six. Which meant his cousin had managed to talk him into it. Or ordered him into it, as the case might be.

Which only added to her panic level. A forced date was even worse than calling it a date when it really wasn't.

She stared at the silk sheath she'd pulled from the closet. It felt too formal—and *way* too date-like—but she also knew the restaurant in the hotel lobby. The darkened interior was full of soft lighting and elegant tables, with small votive candles in the center. And the pretty aubergine shade of the dress always made her feel her best.

"To hell with it." Evangeline shrugged herself into the dress, determined to quit stomping around like an idiot. She had a nice evening planned. On some level, wasn't that enough?

So what was the problem?

But as she turned to stare at her reflection, she knew full well what the problem was.

She wanted the evening to be more.

To mean more.

And she wanted *more* of all of it with Troy.

With quick movements, she ran a brush through her hair and finished her primping with a soft coral lipstick that had been her favorite brand since college and gave herself one last glance in the mirror.

"You haven't been on a date in too long to count. Whether tonight is or isn't a date, go and enjoy yourself."

That admonition carried her out of her bedroom and on into the living room. She'd just reached the couch when her front doorbell rang. The drapes that hung in pretty brocade waves on the window were already drawn, a caution from Melissa before she'd left. That subtle change nearly had her crawling back into the bedroom and diving for the covers, with nothing more than a text to Troy to tell him she couldn't make it, but Evangeline forced herself forward.

She would not hide. Nor would she cower.

Even if she wanted to.

With a quick check through the peephole, she confirmed it was Troy and pulled the door open.

And just like that, Evangeline no longer wanted to hide.

The man that stood on her small front porch was everything she'd imagined as she'd gotten ready—and so much more. He stood there, looking strong and capable and incredibly handsome in the dark slacks and gray button-down shirt.

"Hi."

"Wow. Evangeline." He exhaled her name on a heavy breath before he seemed to catch himself. "You look great."

"Thank you. So do you."

"You ready to get going?"

"Sure. Let me just get my things." She gestured him into her home before turning to get the small purse and wrap she'd left on the chair. It was only as she turned back to face him that she realized his intention.

His heavy footfalls had already echoed away as he marched down the hall toward the kitchen and her back door. From where she stood, she could see him check the locks and confirm all was in place.

The happy bubble of anticipation that had formed as she'd gotten her first look at him fell away. Just like the drawn drapes, she was forced to see the evening for what it was.

Her time with Troy Colton for what it was.

A duty.

Nothing more.

Chapter 14

Troy sensed the change in Evangeline almost immediately, yet had no idea why. She'd greeted him warmly when she'd answered the door, her shy smile shooting sparks through him with all the finesse of a lightning strike.

It was because of those lingering aftershocks that he'd needed a few moments to compose himself before walking her out to the car.

The woman was gorgeous. Her long, straight hair fell, glossy and smooth, down her back. Her arms, sculpted by her active kickboxing workouts, were shown to perfection in the silky confection that covered her. And the slim legs that were already amazing had gone off the charts with the addition of thin heels that put the two of them at eye level.

Had he ever seen a more beautiful woman?

Or one he'd wanted more?

The answer was a resounding no as he opened the passenger-side door for her. He waited for her to slide in, hoping for another one of those smiles, but it never came. Instead, she gracefully slipped in, swinging her feet into the car and keeping her gaze straight ahead.

Determined to have a nice evening, he ignored the deep freeze. He'd figure out what was going on soon enough. And, if he were guessing correctly, he suspected Melissa hadn't given her a particularly big choice in going out that evening.

His fearless chief had come back into the precinct like a whirling dervish, ordering him to get up from his desk and go home to get ready. She'd informed him there was a reservation in his name and that he *would* be taking Evangeline Whittaker out that evening.

Brett had laughed at the set of orders but Troy didn't miss the slight note of panic in the other man's eyes when Melissa turned her serious gaze on him. Troy would have laughed at the unnerved bachelor routine if he weren't being steamrolled into leaving work early and taking Evangeline to dinner.

Which wasn't exactly a hardship.

Troy climbed into the driver's seat and backed out of his spot in front of her home. Part habit, part heightened vigilance, he scanned the parking lot as he drove slowly toward the main road, seeking anything out of place. Satisfied nothing lurked around Evangeline's home, he took his first deep breath as he headed for downtown and the Grave Gulch Hotel.

"I'm glad you could come out tonight." He kept his tone light, conversational, and was completely surprised by the continued cool response.

"Melissa seemed insistent we do this."

"You don't want to?"

He took his eyes off the road just long enough to see her subtle shrug. "It's nice to get out of the house."

Wow, he thought. Chalk that one up to a ringing endorsement. She might have mentioned taking a trip to the grocery store or scraping mud off her shoe.

"I know I'm looking forward to the evening."

When Evangeline remained silent, Troy kept his gaze on the road and focused on the short drive to the Grave Gulch Hotel. At least he'd see a friendly face when Antonio met them at the front desk.

The silence between them was heavy as he drove and it was only as it grew more and more oppressive that Troy realized why. In all that had happened over the past several days, there hadn't been silence. Despite her fear and anxiety, Evangeline had *talked* to him. She'd discussed how she felt and she spoke with him on any number of topics from her work to her family to the external situation they were dealing with in the faceless threat that stalked her.

And now?

Silence.

It was jarring in the extreme, and as Troy thought over the past twenty minutes since his arrival at her home, he racked his brain to come up with what had set her off.

He drove into the hotel parking lot, pulling up to the valet station. Melissa had given strict orders there, too, ensuring his car would be well cared for while he and Evangeline ate. As he handed over the keys, he hoped whatever malaise had settled over Evangeline would fade once they were seated in the restaurant.

Or they were going to have a long night ahead of them.

* * *

Evangeline knew her behavior was terrible. She'd spent enough time growing up to know the damage emotional tantrums—and their counterpart, dead silence—could do.

Yet try as she might, she couldn't muster up any enthusiasm or excitement for the evening. Especially when Troy had made it abundantly clear he saw this whole dinner as a commitment, nothing more.

He did a damn sweep of her home, for heaven's sake. A thorough check of the locks and doors, ensuring no one could get inside while they were gone for the evening.

It wasn't a rational reaction, especially after spending the afternoon convincing herself this evening wasn't a date. Yet at the same time, there was something about watching him inspect her condo that had landed like a cold bucket of water on her hopes for the evening.

Hopes she didn't need to be having.

Yet ones she'd had all the same.

"Troy!" A man she knew to be Antonio Ruiz met them at the maître d's stand at the front of the restaurant. The tall, elegant figure turned toward her, his smile broad. "And you must be Evangeline. I'm Antonio Ruiz. It's a delight to have you dining with us."

"Hello, Antonio. Thank you for having us this evening."

"It's my pleasure. And please consider yourself guests of Melissa and mine."

He led them to their table and Evangeline didn't miss the way several discreet gazes followed them on the walk through the room. She suspected it was due to the fact that she and Troy were guests of Antonio's, but she couldn't deny the feeling of being on display.

After spending several weeks in a mix of isolation and hiding, it was an odd sensation to find herself in view of so many people.

It was only when they were seated at a small table in the back, in a private corner, that she finally began to relax.

Antonio waited until they'd sat, and with a final request that they enjoy the evening, he departed.

"I'm still getting used to the fact that he's about to be Melissa's husband." Troy smiled as he opened the heavy leather menu from its perch on the charger plate in front of him. "We've spent years looking out for this place at the GGPD, ensuring its high-end clientele were always safe while here. It's funny to now think of him as family." Troy glanced over the top of his menu. "And I say that in the best way."

"Melissa seems really happy."

Troy set his menu back down, his smile easy and genuine. "I've never seen her happier. A lot of responsibility rests on her shoulders as chief of the GGPD. Responsibility she's earned and wants. But it doesn't mean that it's not hard. And facing that alone, without a personal support system at home?" He shook his head. "It's a tough life."

Melissa's words from her earlier visit ran through Evangeline's mind.

Troy has borne the brunt of it.

The search for Randall Bowe and all the work to expose the depth of his cover-ups. The ongoing hunt for Len Davison. And the continued frustration that both remain at large.

It can be overwhelming sometimes.

He was deep in the morass that the GGPD was dealing with. Hadn't she seen that herself these past few days? Yet even with the pressure and stress, she'd not seen him crack under it.

No, instead, he did just as Melissa suggested: he bore up under the weight of it all.

She was entitled to her anger from earlier, but did she really want to be petty and ruin a thoughtful evening provided by someone with seemingly the best intentions? Sure, this evening might not be what she'd secretly hoped. But it was still an evening out with an attractive man. A *good* man. One who deserved the simple enjoyment as much as she did.

Wasn't that some of what the past few weeks had taught her? She believed in her work and the long, long hours that she'd put in throughout her career. But the Davison case had also taught her that she wasn't infallible. More than that, her instincts were valuable and worthy, but every situation she found herself in wasn't going to be black-and-white. It was in the shades of gray that the real work happened.

Resolved to look at the evening with fresh eyes, Evangeline picked up her menu. Troy was owed a nice evening, too, and she wanted to be a fun, charming dinner companion.

The word *date* didn't have to factor into it.

And he did look really good this evening. The attraction she was determined to fight was having a hard time remembering the "not a date" part, even as she reveled in being out with such a handsome man.

And in the end, wasn't that something?

Whatever inconvenient feelings she might have for Troy Colton, she couldn't deny how much she enjoyed sharing his company. He was easy to talk to and they had a common bond with their work. She admired his commitment to the job and the focus and dedication that he brought to everything he did.

Her life might be wildly challenging right now, but she wouldn't regret the fact that its temporary strangeness had given her an opportunity to know Troy better. The cop she'd admired from afar, in their limited interactions during court cases, had become a real person.

Tangible.

Human.

And incredibly interesting.

"What are you having?" Troy asked.

"The steak looks wonderful but Melissa already gave me the heads-up that the shrimp scampi was amazing."

"I'm trying to decide myself. And while I love shrimp, I'm not sure I can turn down a steak. Especially when the scents coming from the kitchen are so amazing."

"This really is a beautiful place." She looked around, the dark paneling throughout setting off a bar on the far side of the room that ran to white lighting and yards of glass shelving. Those glass bar shelves glistened like diamonds in the light and she considered what a pretty, intimate setting they'd managed to create here. Grand without being imposing. "I've been here for drinks after work on occasion, but that's been it."

An ADA's salary wasn't designed for steak dinners and lavish appetizers but being here now made her realize that it was okay to indulge every now and again. She worked hard and while she had never regretted going into the district attorney's office, perhaps she'd been a bit too focused on her job and on saving for her home.

"Those look like more serious thoughts than choosing between the filet or the shrimp."

With one last glance at those glistening glass shelves,

she turned back to Troy. "I was just thinking about my life. Before going on leave."

"Oh?"

"I've been so focused on being frugal that I think I might have missed a few opportunities to live a bit."

A trait from her father? He'd spent years launching into a tirade at her mother for the barest infractions, from a splurge on cookies at the market to a new pair of shoes. Had she minimized her needs to avoid a confrontation?

Or worse, looked at any sort of indulgence as so frivolous that it was to be avoided?

"There's nothing wrong with saving what you earn."

"No." She twisted her hands in her napkin, searching for the right words. "There isn't. And I'm proud of the home I worked for as part of that savings."

"So why the sudden sadness?"

"More of my father, I suppose. The strange way he used whatever was at his disposal to control my mother. It was like he always needed to keep her on her back foot. I wonder how much of that I picked up, even subconsciously?"

As the conversation with her mother earlier replayed back through her mind, Evangeline couldn't help but smile. "But on a happier note, I spoke with my mother today and she's seeing someone. A man named Bill who makes her happy and who is from Kalamazoo."

Evangeline shook her head, surprised at how easy that admission came. And how truly excited she was for her mother as she embarked on this new relationship.

"You don't have to brush it off, Evangeline. Those were difficult years. Just because you got out of them and moved beyond them doesn't mean they didn't do damage."

Before she could answer, their waiter came over, balancing a bottle of wine on a tray. "Compliments of Mr. Ruiz."

Although she didn't know the full ins and outs of wine, Evangeline had enough of a working knowledge to know the bottle Antonio had sent them was special. "How lovely."

"May I pour?" Their waiter set two glasses down on the table and made a big show of the wine.

Evangeline gave the man his moment, grateful that the dramatic flourishes gave her a chance to regather her thoughts. Why had she gone there about her parents? As the complimentary wine suggested, it was meant to be a lovely evening out, away from their cares and concerns. Yet here she was, the meal not even served, rambling on about her father and his emotional abuses.

Scintillating conversation, Whittaker.

They waited until their waiter had departed, their orders in hand, then Troy lifted his glass. "To a lovely evening with a beautiful companion."

She felt a flush spread over her skin at his words. "Thank you." She tapped her glass against his, the delicate crystal making that satisfying clink.

The evening flowed from there and Evangeline felt her cares float away on the engaging drift of conversation and food and wine. She'd dated off and on through the years, but in all that time, she couldn't remember a man she'd shared so much with, or whose company she'd enjoyed more.

It made that push-pull of emotion—was it a date? wasn't it a date?—that much more challenging. It was only as their waiter wheeled over the dessert tray that she finally found an answer to both questions.

Did it really matter all that much?

She was out for the evening. Whatever moniker she wanted to put on it, the fact remained she'd had a lovely time. A truly enjoyable evening.

As their waiter wheeled the cart away, with their orders of crème brûlée for her and chocolate mousse for him, Troy's gaze turned serious. "Can I ask you something?"

"Sure."

"Earlier. In the car. I upset you." He stared down at his hands before those hazel eyes met hers, the gaze bold. "Did I offend you in some way? Complimenting you at the door or making you feel as if Melissa forced you to come out this evening?"

Something cracked wide open inside at his honest question. At the fact that he was willing to ask it at all.

"It was the sweep."

He frowned at that, confused. "What sweep?"

"Of my house. Before we left. I thought we were about to go out and you marched in and looked for signs of intrusion."

"And that upset you?"

"No." The answer was out before she could stop it, an unfortunate habit of denying what really mattered to her. With her earlier thoughts about choosing what she wanted in life and making some decisions that could be entirely frivolous in nature, Evangeline forced herself to reconsider. "I mean, yes. Yes, it bothered me."

"Why?"

"I was ready to go out, and you treated the evening like a job."

"But I—" He stopped, genuine surprise still painting his face. "I'd chalk it up to an occupational hazard but that's not fair."

"It's fine now. I'm over it."

"I appreciate you saying that. But regardless of how you feel now, I'm sorry I made you feel that way before."

That was it. A simple *I'm sorry*. Not all the accusations she'd heard through the years, each one lobbed at her mother and, at times, herself, like grenades.

You're overreacting.

That's not what I meant.

You never listen to me.

But never, in any iteration, had there been an *I'm sorry*.

"Thank you." She couldn't quite hide the strangled whisper and reached for the cup of tea she'd requested with dessert. "That means a lot."

As their waiter set down their desserts, Evangeline realized his apology had meant more than a lot.

It had meant everything.

Troy was still reeling from Evangeline's revelation over dessert. He'd been mostly honest with her. It was customary for him to check locks and doors, especially in a location he knew had been breached.

But his walk down her hallway had been about so much more.

Desire.

Desperation.

And an overwhelming sense of despair that his feelings for her were rapidly spiraling out of control. Feelings he had no business having for a woman under his protection and part of an open investigation.

He was a professional, damn it. He knew how to keep his own emotions in check and do the job. And he was good at it. He'd learned the skill early, a coping mechanism to ensure no one would ever have reason to ask him off the force or find a way to push him out of the GGPD.

He was a cop.

It was all he'd ever wanted to be and all he'd ever seen himself becoming.

He'd spent his life accepting that his mother's killer would never be found. Oh, it had never stopped him from following up on leads or reviewing her cold case file with what he hoped were fresh eyes. But it was because of the fact that her case was cold that he'd never wanted to give anyone a reason to think he took the job so personally that he couldn't be objective.

So why now?

And why her?

Evangeline Whittaker needed his help and all he could do was think about getting his hands on her.

So yeah. It was an "occupational hazard" as he'd claimed, marching through her apartment like a man on a mission. But it was more a disguise—a moment to find some much-needed composure—in order to control his raging need for her.

It was why he had put up an argument when Melissa had told him he was having dinner this evening. The protest was token at best, but he had to try.

Only, when faced with his cousin's insistence—and the opportunity to spend an evening with Evangeline—he'd caved pretty quickly.

Some cop you are, Colton.

But wasn't that the problem? He was good at his job. He didn't doubt that. He worked hard and knew the importance of what he did. The emptiness his family still lived with over his mother's murder was something he fought hard every day to ensure other families didn't have to. He couldn't always provide positive news, but he could provide closure.

And for someone in the process of trying to heal, that mattered.

For all those reasons, he knew his badge deserved better. Evangeline deserved better. He couldn't stay focused on her case if he was too focused on her. Hadn't that been proven more than once this week?

Even as he told himself to remain strictly professional, he was also abundantly aware that the genie was out of the bottle.

They had kissed. And spent time together. And even had this evening together.

And she mattered.

In the end, wasn't that really at the heart of it all?

"I hate to leave that wine behind." Evangeline glanced at the almost half-full bottle still perched at the edge of the table. "But two glasses are my limit."

"And one for me since I'm driving." He eyed the bottle, as well, before smiling. "Though to be honest, I'm not sure Antonio will mind. I've seen the wine cellar in this place and our leftover half a bottle isn't making a dent."

"I suppose that's true."

They stood, gathering up their things. In his own inimitable fashion, Antonio had already dispensed with the bill, ensuring Melissa's desire for an evening out was honored. Nor did Troy miss the satisfied smile from across the room where Antonio caught his eye, but he did nothing more than wave goodbye as an acknowledgment. Troy appreciated the dinner, but if Melissa had any inkling how close she'd come to playing matchmaker this evening, he'd never hear the end of it. A sure step in avoiding that was ensuring he didn't tip off her fiancé.

They walked back out and Troy kept his gaze trained on their surroundings. Although he didn't want to let his guard down, he knew the sort of security Antonio ran at the hotel and could at least breathe easy as their car was pulled around to the valet stand with prompt efficiency.

Troy opened the door for Evangeline, helping her slip into the car. His gaze caught hers as he took her hand and something deep and sharp and painful sliced through his midsection.

Did he honestly think he could stay immune to this woman?

She settled into the seat, their gazes lingering, and Troy had to pull away and force himself to walk back around to his side of the car.

Drive her home, Colton. Then get back into the car and drive your lovesick ass home. Look at crime scene photos if you have to, but get her out of your mind and certainly out of your blood.

All very solid direction, Troy thought, as he opened his own door and swung in.

Ridiculously solid, he lamented, as he put the car into Drive and headed for the exit of the hotel.

He'd barely turned out of the parking lot when he heard the sharp intake of breath followed by a piercing scream.

Slamming on the brakes, he turned to stare at Evangeline. Light from the overhead streetlamps at the edge of the hotel property flooded the car and in the glow he could see she'd gone a ghostly shade of white.

Terror glossed her eyes, rapidly transmitting toward him as his gaze tore over her face and upper body.

Was she hurt?

In pain?

"Evangeline!" Her name tore from his lips as he tried to get through the agonizing shrieks.

It was only when that terrified scream fell into a throaty whimper that he saw her gaze actually had a destination.

As his own gaze shifted course, he saw it. The balled-up white shirt on the floor of the passenger seat, streaks of blood soaked into the material.

Chapter 15

"What in the ever-loving hell is going on here?" Antonio Ruiz paced his office from one end to the other. "My valets are trained and they know the penalty for allowing anyone access to a car in our garage."

"We're getting to the bottom of it." Melissa tried to reassure her fiancé but it was obvious she wasn't getting through. The pacing had ratcheted up to stalking a hole into the carpet as he moved back and forth in front of his desk. It had taken Melissa's quiet yet firm order to keep him near his desk and stop him from rushing down to the crime scene in the garage.

Troy could hardly blame Antonio, since he wanted to be down there, as well. But knowing Brett and Ember were there gave him some peace of mind as he kept close to Evangeline and they all waited for news in the office.

She still looked deathly pale, a state that hadn't changed, even with both hands wrapped around a warm mug of tea one of Antonio's assistants had brought in for her.

Her grisly discovery in the car had momentarily stunned him but he'd finally gotten his wits when another patron departing the hotel behind him laid on their horn. Whipping back around into the parking lot, he'd already speed-dialed Melissa to tell her what happened. He'd pulled up in front of the hotel and barked out orders to the valet station to find him a spot to set up in the garage.

The team had complied, the fact they already knew him going a long way toward their cooperation, even before he had his badge out.

Melissa had arrived shortly after, Brett and Ember on her heels.

"What happened?" Brett's question was out before he'd even cleared his car.

"The shirt," Troy had told him. "We got back into the car after dinner and Evangeline found it at her feet on the floor on the passenger side."

"Son of a bitch."

"I know. This is too close." Troy stared at the shirt, still visible on the floor of his car. *Too damn close.*

"Which is concerning all on its own. But worse knowing that shirt's been in play for a few days now." Brett shook his head. "So where's the body?"

The crime scene techs had arrived and were getting set up. Troy was grateful to see Jillian in the mix. She'd do right by the evidence, which meant she'd do right by Evangeline.

Brett had gone to work then, too. He set Ember up with the scent from the shirt and then began the repeated motions, working their way from the car outward, looking for a scent.

Troy had wanted to stay but Melissa's orders, barked at Antonio through her phone to stay put in his office with Evangeline, had sent him running back into the hotel.

Yet even as he ran toward her, determined to shield her as best as he could, Brett's last question rang over and over in his mind.

Where was the body?

When it was just an investigation into a disappearing crime, Troy had been able to keep that thought at bay. They'd reviewed open files for any missing women in the area, but when no one turned up that fit Evangeline's description, they'd moved on.

But now? With the evidence some crime *had* been committed? It was challenging not to follow it all the way through to its natural conclusion.

There was a dead woman undiscovered and unaccounted for somewhere in Grave Gulch.

Pushing that grisly image aside until they had the details from the CSI team and whatever Ember could suss out in the garage, Troy turned his attention back to Evangeline. Her gaze followed Antonio as he crisscrossed his office, but other than her polite thank-you to the man's assistant for the tea, she'd said nothing else.

Which made her next words that much more of a surprise. Her voice was steady and strong as she leveled a question at Antonio.

"Who has access to your garage?"

Antonio stopped and turned at the question. "The valet staff. Hotel staff. Laundry deliveries, too. Big deliveries go through the loading dock but laundry is in the garage as the entrance goes straight to housekeeping."

"Is a badge required?"

"Yes."

"Cameras?"

"Of course."

Antonio nodded before Melissa jumped in. "Ellie's on it and already working with the IT office. If there's something to find she'll find it quickly. There was a limited window of time when someone could get to Troy's car."

Just like the comfort he took knowing Brett and Ember had the garage and Jillian had the forensics on the shirt, he was pleased Ellie was running point on the tech.

And he still hated sitting in the office, away from it all. He knew Melissa felt the same and figured she'd finally give in and let Antonio come with her for no other reason than she wanted to be down in the garage. He'd nearly said as much when Jillian came racing into the office.

"Mel!" Jillian came to a halt when she saw the assembled group. "Even better. You're all here."

"You found something?" Melissa asked.

"The blood. On the shirt."

Troy felt Evangeline stiffen beside him. Before he could ask for more details, Jillian was already excitedly revealing her discovery. "It's not human."

"What?"

The question went up as a collective, all of them talking at once.

"It's a fake." Jillian waved the phone in her hand, tapping the face to pull up a photo. "Look at it."

She set the phone down on Antonio's desk and they all gathered around.

"It's not a person's blood?" Evangeline said, her excitement palpable as she stared at the phone.

Troy heard the distinct notes of hope in her voice and hoped like hell Jillian was right. He didn't doubt his cousin, but after all Evangeline had been through, they couldn't afford to make any missteps here.

"I secured the evidence from the car and was going to take it directly to the lab. I still will, but there was something about the spatter pattern that bothered me."

Troy gave his cousin her due, listening patiently to her overview of blood spatter and the seemingly random nature of what was on the shirt. "But the kicker was when I realized what was missing."

Evangeline's harsh intake of breath had Jillian smiling and nodding, all at once.

"No bullet holes." Evangeline's breath flew out on a hard whoosh. She eyed the phone again before turning her attention fully back to Jillian. "You can see it even in the photo."

"So whose blood is it?" Melissa demanded, snatching the phone off the desk to expand the image of the shirt.

"It's synthetic. Someone wanted this to look pretty damn scary, but the blood isn't human. I'll run full tests on it and log it in evidence, but I'm pretty sure that is not human blood. And based on the integrity of the fabric, no one was shot wearing it, either. The blood spattered like it came out of an exploding capsule. The sort they use in TV shows to fake an accident."

"I don't understand." Evangeline ran her hand through her hair, her gaze steady on Jillian. "I mean, I'm happy no one was shot. Relieved, really. But what is this all about?"

"It's a joke." Melissa's gaze was dark as she set the phone back on the desk. "A nasty one. On you and on all the good cops trying to get to the bottom of this."

Throughout his life, he'd had plenty of experience

with seeing Melissa mad. From family squabbles to workplace blowups, her threshold for anger was something Troy wasn't ignorant of. She was levelheaded and calm and didn't cross that line often, but she was human, too. Add on the high-stress job and she'd been known to lash out a time or two.

But never, in all his life, had he seen the sheer fury that now painted her face. Her crystal-blue eyes had gone dark with it, her slim frame fixed in hard, tense lines. She gripped one of the guest chairs in front of Antonio's desk, her knuckles going white.

It was only after she'd stared at each one of them, Evangeline the longest, that Troy saw that fury channel itself into action. "We're going to find whoever did this and take him down. And if I find out this has anything to do with Len Davison or Randall Bowe, there is no rock either one of them can hide under that I won't pull them out from."

Troy moved close, laying a hand over hers and squeezing tight. "That makes two of us."

Evangeline yawned as Troy turned into the parking lot of her condo. She'd believed getting back into his car would be difficult but she'd been so exhausted by the time they finally reached the parking garage that her fear never took root.

It doesn't hurt, knowing the blood wasn't human.

Which was entirely true, even if she couldn't deny the sheer menace of the situation. Yes, it was creepy to know someone had done such a malicious prank. But it was still a wild relief to know a human being hadn't been harmed in the process.

The various GGPD teams had finally wrapped up in the parking garage about two hours after Jillian's revelation in Antonio's office. And while it had buoyed Evangeline's spirits to know a person was unharmed, those same spirits had taken a second hit when Ellie had come in about an hour later and confirmed she hadn't been successful in finding anything on video.

Antonio's outburst had sent him marching off toward the hotel's IT office, leaving her and Troy behind. She'd encouraged him to go down with the rest of the GGPD but he'd insisted on staying with her.

A kindness she appreciated, even as she warned herself not to get too comfortable with the attention.

While it wasn't definitive proof, whatever she witnessed in the alley seemingly wasn't a murder. A crime of some sort, yes, but not something that had resulted in murder. Melissa had vowed the GGPD would get to the bottom of things, but Evangeline knew the decreased likelihood of a murder meant the already-stretched staff would double down on its efforts to find Len Davison and Randall Bowe.

A move Evangeline not only agreed with but insisted upon. Police resources had to be prioritized where they were most needed and a serial killer at large needed to be everyone's focus.

Even though it meant she'd see far less of Troy.

"I'd like to stay one more night." Troy turned off the car and turned to her. The parking lot lamp was still out but the light she'd left on over her front door gave some illumination to the car.

"You don't have to. I know a lot happened tonight. And I know the shirt thing is creepy and we have to get to the bottom of it all, but I can't tell you how relieved I am that no one was murdered."

"We don't know that."

"No, we don't. But we're a lot closer to thinking

someone's playing a nasty, disgusting prank than anything else."

He still didn't look convinced and Evangeline reached out to lay a hand on his forearm. "You've been so good to me this week. But the GGPD needs you. Totally focused on finding and securing Len Davison." She paused, well aware she'd had a part in that. "I know that better than anyone."

"You don't still blame yourself for that?"

"I do."

"Randall Bowe is responsible for it."

They could go round and round but it wouldn't change anything.

Troy's support of her was sweet and oh-so-caring, but she owned her role in all that had happened. In all the challenges the town of Grave Gulch currently faced. And in the questions the community now rightly asked of its public servants.

He looked ready to argue with her but only nodded. "Let me at least come in and check everything out."

What had seemed insensitive and rote earlier left a new sensation in her chest now. It felt good to be cared for.

Wonderful, actually.

With no small measure of shock—and an amazing shot of clarity—Evangeline realized that she hadn't had that in a long time.

Maybe ever?

Her mother was warm and caring, but so much of Evangeline's childhood was overshadowed by the behavior of her father that those quiet moments with her mother weren't as fixed in her memory.

She'd dated off and on since college, a few of the relationships moving to something steadier and more serious, but she'd always held those men at arm's length. Almost as if the distance could protect her should they turn, their personalities morphing with the same sort of anger and rage as her father had.

It was only now, faced with the innate kindness, warmth and true decency that was Troy Colton that Evangeline recognized all she'd missed.

Or never had to begin with.

And with that realization came one she hadn't expected. Yet now that she recognized it, she couldn't deny it.

She wanted him.

It would be so easy to chalk it up to the stress of the past few days, piled onto the distress of the past few months. A need that could assuage the strain and anxiety and provide a pleasurable reprieve from all she was living with.

But even as she rolled that thought through her mind, Evangeline knew it was an excuse.

The current situation had given her proximity to Troy in a way she'd never had before. And with it, she'd had the opportunity to see all the qualities she'd believed he possessed but hadn't known for sure.

The first time they'd crossed paths in the Grave Gulch County courthouse, she'd seen an attractive man with a strong jaw and sexy smile. As she'd deposed him for cases, she'd seen a man who cared about justice and wanted the best for each and every one of their citizens.

It was only now that she could acknowledge how surface attraction had turned to deep-seated interest. How the knowledge of his professional commitment could make him even more appealing on a deeply personal level. And how attraction, always left on simmer up to now, could leap up and grab you by the throat with sharp, needy claws.

"I'd appreciate that." She took a deep breath and wondered if she could press for more. "Thank you for making sure I'm safe."

He carried the protection even further, asking her to remain in the car until he could come around and get the door for her. It was sweet and chivalrous and the insistent need that had begun thrumming in her bloodstream at the thought of intimacy with Troy began to beat.

His grip was firm as he held her hand, helping her out of the elevated seat of the SUV. She felt her heels hit the concrete and, even with her balance steady, she held tight to Troy at the sudden trembling in her knees.

Did she dare pursue this?

And could she live with herself if she didn't try?

In the span of a few short minutes, they were inside her condo, no external threat detected during the short walk from the car or the time it took to unlock her front door.

Unwilling to stand there twiddling her thumbs, she went to the kitchen while Troy did his check of the house. Surprised to see her hand trembling, she dug out a bottle of water from the fridge. She'd just unscrewed the cap and lifted the bottle to her lips when Troy walked back into the kitchen.

"The house is fine."

She fumbled the water at his unexpected arrival, spilling it over the front of her dress. The thin material was already quite sheer and the water only added to that, the wetness spreading over the top of her chest.

"I'm sorry." Troy's gaze drifted over her breasts before he turned away to grab a towel from where it lay draped over the edge of the sink. "I didn't mean to startle you."

"You didn't."

His eyes remained level with hers as he handed over the towel, his smile sweet and boyish. "You always spill water all over yourself?"

He'd given her the perfect opening and Evangeline recognized this was her shot.

Now or never, Whittaker.

"I'm clumsy when I'm nervous."

His demeanor changed immediately, any lingering humor from her spill vanishing. "You're worried about staying in the house? I checked everything and the doors and windows are secure."

She dabbed at the water stain with the towel, her tone easy. "I know."

"Then what are you nervous about?"

Evangeline set the towel on the counter and turned her full attention to Troy. "That you'll say no when I ask you to stay."

His eyes, that warm, rich hazel, turned a deep gold with desire. He understood what she was asking, but she wanted to make absolutely certain.

More, she needed to. Needed to know he wanted, just as she did.

"With me, Troy. I'd like you to stay with me."

Troy heard her. He even understood her.

But he couldn't believe it was happening.

The woman he wanted more than anything—more than he could ever remember wanting a woman before—wanted him to stay. And there was no way he could act on it.

His job was to protect her. Hell, he'd just done a

sweep of her home, ensuring she wasn't in danger or under possible threat of attack from the nameless, faceless stalker who had set their sights on her. There was no way he could cross the line and sleep with her.

"Evangeline. You know I can't do that." He saw the pulse beating wildly at her throat, even as her gaze stayed level on his. "Even if you are the only thing I can think about right now." He hesitated, before adding, "And the only one I want."

"Why can't we have this? In the midst of all that we've both dealt with, why can't we have this?" She moved a step closer. "Why can't we take it?"

"I have to protect you."

"That's an excuse, Troy, not a reason."

"It's a damn good reason. You said yourself, the GGPD's efforts need to be focused right now. On capturing Davison. On securing Bowe and making him account for his lies. And they need to be focused on what's been happening to you. That shirt tonight isn't the end of things."

He hated to scare her, but if that was what it took to make her see reason, he wouldn't sugarcoat the situation, either.

Oh, who was he kidding? If it was what it took to convince *himself* to keep his head and not give in to passion, then the words were even more important.

"That shirt is an escalation. Sneaking around to place it in my car, knowing you'd be the one to see it? Even more so."

"You think I don't know that? Just because I'm glad there's now a high likelihood a woman isn't dead from a gunshot at close range doesn't mean I'm ignorant of what's going on."

He let out a hard sigh, the frustration of so many unanswered questions more than evident in that hard exhale. "You tell me then, Evangeline. What's going on?"

"Someone has it out for me. Maybe it's someone I prosecuted or someone who's got a problem with the Davison case. Who knows?"

Who did know?

She was the one who hadn't gotten a conviction for Davison, for Pete's sake. And she could be as upset about that as she wanted, but Troy had to believe it hardly made her the first person Davison would change pattern for and come harm.

And Bowe?

In a lot of ways, her use of his data to get Davison off on all charges had reinforced the man's motive. So once again, seeing her as his enemy and stalking her just didn't fit.

Which put him back to more questions with no answers. And a series of incidents that felt off-kilter and *way* off pattern.

"I care about the answer, Troy." She pressed on, her conviction clear, even as she remained close enough to touch. "I care about finding out who's been after me and why these things are happening. But right now? I care about you more. About exploring this need between us. And about letting the rest of the world fall away for a while."

It would be so easy. To simply take what he craved so desperately. To be with her and find a way to get past all the endless questions that roiled in his mind, seemingly without answers.

Because while the mystery of what surrounded her had no answer, in so many ways, it didn't matter.

She was the answer.

To him. For him. And with this wild attraction he'd never expected or anticipated.

From the first night here in her kitchen, he'd had this unrelenting need for her. It kept whispering through him, suggesting she was meant to be in his life.

And meant for him.

Troy knew he stood on a precipice. But as he stood there and saw the need in her eyes—need that matched his own—he recognized something else.

There was nothing on earth he wouldn't do to protect this woman. Nothing he wouldn't do to keep her safe.

Making love wouldn't change that. More to the point, it *couldn't* change that. His commitment to her as a cop was unwavering.

Just like his need.

"I'm still not sure this is a good idea."

He saw victory flash in her eyes, matched by the smile that filled with the knowledge of all that was to come. "I know."

And then there was no more talking. What was the point?

There was only feeling.

Need had already wrapped around them both, but as he pulled her close, his lips sinking into hers, he found that it had shifted somehow. The greedy claws and snapping jaws that had driven him faded, replaced with the gentle need to explore. To touch. To fill them both with pleasure.

It was no less urgent, but it was different. As if the mere act of finally deciding to be with Evangeline had calmed the beast.

Moment flowed into moment as they drifted, never losing touch of one another, even as their clothing was lost somewhere between the kitchen and the bedroom.

A shoe here. His shirt there. Her dress somewhere in the hallway.

And when he finally laid her down on the bed, covering her naked body with his own, he knew joy. The feel of her, so soft to his every touch, was like some sort of happy magic. Troy cupped the rounded curve of her breast, his thumb brushing her nipple, and lost himself in her. Especially when the act pulled sounds of pleasure from her throat and he felt an answering need curling low in the belly.

Want and need were no longer enough. No longer sufficient to describe what she did to him and what he wanted from her.

He wanted all of her.

Every bit she could give him and then he wanted more.

Her hands flowed over his skin, a matching exploration of her own. Over his shoulders, down his triceps, before curling around to his chest. Her touch moved over him, over the hard lines of his stomach, before drifting lower, then lower still to wrap those long, glorious fingers around the pulsing length of him. As she took him in her palm, Troy knew he was lost.

Utterly, completely lost.

"Troy. Now." The words whispered against him, powerful in their simplicity and featherlight against his ear. He reached for the condom he'd set beside the bed and, quickly sheathing himself, moved back into her arms.

They found a rhythm, increasingly urgent as the pleasure built and built between them. He felt her tighten around him, her deep cry of pleasure a match for his own as her release crested.

And as he sank into her, burying himself in the glory

that was Evangeline, Troy knew with absolute certainty why he'd resisted for so long.

He'd believed it was because she deserved better than a guy making the moves on her while she needed help. Then he'd convinced himself that he needed to keep work and personal separate, that his job required his full and complete focus. He'd even told himself that his inability to find a partner in life was a result of the fear for a loved one that had been instilled in him at the earliest age.

All were true.

It was only now—now that he'd made love to her—that he knew what his conscience had only whispered. Because all those things were only excuses. They'd covered up the truth.

He'd been in love with Evangeline Whittaker far longer than he'd realized.

And for all those reasons, there was no way he could have her.

Chapter 16

In the morning, he was gone.

Evangeline knew he would be. She'd mentally prepared for it, even as she'd gone willingly into his arms. But even with that knowledge, she'd given all she felt—all she *knew* down to the depths of her soul—to Troy.

She'd wanted him. And the feeling had been gloriously mutual. They'd spent the night wrapped up in each other. For all the time they'd spent talking since he'd come to her aid on a street downtown, their night together had held little conversation. It was almost as if the words had taken a back seat to action.

She didn't regret it. She'd never regret it. But she'd dearly hoped she'd be wrong about the morning after.

Sitting up, she pulled on a robe and made quick work of her morning routine. In moments her face was freshly scrubbed and her hair was pulled up into a loose bun on top of her head. She ambled down to the kitchen for coffee, touched to see he'd started a pot for her. He'd even had a cup, his mug now rinsed and sitting in the drainboard next to her sink.

All without waking her.

Her gaze caught on the note on the table and she picked it up. It might be cliché, the "morning after" note, but knowing him now as she did, she also recognized it as purely Troy.

Evangeline—
  It's an early day and I need to meet Brett to go over the latest on Bowe. We've been trying to run down Bowe's brother and Brett has a contact who might be able to help.
Troy

As goodbye notes went, it was nicer than most, she imagined. She wouldn't know, exactly, as she'd never received one. But it was clear that he had a job to do and she'd do well to remember that.

A killer was still on the loose, as was the department criminal who'd enabled him. Her night with Troy was a gift for them both. One that had allowed them to escape that for a while. But now, in the fresh light of a summer morning, they had to return to reality.

And she needed to return to some sense of normalcy.

A shower and then a call to Arielle was first on her list. She wanted to set a timeline to return to her job. Because despite the unrest in Grave Gulch and in her own personal life, she needed to be doing something. And sitting home day in and day out wasn't the answer.

An hour later, she returned to the kitchen, hair and makeup done and clad in her favorite work-casual blouse and pressed slacks. She wanted every ounce of confidence she could muster for her call with Arielle and wasn't immune to the benefits of a good session with the eyelash curler.

Evangeline had her phone in hand and was about to ring her boss when the glass face lit up with a call. The number came up, one she didn't recognize. She would have let it go to voicemail, but considering how many people were working on her behalf at the GGPD, she decided to answer. If it was a robocall, she could always hang up.

"Hello?"

"Evangeline." Her name came out in a frightened whisper.

"Who is this?"

"Shh. Shh. He'll hear me."

Hear her? Who?

The voice trembled before the woman continued on. "It's Ella, Evangeline. I live upstairs from you."

Instantly, an image filled Evangeline's mind's eye. The young woman who lived upstairs was small and waiflike and, if she remembered correctly, worked at one of the restaurants downtown.

"Ella. What's wrong?"

"It's him. He's out of control. I'm hiding in the bathroom."

"Who?"

"He's mad. He's in a rage because I broke up with him."

They didn't keep the same hours, and other than their casual conversation earlier in the week, Evangeline hadn't seen much of Ella, but she did remember the day she moved in. She had a large, muscled boyfriend who looked about the same age. Although he hadn't been super-friendly, he hadn't struck Evangeline as a problem, either.

You can't always tell on the surface.

That idea whispered through her mind as an image of her father's face, red and mottled as he screamed, rounded out the thought.

"I'll come up. I can help you."

"No!" The urgency was there, but Ella managed to keep her voice low. "He hit me and split my lip. He'll hurt you, too."

"No, he won't." While she had no way of knowing if that was true, Evangeline hoped she could help defuse the situation and get Ella out of there. "I'm going to call the police."

"No! You can't. He'll kill me if the cops show up."

"All the more reason for me to do it," Evangeline pressed urgently.

"Oh no! He's coming. He's trying to break through the door. He's going to strangle me if he finds me!"

"I'll be right there."

Evangeline disconnected, immediately dialing Troy. She was already rushing out of her door, the baseball bat she kept in her hall closet in hand, swinging around to the landing that held the stairwell to the second floor.

"Evangeline." He answered on the first ring.

Although it seemed incongruous after what they'd shared, she didn't have time for anything sweet or pleasant. "My neighbor. Upstairs. She's in danger. Her boyfriend is trying to strangle her."

"Stay downstairs. I'm on my way."

"I can't do that. He could hurt her."

"Stay downstairs!"

She wasn't going to argue, and while she recognized the reason for the direction, she was sick and tired of waiting while things went on around her. Whatever happened in the end of that alley had vanished because she didn't go down there and engage.

She wasn't letting her neighbor suffer the same fate.

Fully aware of how rude it was, she kept climbing the stairs anyway.

And hit the disconnect button.

Someone needed help. And she wasn't sitting around waiting for someone else to handle it.

Troy slammed his phone on the desk and let out a string of curses as he dragged on his sports coat.

"What is it?"

"Evangeline's neighbor is in the middle of a domestic dispute."

Brett was already up and following him out the door, Ember in their wake.

"I told her to stay put."

"And she's rushing in to help."

The two of them ran for their vehicle outside, Brett hollering instructions to dispatch as they moved through the precinct.

Troy flew through the streets of Grave Gulch, his lights flashing. Brett got on with dispatch the moment they were in the car, Mary's voice echoing through the car speaker.

"I've got two officers nearby en route."

Troy barked out the layout for the condo complex, the access points to the second floor and the likely condo number for Evangeline's upstairs neighbor.

The other officers were already there, their car parked and flashing in front of Evangeline's building as he pulled into the parking lot. Troy swung into the closest spot he could find and leaped out of the car as soon as he cut the ignition.

Panic swam in his veins. For her, for the situation. And for the rising sense of unease that Evangeline would be in the middle of some new mess.

He took the metal stairs to the second floor two at a time, and heard the calm, steady voices as soon as he cleared the landing.

"Ma'am. Nothing is wrong here."

"But he's inside. She's frightened and afraid."

"I'm not afraid. Of anything."

Troy puzzled through the different voices, from Evangeline's rising one to the steady voices of everyone else. It was the same voice someone used when trying to calm an animal or a small child.

And as he came down the landing he could see by the look in Evangeline's dark eyes that it wasn't working.

Her gaze kept darting between the half-open door, filled with a sleepy-looking woman in a T-shirt and short-shorts and two uniformed officers outside the door.

Her hand was white-knuckled around a bat, but the piece remained firmly at her side. "But Ella, you just called me. You said he was coming after you to strangle you. You said you were locked in the bathroom with a split lip."

"There's no one here. I already told you that, like, five times." The young woman still lounged against the doorframe and Troy took in the odd look on her face.

Whatever was going on—and it increasingly looked like Evangeline was wrong again—still didn't match that reaction. Even if Evangeline had imagined whatever had gone on, the woman's casual pose struck him as off.

It also hit him that he'd met her before. Staring up

at the building, trying to figure out the situation with the firecracker fuse.

Ella, he remembered on a rush.

"Officers." Troy moved up to the door, his badge out. He eyed Evangeline, willing her to understand his silent instruction, before turning to the woman in the doorway. "Ma'am. I'm Detective Colton. What's going on here?"

"My neighbor is all freaked out for no reason." The young woman stood taller at his approach, her gaze darting toward Evangeline. "She's been pounding on my door and screaming about letting her in. She woke me up."

"But you called me," Evangeline said from behind and Troy turned once more, his gaze dark.

"I didn't call you," Ella said, her voice rising. "How many times do I have to tell you that?"

Brett and Ember joined them on the second-floor landing and the woman's eyes went wide at the appearance of yet another cop and a dog. "Whoa. Look. I'm not sure what you're all doing here but I didn't make any calls. I was sound asleep up until a few minutes ago and her knocking."

Evangeline must have gotten the message because she said nothing else and Troy ratcheted up the charm. "I'm sorry that you were disturbed, Ms.—" He left it hang there and she picked it up.

"Fields. Ella Fields."

"Ms. Fields. I'm sorry for the inconvenience." He lowered his voice, well aware her casual pose and insistence that nothing was wrong could easily be a ploy to protect the boyfriend. "If there's anything you need, we're happy to help. And if it would set your mind at ease, we can do a sweep of your home."

The woman swung the door wide and extended her hand toward the interior. The layout was similar to Evangeline's and while he couldn't see the full condo from the doorway, it didn't appear as if anyone had gone on a rampage through the apartment. "I have nothing to hide. No one's here."

"We have permission to enter your apartment, ma'am?" Brett stepped up.

"Sure." Ella shrugged. "But just you guys. I don't know what her problem is but I don't want her in here."

Brett moved forward and Troy gestured the officers to follow.

"I'll just take Ms. Whittaker back to her home. Thank you for your time, Ms. Fields."

"Troy!" Evangeline started in the moment he moved up beside her.

"Shh." He let the word out in one quick order and took her hand, giving it a gentle squeeze. "Not now."

He didn't miss the puzzled look on her face but she said nothing further. He retraced his steps back down to the first floor and escorted her to her home. The moment they were through the door, he closed it behind them. "Stay here."

Gun drawn, her swept her apartment, the sudden realization he'd had upstairs looming large in his mind. What if the girl upstairs was a diversion? A way of getting Evangeline out of her apartment so an intruder could get in?

The sweep turned up nothing and Brett's text a few minutes later that Ember hadn't found anyone else reinforced the idea taking root.

As he walked back into the living room, he purposely kept his mind blank, desperate to avoid the images that wanted to take hold. He would not think about the way he'd retrieved his clothing off the hallway floor this morning. Nor would he remember the way they'd used every inch of her big bed, making love several times throughout the night.

"You hung up on me."

"I had to help her."

He wanted to be stern. More than that, he needed to be. She put herself in danger, responding to a call that required the police. But the raw fear that had iced him cold on the drive over needed an outlet, too. Without considering all the declarations he'd made to himself—those uncompromising ones about leaving her alone—that very morning as he rinsed his coffee mug, he pulled her close, his mouth crushing hers.

Evangeline responded immediately, her arms wrapping around him as she answered the deep pull within him.

He did need to walk away. But first, he needed to satisfy himself that she was all right. Needed to feel the life that beat within her and confirm that all his dark fears, the ones that had loomed so large on the drive to her home, hadn't come true.

So he pushed all he felt into the kiss. As if he could convince her how much he cared and brand her at the same time. Because after this, he had to walk away.

She was in his blood now and it was something he never expected. Or needed. Or wanted.

With one final press of his lips to hers, Troy pulled back.

He didn't miss the empty look in Evangeline's eyes. He figured it was a match for how she likely looked this morning when she'd woken and he was gone.

He wanted things to be different. But they couldn't

be. And because of that simple fact, he leaned into the job and used it as a shield to protect his heart.

"Now. Let's walk through this one from the beginning and figure out what's going on."

The morning incident at Evangeline's had put him behind but Troy wasn't quite ready to let it go. Her upstairs neighbor had protested, but Troy had seen Evangeline's call log. He'd taken down the number and the time of the call and hoped it would be enough for Ellie to work her tech magic. If not, Evangeline had agreed to come into the precinct to let Ellie look at her phone.

Which had circled Troy right back to where he'd begun his morning: Randall Bowe.

"Still no luck finding the brother?" Brett asked around a mouthful of sandwich. One of the two he'd picked up on his way back to the precinct from Evangeline's.

"No. I can't find any record of a Baldwin Bowe and I've done some serious searching." Troy took a bite of his meatball sub and considered all the effort he'd put into this case. As he chewed he remembered Brett's offer a few days before.

"How did I forget?" Even as he asked the question, Troy knew exactly how he'd forgotten. Evangeline. She'd been at the forefront of his thoughts, crowding out the work. His cases.

Everything.

Pushing it aside, he refocused on Brett. "You offered to ask your friend. The US marshal who has an inside line to the witness protection program?"

Brett shook his head and grinned. "You haven't gotten to your email yet. Oren got back to us and nothing popped on WitSec."

Troy wiped his hands and turned to his computer, scrolling until he saw the name Oren Margulies. "You spoke well of him." Troy scanned the man's email, the reason for Brett's solid endorsement evident in the crisp, clear words and the genuine offer of help. "I can see why. He's thorough. And doesn't have any detail on a Baldwin Bowe or any hints the man was even considered for protection."

"Another dead end." Brett balled up the wrapper from his sandwich. "There is another angle, though. Would you want to be close to Randall Bowe? The guy's a worm, from everyone's recounting. It's entirely possible Baldwin just doesn't want anything to do with his family."

"True."

Much as he hated thinking of any angle as a dead end, Troy knew Brett was right. The Coltons might be tightly woven and all up in one another's business, but that didn't mean every family was the same.

What also didn't translate was why Baldwin Bowe was so damn hard to find. Everyone had a digital footprint. It was so standard at this point that Bowe's lack of one was a red flag in and of itself. It had become so odd that it might be worth putting Ellie on it to see if she could come up with something.

Which made the woman's arrival at his office door less than thirty seconds later both odd and reassuring. "Troy. Brett. The people I want to see."

She barreled into the office, her trusty laptop in hand as she took the guest chair next to Brett. "Wait'll you see what I found." She angled her laptop so they could both see the screen and tabbed through a few of the apps she had open.

"The number you gave me this morning. It was

shockingly easy to track." She eyed Troy directly. "Like, stupid easy."

"What do you mean?"

"The number that called Evangeline's mobile line? It's the number registered to her upstairs neighbor, Ella Fields. The woman didn't even call from a different phone or try to hide what she was doing."

"Someone could have spoofed the number," Brett interjected, but Troy could see his attention was caught on Ellie's screen.

"They could but based on the logs I pulled from the phone company—" Ellie toggled to a new screen "—there was a call made from that number through those stodgy old phone lines that crisscross Grave Gulch. The girl didn't even use an untraceable cell phone."

"And it was made to Evangeline's cell."

Ellie nodded. "At nine thirty-two this morning."

Which made sense, because Evangeline's call to him had come in four minutes later.

Ellie shook her head as she closed her laptop. "Someone's gaslighting her. That's all there is to it."

Which was the final tumbler in the lock, Troy realized.

He'd questioned the idea and, while not impossible, it had seemed like an awfully complicated way to hurt someone.

But in Ellie's words, Troy knew the truth.

The incredibly simple, *obvious*, truth.

Someone was purposely taunting Evangeline, attacking and undermining her credibility.

As the cloud of confusion lifted, a layer of guilt took its place.

He hadn't believed her. Not fully, anyway. A big part of him might have tried, but there had always been something holding him back, so he'd never fully given Evangeline his trust.

"You mean making her think there's danger when there really isn't?" Brett clarified.

"Yep. Like that old movie. The one with Ingrid Bergman. The creepy husband keeps trying to make her think she's seeing things." Ellie added, "They actually made us watch it in the academy along with one of our domestic abuse workshops."

"It all makes sense. Every bit of it." Troy tried to remain calm, but he couldn't deny the slamming of his heart against his ribs and the rising anger. All at himself.

He'd doubted her. Even when it was clear she was desperate to have someone believe her, he'd held back.

"First the incident in the alley. The weird stuff in her house and the sense of being watched. The bloody shirt. Now the neighbor."

"But who's doing it?" Brett pressed the question. "A woman, and one this soon after his last kill, is a serious break in pattern for Len Davison. And Randall Bowe has no reason to come after her."

Troy was already on his feet. Now that he knew what he was looking for, he had an entirely new approach to keeping Evangeline safe. And it started with the lying upstairs neighbor.

"I don't know. But we're going to find out."

Evangeline tried to focus on the positive call she'd had with Arielle Parks and her boss's agreement that it was time for her to come back to the DA's office and not on the weird incident with the upstairs neighbor.

What was going on with Ella?

The call had been real but so had the sleepy eyes and

disdain for being woken up. But it was also strange the woman had called her. It wasn't like they'd exchanged phone numbers, yet somehow Ella had hers? They'd met the day Ella moved into the condo complex and were cordial to one another when they passed in the parking lot and that was it.

Yet Evangeline was the first one she called?

The ping of a text pulled her away from the puzzle and she couldn't stop the smile as Troy's name lit up the face of her phone. It was a wholly unnecessary reaction, especially given her current situation and the reason he was texting her, but it made her smile all the same.

Got a lead on your neighbor. Can you meet me? The diner just past the edge of town?

She texted back that she could and quickly cleaned up her breakfast dishes. In a matter of minutes, she'd left the house, locking the door behind her. The sense of action felt good. Better than good, she admitted to herself as she navigated her way toward the diner Troy had noted.

She felt more like herself than she had in months. Like she had purpose again.

"That was fast," Troy said as she climbed out of the car. "Things are coming together. Including the fact that your silly young neighbor did call you this morning from her home, just above you."

"That was her number?" Evangeline stared at Troy across the expanse of the hood of her car. Of all the things she expected him to say, that wasn't it. A hello would have been nice, too, but she ignored that spurt of disappointment. "Why would she do that and then pretend she didn't?"

"That's what we're going to find out. Ellie did some quick work on her social media pages and found she works here. She's going to meet us."

Evangeline glanced around the parking lot. "There—" She pointed to a small red compact car. "That's her car."

"I'd normally do this alone but I want her to look at you when I ask her questions."

It was a tactic Evangeline recognized and it made a lot of sense. As of yet, the woman had behaved suspiciously, but they needed to know more. Her presence might be the key they needed to get Ella talking.

"Thanks for bringing me into this. I'd really like to understand what's going on."

"What's going on is that we think you're being gaslighted."

"What?" Evangeline stilled as images of her father's tactics on her mother rushed through her mind. "Why do you think that?"

"Ellie had the idea and it's the only one that fits. You are a strong, competent woman. And all these things that keep happening to you and then vanishing? They're setups."

The wash of relief was palpable, even as the memories of her father's behavior left an oily residue in her midsection. "I'm not imagining things."

He came around the car then to stand in front of her. The hard lines of his face, set in place ever since that last, lingering kiss in her home, finally faded. In its place, his mouth creased into a small smile. "No, you're not. You never were. But someone wants you to think you are." She'd heard of that behavior. She'd even seen it a time or two over her career. Sadistic, psychotic behavior, perpetrated on innocent people to make them feel less-than. And while she was happy to finally have answers, she was angry, too.

How dare they?

Whoever "they" was.

Just like that morning, when she woke with the express desire to call Arielle and get on with her life, that same feeling filled her now. On a nod, Evangeline pointed toward the glass front door, determination straightening her spine with steel. "Let's go get this done."

She walked beside Troy into the diner, her gaze sweeping the room for Ella. Although the diner was large, the post-lunch crowd had thinned out and it wasn't hard to find Ella as she moved around, cleaning off tables and pocketing tips.

"Miss Fields?" Troy approached her, casual and easy. Evangeline had spent enough time with him now to recognize the act and how the smile didn't quite meet those hard cop's eyes.

But anyone sitting around listening wouldn't have known that.

"May we have a few minutes of your time?"

"Um. Well. I'm not due for a break for another half hour."

Troy kept that smile firmly in place, even as his tone remained unbending. "I'm sure your manager won't mind but I can clear it if I need to."

"No, no. The lunch crowd has died down. I'm sure it'll be fine."

Evangeline didn't miss how the young woman's eyes kept darting her way but kept her own smile firmly in place.

Troy led them to a quiet corner of the diner, in a seat Ellie had already grabbed when she came in.

"Who's this?" Ella asked, that cornered look growing more pronounced in her eyes.

"This is Ellie Bloomberg. She's our queen of all technology at the GGPD and she found something interesting this morning with Ms. Whittaker's phone."

"I'm not sure what this has to do with—"

"It seems as if you made a call to Ms. Whittaker this morning," Troy cut her off, pressing his advantage. "A call Ms. Bloomberg was able to confirm quite easily."

Whatever reaction Evangeline was expecting—especially after the sleepy bravado routine this morning at Ella's condo—wasn't in evidence. Instead, her neighbor's shoulders fell as she blurted out, "Damn. I forgot to use that cell phone he gave me."

"Would you like to make a statement, Ms. Fields?"

The young woman's head snapped up. "Am I under arrest?"

"You made a fake phone call with the express intent of harassing someone."

Evangeline stepped in before Troy could add anything further. "I work for the district attorney's office, Ella. I'm quite sure we can talk to Detective Colton's chief as well as my boss and gain their leniency if you can help us with this."

Ella nodded, her eyes filling with tears. "It was a quick hundred bucks, ya know? And it didn't seem that bad at the time."

"What didn't seem so bad?" Troy's voice had gentled and in his compassion Evangeline saw more of what she loved so much about him.

He recognized that the people he was sworn to protect didn't always make the best decisions. But even when they erred, it didn't mean he lost his compassion for them.

"All I had to do was call and rile her up a bit. It was just pretend. Acting, the guy told me." Ella turned her tear-filled eyes to Evangeline. "I really didn't mean to hurt you or upset you. I can see now how I did."

"Do you have any other information?" Troy asked.

"Yes." The waitress nodded, swiping at her eyes. "I have a note in my bag. Let me just go get it."

Ella slid out of the booth to head toward the back of the restaurant. Evangeline figured there was no need to follow her since they knew where she lived. But it seemed odd, anticlimactic, even, to be sitting here waiting for a note.

"She got in over her head," Evangeline started in, curious if Troy would agree. "I meant what I said. I see no reason why we can't figure out a deal. I don't want to press charges."

"Don't be too hasty."

Troy barely had the words out when Ella came rushing back up to the table, a crumpled piece of paper in her hand. "Here. I knew I had the number. He said to call him if there were any problems."

Troy glanced at the small slip of paper before passing it to Ellie, who began tapping on her oversize cell phone. In moments, she had what she was looking for. "It's a local number." With a glance for the young woman who'd helped them, she tapped the piece of paper. "I need to take this with me."

"Go ahead." Ella lifted her hands up, palms out. "I don't want anything to do with it."

They wrapped up quickly, getting the details of how Ella was approached and a description of the guy who'd paid her. Other than making the young woman even more scared than she already was, there was little to be gained after getting the details.

The waitress was obviously remorseful and while Troy might not be quite ready to let her off the hook, Evangeline had worked long enough in the DA's office to recognize young and naive over criminal any day.

What still remained was what was going on with the person who put her neighbor up to this.

Ellie turned to them when they got into the parking lot. "I didn't want to give her any more details, but that number appears to be tied to some of the back-end operations of a local restaurant. I got the type of business off of their tax filings."

"What restaurant?" Troy demanded.

"I can't see it on my mobile device. I need to dig into the computer back at the office. Shouldn't take me long to get it for you."

Ellie was already climbing into her car to head back to the precinct.

"I'll let you go, then." Evangeline dug her keys out of her purse. "Thank you for including me in this. And for your kindness to Ella."

"She's not out of the woods yet."

"She should be. She did a stupid thing. She's young and she saw the money and thought it was a phone call."

"She committed a crime."

Evangeline let out a hard sigh. That stony, stoic look had returned to his face and suddenly, she wasn't able to face it any longer. They'd made love the night before and while she wasn't expecting declarations of everlasting devotion, his lack of acknowledgment stung. Terribly.

"Please let me know what you find out about the phone number."

He only nodded and it took everything inside of her to get in her car and keep the tears at bay.

The drive back to her condo passed in a blur of tears

and sobs and the deep desire to climb into her bed and pull the covers over her head.

How had she been so stupid? Because as she drove the winding miles through Grave Gulch back home, she knew the truth. She'd fallen in love with Troy. Beyond her better sense or any modicum of reason, she had and there was nothing to be done for it.

Swiping at her eyes, she dashed away what was left of the tears. She was stronger than this. Hadn't the past week shown her that? Hell, the past few months. She'd get past this and move on and someday she'd find a way to stop thinking about Troy Colton with every fiber of her being.

But that day wasn't today, Evangeline admitted as she got out of the car and walked to her front door. She slipped the key in the lock and only barely registered the ease with which the door swung open, even before she turned the key.

If she weren't distracted, maybe, she'd have reacted differently when a big, beefy hand clamped around her wrist and dragged her inside the house.

But she couldn't even summon a scream as a second hand clamped over her mouth.

Chapter 17

Troy could still picture Evangeline's face a half hour later as he tried to work his way through a response to Oren Margulies. The US marshal had been kind enough to offer to answer any additional questions Troy might have and Troy wanted to see if the guy had any insight or experience that might help them find Baldwin Bowe.

Even as he typed, then deleted, then typed some more, Troy couldn't find his focus.

All he could see was Evangeline's face when she turned away from him in the parking lot and got into her car.

He'd hurt her. That much was evident. More than evident, he admitted to himself, because he knew it was purposeful. And much as it pained him to do it, he needed to begin making the break with her.

The discovery of the gaslighting had broken the case open and now that they had a phone number they were running down, he and Brett would go deal with the restaurant owner and get the entire situation resolved. This nightmare she'd been living in would all be over.

Just like him and Evangeline.

It was the right thing to do. More than right, he considered as he typed another paragraph to Margulies. The Davison and Bowe cases needed his full attention.

His full focus.

So why did he feel so miserable?

"Ellie got us a name and an address." Brett's voice flowed into the office a few beats before he walked in. "Sal Petrillo. Guy owns That's Amore, an Italian restaurant downtown."

Troy knew the place. He'd been there on a few dates and had done takeout a time or two. "I know it. It's been there a few years. Guy opened it after moving down from Detroit, best I remember."

"Your intel matches Ellie's. She also said she's heard rumors the reason Petrillo moved down from Detroit was that he had some debts up there he never really paid off."

Troy hit Send on his email. "Oh, he does?"

"Since I've learned in the very short time I've been here that Ellie is always right, who am I to argue?"

"You learn fast, Shea."

"I like to think so."

Troy texted Evangeline to see if she knew anything about the restaurant or had any run-ins with its owner. As he hit Send, a small shot of remorse filled him at the simplicity of the text and the way he'd shot out an order to text back, but he had to ignore it. He needed an answer and he wasn't composing damn love notes.

In a matter of minutes they'd arrived at the restaurant and Troy looked around as he got out of the car, pushing the text to the back of his mind.

"It's not that far from Evangeline's alley."

"No, it's not." Brett pointed in the direction of the row of buildings that spread before them. "I'd say one major block over, give or take a few storefronts."

"Right you are."

Troy considered it as they walked up to That's Amore. A neon Open sign was lit over the door and they walked into the scents of tomato sauce and baking pizza. Although this place didn't back up to the alleyway where Evangeline saw the purported shooting, it would be easy enough to squeeze through a few buildings to come out to this one.

Again, he filed it away as a hostess greeted them. "Can I help you? The dining room's closed until dinner but we can still do take-out orders."

"I'm actually looking for someone." Troy shared the number that had been included on Ella's note. "I have a number and I understand it's associated with this restaurant."

For the first time the woman looked uneasy and Troy pulled out his badge, as did Brett. "We need to know if you recognize it."

It had been a deliberate gamble, but they'd not called the number in advance, instead hoping to catch the owner here. The hostess's response confirmed it was the right one.

"Yeah, that's Sal's number. He's the owner. He's in the back. I'll just go get him."

"Clumsy move to use his phone and to get dumb kids to make calls for him," Brett observed as he moved around the small waiting area. There were a few framed newspaper articles on the walls, the sort local restaurants put up to affirm they were part of the community. Troy scanned them for any insight into the mysterious Sal and it was only as his gaze alighted on the last one that he recognized the image.

From the sketch his sister had done.

He was about to call Brett over when the hostess walked back out from the kitchen.

"I'm sorry, Detectives, but Sal left, apparently. Right after the lunch rush wrapped. Or what passes for it these days."

"Do you know where he went?" Troy asked, that same uncomfortable feeling that had ridden him in his office flaring high like a bonfire.

The woman shook her head. "I don't know."

Troy grabbed his phone from his belt to check. No answering text from Evangeline filled up the screen. He turned to Brett, his gut screaming that they already knew the location of the elusive Sal. "Let's go."

Evangeline struggled against the bonds at her wrist but didn't dare move too fast. The big, beefy man who'd been at the heart of all that had happened to her was surprisingly quick and had done an even quicker job jamming her into a kitchen chair.

One that he'd already rigged with a bomb underneath.

One he'd told her about as he slammed her into place, tying her hands behind her.

Thoughts raced around in her mind as she desperately tried to come up with a plan. She had no experience with bombs but based on the gingerly way he'd maneuvered around her once he had it set, she had to assume the situation was sensitive.

And highly deadly.

"Why are you doing this?"

"You've ruined my life."

"Me? I don't even know you."

It was the wrong thing to say and it had his ire flaring, his face turning a mottled shade of red. "You've ruined my business. It's your fault that piece of scum is out on the streets. No one's willing to go out anymore. I was getting by on a shoestring as it is. And now they've found me."

"Who found you?"

He turned bloodshot eyes, buried deep in his face, on her. "Some guys I owe money to back in Detroit. I guess I didn't run far enough away. Figured this dump of a town would be plenty of protection. Why would anyone look for me here? I'd get back on my feet, run a good business and make my money back, and then I could pay what I owe."

While she took serious offense at hearing her home characterized that way, antagonizing him wasn't going to help the situation. "I can assure you, I'm as upset as you about the murders. I was put on leave because of the Len Davison case and I'm heartsick to know he's killed more people."

"Keep your sob story to yourself. My business is down fifty percent. No one can pay off a loan when they can barely pay the rent. And that's damn hard when no one wants romantic dinners when a killer is on the loose. All the publicity your case drummed up for the loser put me smack in the crosshairs of my loan sharks. One of 'em saw me on TV, standing in front of my restaurant waving away those damned protestors."

Evangeline had no idea how the man had twisted the story around to suit himself, but it was obvious he had.

Even more obvious: Whatever story he'd told himself had become his truth.

Her legal case with Len Davison, terrible as it was, had no bearing on unpaid loans to unsavory people. And if she'd hoped that sharing her sob story would build a kinship between them, she was sorely mistaken. His eyes only turned meaner. "Figured the cops would ignore you and think you were crazy. Make it all so easy for me. Only they've gotten closer than ever."

"You were the one behind it all?"

"Figured I'd have some fun with you for a while. You've given me enough sleepless nights. Thought I'd toss some your way."

Although she had little hope she'd be successful, Evangeline tried once more. "Look. I'm sorry your business is failing but I'm sure we can figure something out. Make a deal or something. I'm part of the county DA's office and I'm sure we can work with the city to help with some of your mounting financial problems."

He laughed hard at that, the mirthless sound seeming to rattle around the kitchen. "Just like every other lawyer I've ever known. You think you can talk your way out of everything. Only, you can't."

As she stared at him, Evangeline knew the truth.

She couldn't talk her way out of this one. Just like she couldn't run far enough away from the bomb, even if she did manage to get her hands free.

And no one knew she was here with a madman and a bomb.

No one at all.

"The shades are drawn." Brett sized up the front of the condo from where he and Troy sat in the cruiser. Brett was in the driver's seat and Ember rode in the back. And Troy felt like a caged animal in the passenger seat.

"I need to get in there."

"We need to assess the situation and get backup."

Backup Troy had already been assured was on its way.

"We're going to start with a perimeter search with Ember. See if she picks up a scent."

"You can't ask me to wait that long."

"I'm asking and I'm telling." Brett turned to face him fully. "It's what partners do. You have to trust me. I know what I'm doing. And I trust my K-9 to tell me what's going on."

Brett had already picked up the stained white shirt from the evidence room before heading out to Evangeline's. He reasoned that the lingering scents on the clothing would be enough for Ember to suss out if Evangeline's stalker was here.

Troy knew it was the right approach. He had nothing to go on except the lack of response to a text. If they went in guns blazing and she was in danger, they could do more harm. If they sat it out and ignored every clamoring nerve ending that said she was in danger, she could be hurt then, too.

And then he'd never get to tell her he loved her.

That thought lodged in his chest like an immovable boulder, heavy and suffocating.

He loved her.

And he had to get the chance to tell her.

"Ember will be quick and then we'll know what we're dealing with."

Troy nodded and got out of the passenger seat. Brett had parked several spots down from Evangeline's front door, hiding them from immediate view of anyone peeking through the blinds in her front window.

With careful precision, he folded the shirt so that the stains were on the interior and the areas of the shirt untouched by blood could be sniffed by Ember. Troy feared that even with those precautions the synthetic blood would act as a block to Ember catching a scent, but Brett didn't seem to harbor the same concerns.

After sensitizing Ember with the shirt, Brett gave his orders and she was off.

She moved around the front, sniffing along the perimeter of the building. It was only as she got to the edge of Evangeline's condo that she stopped and sat.

Brett heaped praise on her before pulling her away from the front door. "Let's head around back."

As his partner suggested it, Troy recognized the benefit. Sal might have lurked around the front of the house but if they could get behind the building they'd likely have a better shot at catching him unawares.

Troy visualized Evangeline's home and the layout from the back door to kitchen, then on down the hallway to the living room and bedrooms. If they could catch him unaware...

They moved as a team down the front of the condo building, around its side and then to the common area on the opposite side of the condo complex. The summer day ensured there were a few people out but all seemed to be focused on sunning themselves. As Ember continued smelling the perimeter, Troy heard the quiet step behind him.

His sister Grace moved up beside him.

"You shouldn't be back here."

"I got the call. I'm here." Her words along with the mulish expression shut him down before he could get a head of steam going. He still struggled knowing his baby sister was a rookie but he had to trust in her training.

Had to trust in her.

He quickly directed her and her partner to get the sunbathers off the property and away from the back of the complex. Grace nodded, clearly intent on answering his request immediately, before she turned back. "We're pulling for you and her. All of us. Oh, and there are three more pairs of officers out front waiting for instruction."

"Thanks."

With his sister's words still ringing in his ears, he caught up with Brett. And stilled when he saw the wide-eyed look his partner gave the K-9 as she sat abruptly, her face turned toward Evangeline's back door.

"Did she find something?"

"Yeah."

"Evangeline?"

Brett's expression was perfectly neutral. "Ember found a bomb, Troy. Based on where she's perched, it's through that door."

"The bastard has a bomb? What if she's wrong?"

"She's not wrong." Brett shook his head. "She's trained for this. That nose is never wrong."

Troy wanted to rant and rail and say that no system was infallible, but he knew it was useless. Brett trusted Ember and he trusted Brett.

And Ember knew her world through smell. His sister Annalise was a K-9 trainer. Hadn't she bragged about her dogs through the years? Their ability to scent off the most minute detail?

Brett pulled Ember away from the door, setting them

up a few yards down to avoid being heard. "We need to call in the bomb squad. Now."

"We don't have time for the bomb squad. He's got her in there and he's got no reason to keep her alive."

Brett considered for a minute before nodding. "I know how to dismantle it and I've got gear in the car. I know it's precious minutes but it's the best I can give you."

Troy nodded and was already on the move. He waved Grace over since she was closest, her partner still rounding up sunbathers, and gave her the details as they walked.

"You can't go in there," Grace argued.

"I don't have a choice."

"Mom will kill me if anything happens to you," she finally muttered before pulling him in a tight hug. "I'll radio the rest of the team out front."

Brett stepped in, handing Ember's leash to Grace. "Keep her as far away as possible."

Grace did as requested and moved off to join her partner, Ember obediently following. Troy and Brett jogged to the car and Brett gave a set of orders as they dragged on the gear.

Troy didn't doubt for a minute what he was doing, but as they headed around the back of the building to make their entry, a big part of him kept expecting to hear an explosion. Kept waiting for the reality that they weren't fast enough.

"Remember," Brett said as they got to the back door. "He's not pulling any trigger until he's out of there. Nothing about his behavior has suggested suicide mission up to now."

It was an oddly comforting thought and Troy hoped like hell Brett was right.

The life of the woman he loved depended on it.

As he reached for the doorknob, intent on picking the lock, he felt the door turn in his palm.

One hurdle down.

It looked like the bastard was aiming to make a quick escape.

Evangeline hated the helpless feeling that had washed over her. The raw fear and the endlessly cycling thoughts of Troy, her mother and how much she wanted to be alive to talk to both of them again.

Yet even with the panicked thoughts, another flew through her mind on the same loop. She'd believed herself helpless these past few months, too.

And she couldn't have been more wrong.

It was only now, strapped to a bomb, that she understood how strong she had really been. How much power she actually had to make a difference, the case against Len Davison be damned.

And how much she had to live for.

The man—did she even know his name?—had stalked around her a bit more, checking a few things on the chair and grunting as he bent his bulk over to look at the wiring before standing back up and looking at a small device in his hand.

A detonator?

The raw terror that had kept her on high alert spiked once more and Evangeline was shocked that she didn't leap up off the chair from the sheer rush of it.

But it was when he took a few steps back and stared her dead in the eye that Evangeline realized there was nowhere to go.

And nowhere to hide.

So she might as well get her answers.

"How'd you do it?"

"Do what?" His voice was gruff but she saw the slightest flicker of respect in his eyes. Like he admired that she'd finally started asking questions.

"The woman. The alley. That looked awfully real."

He guffawed at that—actually laughed—and Evangeline fought the need to scream.

"You mean my little acting job. It was easy to pull off. Been acting since I was a kid. I know all the tricks and I even do a decent make up job. It's how I got out of Detroit in the first place.

"I'm real good, too."

"Good enough to hide DNA?"

"That's easy," he said and waved a hand. "Pour a few cans of soda on the ground and you wash away any DNA left behind. Or you leave it so sticky, no one's finding anything."

Evangeline struggled to take it all in, but figured it was better to let him talk. As long as he was talking she was alive and that counted for something.

It had to.

"You really should take more care in your surroundings. You were easy to follow and it was even easier to break into this place. Ground floor." He shook his head and Evangeline knew in that moment that if her hands were free she'd have smacked him.

"I had my friend all set up and she wore a blood packet. All we needed to do was get your attention and then the rest was easy. We ginned up that fake fight and you fell right for it."

"That was fake blood?"

"Fake blood. Fake fight. Most of my waitresses want to be actresses anyway. A few hundred bucks and a day off." He shrugged. "Easy."

For a moment, she thought he was going to tell her more about the fake play he'd put on in downtown Grave Gulch.

Which made his next comment that much more surprising.

"This was never my intention, you know. Hurting you. At least, not at first."

"Oh no?" She heard the quaver in her voice and hated it, but couldn't help it around the adrenaline jangling her system.

"It's just all gotten to be too much. I was so close to paying off my debts. Living without that hanging over my head, until you let that guy go free. And I finally realized, someone else has to suffer, too. You know?"

He turned on his heel then and left. As if that was somehow an explanation for what he'd done. Or a reason she should blithely accept his justifications while she sat strapped to a bomb.

She nearly let loose the scream that was building in her chest when she saw the flash of movement through the doorway to the kitchen. A loud grunt echoed from the direction of the living room as Brett Shea raced into the room.

"Evangeline! Don't move!"

He was by her side immediately, his attention fully focused on the chair.

"He's got a detonator. You have to leave! Now, Brett! You and Troy. You have to leave!"

"We're not leaving without you."

"But he's going to blow us up."

"Troy's got it."

"You—" Her voice trembled, raw in the throat from the urgency of it all. "You need to go help him."

Brett nodded, understanding the import of her words.

But it was the ones that came back to her that gave her the first kernel of hope. "He's got a lot of incentive to ensure we're all walking back out of here."

Troy slammed a fist in Sal's gut, the impact ringing through his wrist and up his arm. Damn, but the bastard was a grizzly bear. He was paunchy but big and he had a lot more power behind him than Troy expected.

He also had a detonator.

Brett had already shouted it from behind him as he sought a way to get at the detonator.

Troy wanted to scream at his partner to go to Evangeline, but for the moment, that detonator required their full focus. The presence of the police ensured the guy knew he was caught.

Which meant he had precious little motivation to keep them all alive.

Troy dodged a jab at his kidney but took a beefy fist to the ribs that nearly had him doubling over. It was only the reality of the stakes that kept his hand still locked hard on the man's wrist, unwilling to give him any opportunity to press the button.

Brett moved in closer and Troy grunted as he tried to keep Sal pinned. But it was Brett's quick stomp on the man's exposed arm that ultimately did it. The combination of Troy's hold on the wrist and Brett's boot to the elbow had Sal screaming in pain, his fingers opening.

Brett snagged the detonator and raced to the kitchen. Troy moved equally fast, taking the temporary advantage and using it to turn the man over and dragging his hands behind his back. Sal's Miranda rights were already falling from Troy's lips as he tugged the handcuffs tight over those two meaty wrists.

Satisfied Sal was subdued, he opened the front door,

his hands up. It was only when he got an "all clear" shout from Melissa, holding the line across the parking lot, that Troy screamed further orders.

"Stay where you are. Suspect is subdued but the bomb is still live."

Melissa's pale visage was the last thing he saw before he turned and ran toward the kitchen.

"Just a few minutes more, darlin'." Brett's voice was steady and calm and Evangeline figured it was costing him a lot to stay that way. And she wanted to believe him. She wanted to sink into that calm, reassuring voice and lose herself there.

Only she couldn't because he was stuck under her kitchen chair, in close range of a bomb and Troy was sitting beside her at the table, his hand cradling hers.

"You need to leave. Please leave," she'd asked, over and over, but the stubborn man refused to move.

Both men had put on bomb vests, after freeing her wrists and settling one over her, but it wasn't enough. They needed to leave. It pressed on her, preying on her mind in an endless loop until a well of sobs finally took over, the adrenaline coursing through her body obscuring anything but the desperate prayer that they'd leave her and save themselves.

The sobs continued as she was lifted from the chair, wrapped in Troy's arms as he walked her out of the house to the ambulance waiting in the parking lot. And they kept on when he climbed in behind the paramedics, riding with her to the hospital.

Later, she'd learn that Brett had executed the bomb's defusion perfectly. She'd also learn that the bomb squad had come in for a formal sweep of her condo and all the other homes in her complex, declaring the entire facility safe. She'd even learn the name of the attacker, Sal Petrillo.

But all of it seemed so distant and foreign as she lay in the big hospital bed, machines beeping around her long into the night.

Troy stretched from his position on the chair beside Evangeline's bed. He'd wanted to call her mother but had ultimately waited until morning. He knew she'd kept the news of her ordeal quiet and since it had been so late by the time she was fully checked out and brought to her room, he made the decision to err on the side of fresh morning light.

The doctor couldn't give him much beyond the reassurance that she'd experienced a major trauma but would be all right with some time. So he'd stayed and waited and wondered how he could help her until her mother had shown up.

And after giving the kind woman with the even kinder eyes—Evangeline's eyes—the details, he left. And went back to the precinct to write everything up. A steady stream of people came in to greet him throughout the day, all doing a mix of checking in and getting the latest on what had gone down. It was only when he finally confirmed that he'd tell everyone everything but he needed some quiet that the line outside his door finally died down.

Which was when Melissa showed up.

"You didn't follow protocol yesterday."

"No, I didn't."

"And because of that, you saved her."

It was high praise from his chief. But it was the understanding in her eyes that was all family. Melissa closed his door before crossing to the chairs in front of his desk. "You doing okay?"

"Sure. It's the job. We're just fortunate those days are few and far between."

Not that he'd ever been part of a bomb defusion six inches away from his body. And certainly not one for the woman he was in love with.

Which only added to all the reasons he needed to walk away. He'd been a detective on cases that Evangeline prosecuted. One of those cases involved the town serial killer. Davison had to be Troy's full focus right now.

"I know you, Troy Colton. Why are you torturing yourself about this? And why aren't you with Evangeline?"

"We need to stop spending time with each other. It's as simple as that. We both have jobs to do, even if the past few days have made us lose sight of that."

"Jobs? You both almost died yesterday."

"But we didn't."

"Troy—" His name hung there and much as he wanted to just send her away, he finally gave in. Throwing down his pen, he gave his cousin his full attention.

"You didn't see her in that chair, Mel. The fear in her eyes. And the adrenaline crash when the dam finally burst. She was in danger and has been all along and I spent half the time doubting her. Our jobs are too much at odds with one another. I knew it from the start and this has only proven it."

"That's bs and you know it."

"Is it?" He might be sick of his own thoughts but he didn't need his family's interference, too. "How is it bull? Tell me how our professional lives haven't complicated the situation."

"It doesn't matter if things got complicated. The point is that you care about each other." He saw her grow still before she pressed on. "That you love each other. That doesn't come along every day and to hell with some job standing in your way."

"What good did that do my mother?" The words tore out of him, landing between him and Melissa with sharp, spiky edges. "She needed attention. She needed justice. But someone, somewhere dropped the ball. That's why her murder is unsolved to this day."

"You know as well as I do, we don't close every one of them. It's not a statement on the work, Troy. It's a reality of the job."

That might be the case but he'd spent a lifetime living with that reality. And he couldn't stand the fact that his closed-mindedness and his inability to see the bigger picture of what was happening had nearly gotten Evangeline killed.

"The job takes everything. It's just the way it is," he said.

"I'm sorry you feel that way." Melissa stood then and walked out of his office, leaving him to the empty thoughts that swirled in his mind, refusing to calm.

A week. Evangeline had been home a week. Her mother had fussed over her, making her favorite foods and sitting up talking with her late into the night. It had taken a few days but her mom had finally approached the question of why Evangeline had kept her in the dark about the leave of absence from her job.

After a lot of tears and "I'm sorrys," Evangeline had finally shared the truth. That she was afraid of upsetting the new life her mother had built.

After getting a stern talking-to, full of Dora Whittaker's abundant love and frustration, Evangeline could only laugh. How had she thought her mother couldn't handle the truth? It was only after that storm passed that her mom had moved on to the subject of Troy.

Since that subject did nothing more than get Evangeline's own ire up, her mother had ultimately changed the subject.

And now here she was.

The entire GGPD had checked in on her, Melissa at the front of the line. Brett and Ember had showed up with lunch one day earlier in the week. Grace and Ellie and Jillian had all come to see her, as well.

But Troy had stayed away.

Everyone diligently avoided mentioning his absence, but it loomed large all the same.

Which was why Evangeline ultimately moved on. The thoughts that had swirled so strong and sure during the experience with Sal Petrillo had morphed into purpose and, finally, action.

She loved the time she'd spent at the DA's office, but it was time for something new. Through the years as a prosecutor she'd seen any number of women who'd been through similar situations as her mother. Families that had been torn apart by violence, physical and emotional, and who needed help and support to get back on their feet. It was something she'd thought about for years, but it finally felt like the time to make a change.

She'd given Arielle plenty of time in her resignation letter, but effective two weeks from now, Evangeline was beginning the courses needed to become a licensed social worker. It would be hard work to juggle the courses and her ADA job, but it was time to make a change.

Time to make a difference in the community in a new way.

It was a decision that felt right and good and she was ready to get started.

But first, she needed to close the current chapter of her life.

On the drive into downtown, she took in the familiar street signs and buildings she'd seen her entire life. Despite Sal Petrillo's crimes against her, Grave Gulch was a good place to live. A good place to work and to build a life.

Evangeline was determined to find both.

She pulled into the parking lot at the GGPD and headed into the precinct. The steady hum of activity she always associated with the place was in full swing and she saw an active bullpen.

"Can I help—" Mary Suzuki broke off with a broad smile. "Ms. Whittaker. It's good to see you. I'm so glad to see you're doing okay."

"Thank you. I wanted to see if Detective Troy Colton is in?"

"He is. Let me call him." Mary was about to dial when Melissa materialized at the front desk.

"That won't be necessary, Mary. I'll walk Evangeline back."

"Oh." Mary's eyes widened as she keyed in to why their chief was stepping in. "Thanks, Chief."

Melissa gestured Evangeline through the door beside Mary's desk, walking her through the bullpen. "I hope you brought your boxing gloves."

"They don't match my outfit," Evangeline deadpanned, even as she caught onto Melissa's meaning a lot quicker than Mary had.

"A solid choice, by the way. And those heels are awesome." Melissa patted her back, giving her an encouraging smile as they reached Troy's door. "No mercy."

The obvious support buoyed her, giving her the final push she needed to get into Troy's office. She had dressed carefully and the other woman's notice added an extra shot in the arm.

Now or never, Whittaker.

"Troy. I'd like a few minutes."

He looked up from his desk, the circles under his hazel eyes an obvious and outward sign of his exhaustion. "Evangeline."

"You've been quiet this past week."

"I've been trying to catch a killer."

"I understand. Which is why I don't need much of your time." She turned and closed the door behind her. Whatever the outcome of this discussion, it was between her and Troy and no one else.

"I came to tell you a few things."

She saw his mouth open in question but he quickly snapped it shut, saying nothing.

"I finally stopped crying. It took a few days, but I got it out of my system."

"I'm sorry you had to go through that."

"I'm not. Those tears gave me a lot of clarity. Some things I hadn't been willing to admit or address in my life."

His eyebrows narrowed in question, adding additional creases to those dark circles. "Clarity on what?"

"I'm no longer interested in working for the DA's office. I've had a good run but I think my talents can be put to better use somewhere else."

"That's a loss for Arielle and for Grave Gulch."

"I don't think so and neither does she. I'll see out all my current cases for the foreseeable future, but I'm starting classes in a few weeks. My new focus will be social work. Hopefully I can help people before they find themselves in need."

"Congratulations."

"Thank you. But to be honest, that's not why I'm here."

"Why are you here, Evangeline?"

"I thought it was important to tell you that I love you."

"I don't—"

She held up a hand. "I don't expect you to say it back. I also don't expect you to do anything about it. But I do expect that you won't lie to me."

She saw the flash of heat in his eyes. Good. The jab hit its mark and she didn't even need boxing gloves to do it.

"I haven't lied to you," he said.

"Then you've lied to yourself."

As more anger flashed, Evangeline knew she'd landed another direct hit.

"You've somehow convinced yourself that the calling you have for your job means you can't have a life. And that's a steaming pile of crap."

"It's true."

"No, actually, it's not. Do you want to know how I know?"

She saw it then. The moment when everything shifted. When the walls he'd put up to protect himself began to crack. "How do you know?"

"Because I was there, too. I believed more of my father's lies and abuses than I realized. I convinced myself that I didn't have what it takes. Or that I had a hand tied behind my back because I always had to prove myself. That I was emotional. Or hysterically reacting to a situation. I wasn't, but I forced myself to remain calm and dispassionate to make my choices."

She let out a hard sigh. "Because of it, I let Len Davison slip through my fingers. I read the data but I didn't truly read the evidence."

"I've told you from the start that's not all your fault."

Oh, this sweet, sweet man, Evangeline marveled. Still singing that tune.

"But you see, Troy. It is my fault. That's what I've had to come to accept. That data and details are just that. Items that sometimes add up and sometimes don't. It's what's inside—" she moved closer, laying a hand on her chest "—what's in here that matters."

"Why are you telling me this?"

"Because you've convinced yourself the only way you can honor your mother is to keep the cop separate from the man. But it's the man you are that makes you an amazing cop. One your mother would be proud of." Evangeline doubled down, full well knowing it was the truth. "One she *is* proud of."

He came around his desk then and stood before her. "I can't be someone I'm not."

"I'm not asking you to."

"Then what are you asking?"

"That if you love me you'll take the chance on us. That you'll fight for us. And that you'll still be Detective Troy Colton every day, too."

Whatever lingering ire filled his eyes vanished, replaced by a haunting vulnerability that skewered her clean through. "What if I don't know how?"

"We'll figure it out together."

He closed the remaining distance between them, pulling her against his chest and bending his forehead to hers. "I do love you."

"I love you, too."

He lifted his head, his gaze never leaving hers. "Do you think it's enough?"

"I think it will always be enough."

And as Evangeline's lips met Troy's, she knew, with absolute certainty, that she was right.

Epilogue

Troy stared at his bride-to-be across the expanse of the restaurant at the Grave Gulch Hotel and considered how far they'd come in only a few weeks. The night he and Evangeline had shared here, having dinner, had been something special. Until it wasn't, as Sal Petrillo had lurked in the shadows.

But no matter how scary that evening was, it had been the catalyst to crack Evangeline's case wide open and ultimately bring them to this moment.

He would have preferred they'd gotten here without the risk to her life, but now that Petrillo was in their rearview mirror—and awaiting trial in Grave Gulch County—Troy had begun to breathe easier.

Evangeline mingled around the room, Desiree excitedly chattering beside her as she introduced Evangeline to their assembled guests.

"Has she met the family yet?"

Troy turned toward his brother, Palmer, and they clinked the tops of their beer bottles to one another in greeting. "She's getting there. Every time I think she's met everyone, someone new pops up and I realize I'm wrong."

Palmer laughed at that, lines creasing the skin around his vivid green eyes, tanned from all the time he'd spent outside on his ranch. "There's always another Colton to meet."

Troy eyed his brother and realized that he'd seen Palmer staring in the direction of Soledad de la Vega more than once this evening. The fraternal twin of Dominique de la Vega, their cousin Stanton's fiancée, had been invited to join them all for the evening.

With a nod to the beautiful baker, Troy pressed Palmer, "You see something you like?"

"Come on. You know me. I'm a perpetual bachelor."

Troy heard his brother's words but didn't miss the distinct notes of longing before Palmer shut it down. Nor did he miss Palmer's rush of excuses to head to the bar for a refill when Dez and Evangeline walked up to join them.

"Did someone say bar run?" Desiree smiled, linking her arm with Palmer's. "Count me in."

Troy put his arm around Evangeline, taking joy in how simple it was to pull her close as Palmer and Desiree headed for the bar.

Why had he fought this for so long?

It was a question he'd likely ask himself for many years to come, only there was another part of him that knew the answer. Until the past few weeks, he'd admired Evangeline from afar, but had never really gotten to know her. His interest, up until then, had been superficial at best.

But now…

Now he knew so much more. And even better than the knowing, he recognized that they'd have a lifetime of learning all there was to know about one another. It was a heady thought, one that caught him unawares at the oddest moments.

Yet as he stood there, looking out over the room full of the people he loved, he had to admit that his sister had been right all along.

Love did find you at the most unexpected times.

As he bent to press a kiss to Evangeline's forehead, Troy knew another truth. One he'd had to learn for himself.

When you found it, you needed to hang on with both hands, and never, *ever* let go.

* * * * *

Check out the previous books in the
Coltons of Grave Gulch series:

Colton's Dangerous Liaison *by Regan Black*
Colton's Killer Pursuit *by Tara Taylor Quinn*
Colton's Nursery Hideout *by Dana Nussio*
Colton Bullseye *by Geri Krotow*
Guarding Colton's Child *by Lara Lacombe*

And don't miss Book Seven

Rescued by the Colton Cowboy
by Deborah Fletcher Mello

Available in July 2021 from
Harlequin Romantic Suspense!

COMING NEXT MONTH FROM

ROMANTIC SUSPENSE

#2143 COLTON 911: SECRET DEFENDER
Colton 911: Chicago • by Marie Ferrarella

Aaron Colton, a retired boxer, hires Felicia Wagner to care for his ailing mother. Little does he know, the nurse hides a dangerous secret and could disappear at a moment's notice. Does he dare get too involved and ruin the bond building between them?

#2144 RESCUED BY THE COLTON COWBOY
The Coltons of Grave Gulch
by Deborah Fletcher Mello

Soledad de la Vega has witnessed the murder of her best friend. Running from the killer, she takes refuge with Palmer Colton. He's been in love with her for years and doesn't hesitate to protect her—and the infant she rescued.

#2145 TEXAS SHERIFF'S DEADLY MISSION
by Karen Whiddon

When small-town sheriff Rayna Coombs agrees to help a sexy biker named Parker Norton find his friend's missing niece, she never expects to find a serial killer—or a connection with Parker.

#2146 HER UNDERCOVER REFUGE
Shelter of Secrets • by Linda O. Johnston

When former cop Nella Bresdall takes a job at a domestic violence shelter that covers as an animal shelter, she develops a deep attraction to her boss. But when someone targets the facility, they have to face their connection—while not getting killed in the process!

HRSCNM0721

Love Harlequin romance?

DISCOVER.

Be the first to find out about promotions, news and exclusive content!

Facebook.com/HarlequinBooks

Twitter.com/HarlequinBooks

Instagram.com/HarlequinBooks

Pinterest.com/HarlequinBooks

YouTube.com/HarlequinBooks

ReaderService.com

EXPLORE.

Sign up for the Harlequin e-newsletter and download a free book from any series at **TryHarlequin.com**

CONNECT.

Join our Harlequin community to share your thoughts and connect with other romance readers!
Facebook.com/groups/HarlequinConnection